MURDER IN THE FAMILY

A Golden Age Mystery

MURDER IN THE FAMILY

A Golden Age Mystery

G.G. VANDAGRIFF
AND DAVID P. VANDAGRIFF

Dedicated To
Neve Marguerite Bailey
Our Granddaughter

Chapter One

Lostwithiel, Cornwall, England
Tregowyn Family Chapel
December 1935

"Harry! What are you doing here?" Catherine said to her bridegroom as he entered the robing room off the vestibule of the old chapel. "You're supposed to be out at the front of the chapel! You're not meant to see my gown!"

"Sorry, old thing," Harry said looking about as though he had lost something and not paying attention to her at all. "You haven't seen my uncle, have you?"

"Uncle Jonathan?"

"Yes. My best man. He's not shown up."

"Oh, Harry! You'd best get back where you belong before everyone thinks you've got cold feet. My mother will be having vapors!"

"Right. He must have had car trouble. Perhaps the old Hispano Suiza wouldn't start. I'll have the pater stand in for him." He finally looked at her. "I say! You look devilish fine! You're an out and out stunner, darling."

She grimaced at him. "Pretend you didn't see."

Grabbing her about the waist, he kissed her before he left. "I'll see you at the other end of the aisle!" he said over his shoulder.

Where was Uncle Jonathan? Catherine tried to compose herself. She'd always dreamt of being married here in the family chapel. She loved its weathered granite walls and slate roof, now mostly green with moss. A thick Celtic cross, predating the chapel by centuries, stood nearly upright near the entrance beside an ancient stone well. There was a legend of an unnamed saint who had stopped to refresh himself on a journey and left a blessing that the well would never run dry.

These thoughts centered her. What did a missing best man matter in the scheme of things?

I'm getting married to Harry today.

She smiled, and suddenly her nerves fled. Catherine had been a little worried about the Juliet cap, which fitted snugly over her head and tied under her chin. It wasn't the intriguing veil she had wanted, but when one had been in a life-threatening car smash, one might be expected to have patches of baldness from where one had stitches. She reminded herself that she was lucky to be alive, and Dot, her maid of honor, had been a wizard with her eye makeup. Catherine's large velvet brown eyes were her best feature.

Catherine fished her gold wristwatch from her decolletage. It was Harry's wedding gift and she had wanted to keep it close. But her mermaid silhouette wedding gown had no pockets. Five minutes late. Her mother must be having kittens.

Catherine had been swamped by details all day, but when Wagner's wedding march began to play on the chapel's small pipe organ, it jerked her into the present moment.

Her knees quaked at the enormity of it all, and it was only with the greatest difficulty that she moved forward through the chapel doors and down the aisle. Narrow stained-glass windows let in a peaceful light. A white satin altar cloth with a stitched golden cross partially covered the granite altar stone that stood at the front of the church.

Unfortunately, her father was not well enough to take the traditional post by her side during this historic walk, but he was seated in his wheelchair in the front row. If not precisely beaming, the baron was at least smiling slightly at the sight of her.

Her mother beamed, however. She had come to know Harry quite well as the three of them had shared Catherine's small flat for the two weeks he was confined to a hospital bed in her sitting room. Harry had won her mother over with his good nature. Even while he was in pain, he had maintained a sunny outlook.

Now he stood at the head of the nave, and his smile was all for her. The bouquet in her hands quaked as the magnitude of the ceremony settled on her.

Forever afterward she would remember the moment when Harry extended his hand to take hers while she accomplished the last two steps of her journey.

The words from the Book of Common Prayer were pronounced solemnly by the family chaplain.

"Dearly beloved: We have come together in the presence of God to witness and bless the joining together of this man and this woman in Holy Matrimony."

Harry squeezed her gloved hand in his, and warmth infused the ice in her that had kept her separate from all the people in her life so it wouldn't hurt that they were almost never there.

". . . The union of husband and wife in heart, body, and mind is intended by God for their mutual joy; for the help and comfort given one another in prosperity and adversity; and, when it is God's will, for the procreation of children and their nurture in the knowledge and love of the Lord. Therefore, marriage is not to be entered into unadvisedly or lightly, but reverently, deliberately, and in accordance with the purposes for which it was instituted."

The scent of Harry's spicy cologne, the sharp sweet smell of the Lilies of the Valley in her bouquet, and the homey mustiness of the old chapel combined to anchor her in the present moment. Peace washed over her, and she heard the rest of the service in a dreamlike trance until those final words: "I now pronounce you man and wife."

Harry's eyes were soft as he leaned down to kiss her. The last of her frozen separateness melted away. Dazed, she took his arm for the walk back down the aisle, surprised that her legs could hold her. Harry walked with the aid of his smart new walking stick in his left hand—the only visual reminder that his leg had been badly broken just two months ago.

Rice rained over them. Harry smiled. Everything was perfect.

* * *

The wedding breakfast for the Tregowyn's fifty guests took place in the ballroom of the manor. The ballroom's most prominent feature was a large curving double-staircase that descended from the second floor down to the ballroom floor. It was a wonderful place for a grand entrance. As she walked down the staircase, Catherine didn't feel quite real. She was the embodiment of dreams she had nurtured since childhood.

Six large crystal chandeliers lit the room, brightening a room otherwise lit only by the gray day outside. White tablecloths reflected the light and gleamed with the Tregowyn family silver. A small army of local servants on loan from neighboring houses had polished the parquet floor to near perfection.

As Catherine and Harry made their way down the staircase, the guests raised their champagne glasses and toasted the young couple.

Uncle Jonathan did not appear for the wedding breakfast. At first, Catherine only noticed this absently as she enjoyed the frivolity around her.

Harry's mother, Dr. Sarah Bascombe, was usually the soul of calm. But today, she was not quite her serene self. Catherine saw her whisper something to her husband, whereupon he left the table, apologized briefly to Catherine's mother, and left. At this, Catherine began to grow concerned.

Jonathan had a holiday cottage in St. Ives which was only thirty-odd miles away on the northern coast of Cornwall. During the past week since Harry's uncle had arrived from London, he had made the drive to Tregowyn Manor several times in his cream-colored Hispano Suiza. The latest visit had been just last night for the family dinner.

The only explanations Catherine thought of were dire—sudden illness or a car smash. Jonathan had seemed the soul of reliability. This concern put a damper on her appreciation of the celebrations.

Later, just before she and Harry departed for the train station, Harry's father arrived with word that Uncle Jonathan had gone missing. He was nowhere to be found. To this was added the fact that three of his bachelor friends and an angry Italian woman awaited him at his cottage.

Harry's father was quite obviously shaken, and not only by the news about Jonathan. "The Italian woman is a glamourous creature, and of all things, claims to be Jonathan's wife! She is something to him, that's for certain, for she possesses two children of his—the boy is Jon's exact image." Harold Bascombe wiped his sweaty forehead with a handkerchief though it was a cold day.

"She is on the warpath," he said to Harry. "Apparently, your uncle placed the children in English boarding schools earlier this year against her wishes. She came to retrieve them, now that the term is at an end. She is all ready for a showdown with Jonathan. She proposes to take the children back to Italy with her permanently. She even brought her nanny, though one would never take her for such. She is another glamorous lady."

Uncle Jonathan had always been thought to be a confirmed bachelor with a proclivity for a variety of beautiful women. Catherine agreed that it was all most mysterious.

* * *

Some hours later, Harry and Catherine were standing at the rail of HMS Aurora watching Southampton port recede in the distance as they began their sea journey to the Costa del Sol in southern Spain.

"Well, darling," said Harry in robust tones, "can you believe the sun is actually shining somewhere in our near future?"

"I can't wait!" she said. "But do you suppose something dreadful has happened to your Uncle Jonathan?"

"Perhaps he has just fled the charms of that woman who claims to be his wife," Harry said. "Jolly strange, that."

"Tell me about your uncle," Catherine said. "Is he prone to rash undertakings?"

"You mean marriage?" he asked, putting a fingertip up to her lips.

"Yes. Not everyone is as brave as you." He kissed the dimple in her cheek. "Well, I wouldn't have said so, but he's a bit of an adventurer. He ferrets out Renaissance masterpieces from old barns, attics, and ancient monasteries in Italy and then restores them. Even if he only finds one every year or two, he reaps fabulous profits. I used to join him on his trips to Italy during my Oxford holidays. Unlike his London days, there was nary a hint of a woman in the background."

Catherine smiled at him. "You're a bit of an adventurer yourself. Now I know where you get it from."

He winked and put his arm about her waist, pulling her close. "Faint heart ne'er won fair lady," he breathed into ear. "Speaking of which, our bridal suite awaits."

* * *

Catherine couldn't have told anyone much about the coast of Western Spain. She was lost in Harry's considerable charms for the three days it took for them to sail to the Costa del Sol. They disembarked at Málaga and took a taxi to the Moorish-looking Grand Hotel on the seaside. Unbelievably, the temperature was close to 90 degrees. The sights and the heat combined to take Catherine's breath away. This was the first time she had visited such a foreign-looking place.

For the next week, they thought not at all of Uncle Jonathan, but sunbathed, ate their fill of seafood, and strolled down the old streets of the city. Harry could not convince her to go to the bull-fights, however.

They visited the Alcazaba, an ancient Moorish fortress visible from any location in the city and the Cathedral, still lacking a south tower because its building funds had been raided to support the American War for independence fought against the British. Catherine's personal favorite was the Parque de Málaga, still lush and green during Britain's winter months. There she let herself bake in the glorious sunshine, breathing deeply with satisfaction.

When they reluctantly boarded the HMS Ulysses for their return trip to England, Catherine sported a slight tan and Harry an outcropping of freckles. Catherine had visited the street market where she bought a straw sunhat and matching bag which she filled with gifts for their families and Dot.

Catherine wondered if they were truly ready for a gray December in Oxford and real-world responsibilities. It had been a glorious honeymoon. As they stood at the ship's railing and watched Málaga recede, Harry said, "I vote that we come here every year for our anniversary."

"I second that motion," said Catherine. "But I fear we will never have such a perfect holiday again. It's just impossible to enjoy such happiness more than once in a lifetime."

"You are sounding depressingly British," said Harry. "You want to watch that."

"I am just glad we took so many photos. But no one will believe how turquoise the ocean was," she said wistfully. "Or how golden the sunsets."

* * *

To their surprise, they were greeted at Southampton by Harry's parents.

"You look like you've thoroughly enjoyed yourselves," said Sarah Bascombe. Turning to her husband, she said, "Darling we must sail away to Spain as soon as this business with Jonathan is over. I need it, desperately."

"Business with Jonathan?" Harry asked. Catherine felt her sensible Oxford self begin to reclaim her.

"Yes, darling," said Sarah. "That's why we've come to meet you. We know you were planning to spend the rest of your holiday with us in Hampshire, but you must go back to Cornwall. Catherine's parents are expecting you." It was only then that Catherine took in the gray circles under her mother-in-law's eyes and new lines about her mouth. "Your angel mother is also keeping us. We just drove down from Hampshire yesterday."

"Where did Jonathan disappear to?" Catherine asked.

Sarah held a handkerchief to her lips, trying unsuccessfully to hold in sudden sobs. "I'm afraid he's dead. A fisherman found him yesterday. They're saying it's suicide, but of course, it isn't," said Harry's father with his hand on his wife's shoulder. "He was in his prime and doing what he loved. It was an accident, most likely."

Catherine felt Harry go rigid beside her. "Oh, hell," he expostulated. "I'm so sorry, Mother," said Harry. "Where was he found?"

"At the bottom of a cliff near St. Ives not far from his cottage," said his father. "The beach is only accessible by sea, and his poor body had been washed into a cave. I'm afraid your mother had to identify him. It was ghastly. He'd been in the water for almost two weeks."

Catherine wrenched her thoughts away from Spain and the delights of her honeymoon. They were really and truly home. And, oh, poor darling Harry. She had never seen him so shaken.

Chapter Two

"Cat!" her mother exclaimed upon their arrival at Tregowyn Manor. "You look quite suntanned! And rested for once." She hugged her daughter awkwardly. These mother-daughter embraces were a fairly new thing, and they were both still adjusting to them.

The baroness sobered as she turned to Harry and placed her hand on his arm. "I'm sorry about your Uncle."

His manner stiff, Harry thanked her. Catherine watched as he clenched his jaw. A muscle flexed in his cheek.

"Where is Father?" Catherine asked.

"He's having a lie-down. I'm afraid the news about Jonathan was a shock he wasn't prepared for. He is having his dinner on a tray. But you can go up and see him. It will do him good," her mother said. "Jonathan's solicitor rang," she added, speaking to Sarah Bascombe. "I saw the story about his death. It was in the *Times*. I'm afraid one of Jonathan's household must have spoken with the press and told them you were staying here."

The usually calm Sarah Bascombe looked dithery as she hunted in her purse. "Did the solicitor leave his number? I'm afraid it's gone straight out of my head," she said.

"Darling, I will ring him for you. You have enough to deal with at the moment," said Harold, Sr., patting his wife's shoulder.

As though to prove his point, the Tregowyn's butler entered

the sitting room. "The police are in the house," he said, his words clipped with disapproval. "They wish to see Dr. Bascombe."

"Police?" Sarah Bascombe's voice quivered. "I presume they mean me and not Harry."

"You may see them in my husband's study," said Catherine's mother with tact.

The doctor clutched her husband's arm and looked into his face. Catherine had never known her mother-in-law to not be up to the task.

"I think we'd better come with you, Mother," said Harry. "This doesn't sound like anything you're prepared to deal with."

"Nonsense," said Sarah, straightening her spine. "But I should appreciate the support."

"I'll come, too," said her husband.

"That will be quite a crowd for the study," said the Baroness. "Perhaps you should just bring them in here, Davies."

A stout man in an overcoat, carrying a bowler hat came into the room, followed by a tall thin man with a mustache. One look at the bulldog face of the shorter man was enough to tell he was the lead detective here.

"I'm Inspector Ross," he said. "This is Detective Curtis. Dr. Bascombe, I'm afraid we have some disturbing news. The medical examiner has completed his autopsy on your brother, and he found evidence of murder. I'm sorry to say, there was a small wound on his back, made by a very thin knife. It pierced his heart, leading us to the conclusion that he was knifed before being pushed over the cliff onto the beach. There will be an inquest on Monday."

Sarah gasped and sank into a chair. Her husband, Harold, put a hand on her shoulder.

Harry reached for Catherine's hand. His had begun to shake.

"This is rather a shock," Harold said, his eyes reproving the detectives.

"Murder is shocking," the policeman said. "We don't have many in St. Ives, but I investigated several murders when I was serving as detective in Plymouth. Now. I understand there was a wedding taking place here and that the deceased was to have been the best man. What time was the wedding?"

Catherine's mother said, "It was at eleven o'clock a.m. on Saturday, the 14th. We had a family gathering the night before and Jonathan was present for that. We had no inkling that anything was wrong."

"The M.E. tells me that the body was in the water for approximately twelve days. He can't make it any more specific, apparently. So Mr. Haverford was killed either on Friday night of the 13th after returning from Lostwithiel or Saturday the 14th sometime in the morning prior to the wedding. Since his stomach was empty, I believe the murder took place in the morning before breakfast. We shall be interviewing the witnesses who were staying in St. Ives to determine the last time he was seen alive at his home."

"My husband and I were staying here at Tregowyn Manor," said Harry's mother. "As were the bride and groom."

"Jonathan dined here the night before the wedding," said Harold. "He left around midnight."

"Dr. Bascombe," the policeman said, pulling a card out of his waistcoat. "Here is my card with my telephone number. Please ring me with anything you think may be relevant to the murder. Oh! One thing I forgot to ask. Were any of the guests at Caravaggio House--Mrs. Haverford or Mr. Haverford's friend, Mr. Milton-- invited to the wedding?"

The doctor spoke up. "Mrs. Haverford?" Her words rang with shock. "To my knowledge, my brother was not married! Who is this woman?"

Inspector Ross raised an eyebrow. "She is Italian. She claims your brother was her husband and the father of her two children. She comes from Milan. I'm afraid she is rather hysterical over your brother's death."

Catherine watched as Sarah Bascombe's face mirrored her outrage. "I'm sorry for her," the doctor said finally. "But I find it difficult to believe she was actually married to my brother. I had no clue that Jonathan had guests. I can assure you that neither she nor the other man you mentioned was invited to the wedding." She paused and put both hands up to her face. "Murder. I can't take it in. That woman must have done it. We knew someone was there claiming to be his wife, but I must tell you, he never told us he was married."

Catherine looked at her husband. His face was blank with shock.

"I am sorry for it, Doctor," said the inspector. His voice was gentler as he said, "If you would like to view the body, you may do so. The M.E. is at Edward Hain Hospital in his laboratory next to the morgue."

At the final nature of this fact, Sarah broke down in silent sobs, holding her sodden handkerchief to her face. Harry's father put an arm around his wife and drew her close to his side.

Catherine took Harry's hand in both of hers and squeezed it.

"You have our condolences," the policeman said quietly, his bulldog face softening. "We will leave you now." He and his silent partner left the sitting room.

"Tea," said the baroness, pulling the servant's bell. "A nice cup of tea will soothe you, my dear." She turned to her daughter, "Catherine, you and Harry are in the Blue Room. Dinner will be served early at seven o'clock because we thought you would be starved. Now, I only hope we can eat."

"I'll just have some tea and then I'll be off for St. Ives," said Sarah. "Don't hold dinner for me. I'm going to view poor Jonathan's remains."

"I shall go with you, Mother," said Harry. "I should like to see him."

"Whither thou goest, darling," said Catherine. "I go, too."

Her mother said, "I'll put dinner back to nine o'clock then."

Harry and Catherine joined his mother and father in the Bentley, and they drove for close to an hour to get to the hospital. No one said much during the journey, but Harry held Catherine's hand in such a firm hold she could tell he was emotional.

When they arrived at the hospital, Catherine decided to wait outside the lab after all. She was too new a relation to intrude on their grief.

They were not gone long. Harry emerged looking shaken but determined, and his mother was even more pale and red-eyed. Harold, Sr. moved stiffly and looked straight ahead, clearly working to contain his emotions.

"Now," said Dr. Bascombe, I should like to meet Jonathan's supposed wife, if the police haven't arrested her."

"He did plenty for me during his lifetime," said Harry. "I'm afraid I think the inspector to be a puffed-up poser. Catherine and I will find out who did this to him. Even if it was his wife."

* * *

The police vehicle was parked outside when they arrived at Harry's uncle's cottage. Catherine thought it was ridiculous to refer to Caravaggio House as a cottage. Made of rough-hewn local granite, it had clearly been built to withstand the strongest north winds off the Celtic Sea. The thick slate roof was similarly stormproof. A Cornishwoman born and bred, Catherine thought it reflected the doggedness of the Cornish character.

She had a hunch that the local police would prove to be just such Cornishmen, and knew it wasn't wise to interfere with their interrogations at this point. She said as much to the others.

"I agree," said Harold, Sr. "My dear, this is not the best time, I think."

"Nonsense," declared his wife, stepping briskly up to the door. She opened it without knocking. Catherine was seeing a new side to her mother-in-law. Previously, she had been nothing but gracious and nurturing. Now that she had recovered from the shock, she was intrepid.

The cottage had no entryway. It opened right onto the sitting room. A huge granite fireplace was set into a free-standing brick wall that divided the cottage between the sitting room and what

Catherine supposed was the kitchen. Sitting before a roaring fire was a man with slicked-back blond hair, reading the newspaper.

"Hullo!" he said jumping to his feet.

Harold strode in and offered his hand. "Harold Bascombe," he said. "I'm Jon's brother-in-law. This is my wife, Dr. Bascombe, Jon's sister, and here is our son, Professor Bascombe and his wife."

"Roderick Milton," the man said. "I was a great friend of Jon's. I stayed on after the wedding weekend when Jonathan was found missing. Dr. Bascombe." He offered his hand to Harry's mother. "I have been helping with the search." He extended his hand to Harry's mother who shook it. "Let me offer my condolences. This is a bad business. I have known Jonathan since I was eight years old. It will take a while before this even seems real."

"I remember you!" Harry's mother said. "You were at Harrow with Jonathan. You came home on holidays with him."

"Yes. And you ran wild with us. I wasn't sure you would remember me."

"Did *you* know my brother was married?"

"Not a clue," Mr. Milton said. Looking over his shoulder, he said in hushed tones. "I don't believe he was, whatever the woman says. I stayed on to make certain she didn't abscond with the plate."

Catherine liked the looks of Jonathan's friend. He seemed quite genuine. The coziness of the room gave no hint that anything was amiss. Certainly not a murder! From the carpets to the Queen Anne furniture, everything was colored in a soothing Tuscan palette—apricot, biscuit, and silvery olive green. Could those paintings possibly be originals? She wandered over to the two Renaissance portraits hanging on the walls beneath the heavy oak beams.

At that moment, a pretty dark-haired little girl stuck her head into the sitting room. "Who is here?" she asked of Mr. Milton.

"Mr. Haverford's people. Come in and I'll introduce you properly."

"Why do you always call him that? He's my papa!" The child's eyes flashed. Catherine made her out to be about eight years old.

"Dr. Bascombe, Mr. Bascombe, Professor Bascombe, and Mrs. Bascombe, this precocious creature is Adriana. She's down from school for the Christmas holidays."

The girl shook everyone's hand with a solemn expression on her face. "How do you do?"

"Adriana attends St. Anne's. She's in her first year." Roderick Milton said. "Where is that scamp of a brother of yours?" he asked Adriana.

"Teasing the cook. When do you suppose we shall eat dinner?" the girl asked.

"Now then. Don't be rude. Sit down and mind your manners," said the blond man.

"Why are you here?" the girl asked them.

Dr. Bascombe answered, "We came down to meet your Mama. I'm Mr. Haverford's sister."

"Mama is with the p'leece. In Papa's study. I think they want to know where Papa is. He's missing. They've been here before."

Catherine thought Adriana a beautiful child with her olive skin, dark brown pigtails and disconcerting blue eyes. "When was the last time you saw your Papa?" asked Catherine.

"I haven't seen him since the day we got here. He promised to take me out for tea, but he never did. He disappeared. Mama's very sad. She cries all the time. Even Nanny's sad."

At that moment, a stripling of a boy in trousers that had become too short entered the room. From the one time she'd met Jonathan Haverford, she determined this boy with his light-haired English good looks took after him. "Hullo!" he said. "Who are you?

"I am your aunt," said Sarah. "You look very like your father. He was . . . uh is my brother." She introduced the rest of them. What is your name?"

"I'm Giovanni. You can call me Jon. Everyone does except Mama." He turned to Mr. Milton and said, "Cook says to come for dinner. It's crab again."

The man said, "Tell cook you and Adriana may begin, but I shall wait for your Mama."

Scampering out of the room, Adriana informed them, "I love crab!"

The door to what Catherine supposed was the study, opened and an absolutely smashing brunette made her entrance. Smooth, graceful, and soigné, Jonathan's "wife" raised a brow. "Hullo," she said, "I am Elisabetta Haverford. Are you waiting for me?"

"Yes," said Sarah. "I am Sarah Bascombe, Jonathan's sister." She introduced the rest of her company.

"How good of you to come," said the woman, sounding as though she were a queen granting an audience. "This is a very sad business. I cannot bring myself to tell the children. They will be heartbroken. They loved their papa."

"How old are they?" asked Sarah.

"Giovanni is ten. Adriana, eight."

"You really need to tell them, Betta," said Mr. Milton. "It's not a kindness to leave them in the dark."

She snapped, "Rodrigo, they are *my* children. Italian children, no matter how English Jonathan tried to make them. I will tell them in my own time. Then we will go home to Italy, and they will be taught at home by tutors, not sent away in the barbaric English manner. And Italian children know how to grieve. They do not have the 'stiff upper lip' like you British." By the conclusion of this speech, the woman was fighting tears. Mr. Milton sighed and handed her his handkerchief.

Catherine intervened, "Where do you live in Italy?"

The beauty made use of the handkerchief and seeming to have her emotions under control once again, she strolled to the huge fireplace where she took a cigarette with shaking hands from the box on the mantel. "We live in Milano. I prefer Sicily where I grew up, but I am a fashion model. The fashion houses are in Milano."

"Ah," said Catherine. This woman was very slick. She was trained to appear graceful in every movement. Catherine had never seen anyone light a cigarette with such artistry. "Did you come to England for the Christmas holiday?"

"No. I came because I planned to convince Jonathan to give me back my children. I was on a shoot in Paris when he took them away to boarding school. They have written me how miserable they are. They begged to come home. I do not approve of the British way of raising children. I will not send my children away to boarding school when they are little more than babies! Jonathan was quite disagreeable about it."

Another beautiful woman glided into the room. This one had reddish blonde hair coiled in a chignon. But her face, though lovely and fine-boned, did not have the brilliance of Elisabetta's. "The children. They want you," she said in heavily accented English.

Elisabetta said something sharp in Italian, and the other woman left in a hurry. "The children's nanny," she said. "I must go to Adriana. She can scarcely let me out of her sight now that we have been reunited. It was a pleasure to meet you. I will be arranging a Funeral Mass for Jonathan this weekend. Then we must return to Italy. I have work."

"I say," said Harold Bascombe. "Jonathan was not Catholic. My wife has her heart set on an Anglican service at Jonathan's home chapel in Hampshire."

"Jonathan will be buried according to my wishes. I am his wife, after all," Elisabetta turned to leave the room.

"Are you?" challenged Harold in a hard voice Catherine had never heard before. "I'm afraid I have some questions about that."

The scornful eyebrow went up again. "We are at the end of this discussion."

Harry asked, "Have you discussed your plans to leave for Italy with the police?"

"Pfft," she said with a dismissive gesture. "They do not matter."

"I'm afraid they matter quite a lot," said Mr. Milton. "This is no ordinary death. It's murder. The police surely told you that.

Someone killed Jon. And the wife is always the most obvious suspect."

Elisabetta's eyes flashed. "Oh, but I think they are very interested in what I had to tell them about you, Mr. Milton." With those words, she made a dramatic exit.

His fair complexion grew red, and he clenched his fists, "You little tart."

"Pah!" replied Elisabetta before she turned and left the room.

Catherine had her first inkling that Mr. Milton might not quite be the gentleman he seemed at first blush. And then there was Jonathan. If he was married to this beautiful Italian, why did he keep it a secret?

* * *

Evidently having finished their interrogations, Inspector Ross and DC Curtis came through the door to the kitchen. He had Jonathan's wife with him.

"Now, if I didn't make it clear before, Mrs. Haverford and Mr. Milton, you need to remain here in St. Ives until you receive our permission to leave. To that end, I will need your passport, Mrs. Haverford. It will be held in our safe at the police station with other evidence."

"My passport!" cried the model. "But I must get back to my work! I have a shoot scheduled next week in Greece!"

"Nevertheless, you will stay here. Would you get your passport for me, please? Also, those of anyone traveling in your company—maid, nanny, etc."

"But this is cruel! Never have I been treated this way! I will speak to your superior! And if he will not help me, I will speak to the Italian ambassador! He was a friend of my husband."

"Very well. My supervisor is the Detective Chief Inspector. His name is Gomes. Now, if you will get the passports for me, please, we will be able to take our leave."

Elisabetta said something unpleasant in Italian and stormed up the stairs. Catherine marveled that the staid Englishman she had met had ever been married to such an emotional prima donna.

The Inspector turned his attention on Mr. Milton. "You said you were down here the week before the murder with friends. If you could give me their names and addresses, I will contact them. They will need to be questioned and to give evidence at the inquest."

Mr. Milton looked a bit uncomfortable. Patting his pockets, he found his pipe and drew it out. "Well, there was Lawrence, Lord Fawcett. He lives in London. He's an investment advisor. I have his telephone number." Patting his pockets again, he came up with a small black address book. He rattled off a string of numbers.

"Anyone else?" asked the policeman.

"George Baxter. He's an art dealer like Haverford." He paged through his little book and gave DC Curtis another number. "I understand that Baxter is Jon's executor as well as his trustee. He is coming down on tonight's train."

"And how were the four of you connected? Did you know each other well?"

"We were at school together—Harrow. Then we all went to Oxford. Different colleges, but we remained close. None of us is married at the moment, which means we get together frequently. I fancy myself a bit of a chef and I feed everyone. We're also keen card players, and of course, chat horse racing and whatever else catches our fancies."

Catherine wondered why Mr. Milton was babbling. Why was he nervous about his group of friends? What was his profession?

She and Harry were sitting together on the apricot-colored sofa. He took her hand and squeezed it. Did she really want to get involved in this case? How competent were these rural policemen? She wondered what Harry felt about it. She missed the intimacy she had enjoyed with her husband on their honeymoon. How did Harry feel about getting involved in a case that involved his family? His face was a grim mask.

She thought of the children who had just lost their father. If they had a nanny, Catherine assumed that their mother spent much of her time away from them. Would Harry's uncle have wanted them to return to Italy upon his death?

On the other hand, Catherine certainly knew what boarding school could be like. She had hated it when she was their age. She agreed with what Elisabetta had said about boarding school for the young. She remembered those years through a miasma of gray. And though the fire was burning hot in the huge fireplace, when she thought of school, she was always cold. And her hands felt chapped. If it hadn't been for her friend, Dot, the whole experience would have been awful. But she and Dot had formed a close friendship that had burned brightly in the bleakness.

Did these children have any close English friends? Catherine felt that she should ask them. She hoped they did.

The Inspector was asking Mr. Milton, "You wouldn't happen to know Haverford's solicitor, would you?"

"Yes. It's a Mr. Brundage in London. I rang him as soon as Jon was found. I was worried about what damage that Italian bag of tricks could do. Turns out the will has provisions which need to be addressed immediately following Jonathan's death. The lawyer will be down tonight. He plans to pay the widow, or whatever she is, a visit tomorrow morning."

Harry's mother was busy writing on the back of a visiting card. She handed it to Mr. Milton. "I would appreciate it if you could tell the solicitor that I would like him to ring me. I am staying at the Tregowyn's in Lostwithiel. He may have tried to ring me in Hampshire."

The detective inspector took Sarah's visiting card just as the front door opened and the angular form of Patricia Buchanan burst into the room on a blast of frigid air.

Chapter Three

Catherine knew Mrs. Buchanan only because she had met the woman at the wedding two weeks before. She was Jonathan Haverford's other sister. Her surprise at seeing a gathering in her brother's cottage was obvious.

With her forehead drawn in a frown, she asked, "Who are these men, Sarah? What are you all doing here? Surely you're not all here for the reading of the will!"

Sarah introduced the police to her sister. "I'm sorry to tell you, darling, but it seems Jonathan's death was murder. He was stabbed before he fell. We only found out a few hours ago. These policemen are investigating the crime." Patricia Buchanan was speechless.

"Come in and sit down," Sarah said. "I suppose Jon's estate will run to a glass of brandy. Harold, will you fetch a drink for Pat?"

"You were here for the wedding, Mrs. Buchanan?" asked Inspector Ross.

"Yes. Harry is my nephew," the woman said. "First an Italian wife and two children. Now we find out Jon was murdered. Whatever is next?"

"Next we will find the murderer," said the inspector. "Perhaps you can help us."

"Not this minute," Mrs. Buchanan said. "Give me some time to take this all in." She accepted a glass of brandy from her brother-in-law's hand, put it away in two gulps, and handed it back for a refill. Catherine had never understood the attraction of brandy in a crisis. She found it nasty.

The woman had struck Catherine as rather hard-bitten and difficult when she met her at the family dinner the night before her wedding. She was as different from Harry's mother as anyone could be. Her questioning of Harry over how Catherine and he had met had felt like an interrogation.

"If you would please come with us to the study, we can get the questions over with and then you can visit with your family," said Inspector Ross.

"I'll come when I'm darn good and ready!" Mrs. Buchanan snapped. "Harold, I'd like another brandy. There's a pet."

But Harold only said, "You'd best go get it over with. Were you planning on staying here with the Italian woman?"

"She's still here?"

"Of course. I wonder why you didn't tell us about her at the wedding," Sarah said.

"I didn't want to ruin your day, Sarah. It was such a lovely wedding."

"Well, where are you staying?" her sister asked.

"Here, I think. Where are you?"

"The Tregowyns are kindly putting us up. You'd best go to a B & B in town."

Her anger flashed. "I don't have that kind of money. I'll have to stay here. There are four guest bedrooms, as I recall."

At this point, Harold said, "You have met Mr. Milton, I assume?"

This was the final straw, as far as the Inspector was concerned. "This isn't a garden party. It's a murder investigation, and you, Mrs. Buchanan, will come with my detective and me. Now."

"That's Dr. Buchanan!" Patricia flushed bright red and began mumbling to herself, "The nerve. Who does he think he is anyway? Probably the son of a blacksmith."

"Watch it!" said Ross, as his DC firmly grasped her elbow and steered Patricia into an adjoining room, firmly closing the door.

* * *

By the time Patricia's interview was over, Catherine was very hungry. She had already rung her mother to tell her that they had been held up. When she told her of Dr. Buchanan's appearance, her mother asked if the woman needed a place to stay. Heartlessly, Catherine told her mother that the situation was under control. There is no way she'd have Harry's impossible aunt at Tregowyn Manor. Things were fraught enough with Harry's poor bereaved parents there.

After listening to all of Patricia's complaints about the police, the party was finally ready to extricate themselves from Caravaggio House.

It was so dark on the road home to Tregowyn Manor that Catherine and Harry were able to enjoy a little kiss and a cuddle in the back seat. Catherine felt the need to comfort her husband. When they arrived, dinner was ready. Being so close to the ocean, her family enjoyed seafood often. Tonight, they had fresh lobster with hot rolls, fried potatoes, and peas from the hothouse.

Catherine was very concerned about her father when she saw him for the first time since she had returned. He was not his robust and blustering self and hadn't been since his heart attack last winter. He seemed to be fading away. Though they had never been close, she missed him.

Despite her other concerns, Sarah Bascombe kept a professional eye on Catherine's father. After they were finished eating, he thought he would retire, but consented to having Sarah just listen to his chest with her stethoscope.

Catherine hovered nearby during the procedure. Accustomed to reading Sarah's face by now, she could tell that the woman was concerned. Catherine nodded to her mother, then pushed her father's wheelchair into the room that had been refitted as a downstairs bedroom.

"Goodnight, Father," Catherine said after kissing his cheek. She pulled the bell rope for his man, Stebbins. "Here comes your valet. I will see you in the morning." Walking out of the room, she reflected on how sad it was that she and her father had not built a relationship over the years. Now it was too late.

* * *

When Harry and Catherine were finally alone in the blue bedroom, they came together in a passionate embrace. Catherine loved the feeling of being crushed in her husband's arms, especially now when she could tell he was hurting. When Harry finally took a breath, she said, "Darling I've been dying to talk to you about this all day long! What do you think about your uncle? Why would he have a secret marriage, especially when two children are involved?"

"I find that bit just as difficult to understand as the fact that he was murdered," Harry said. "I always thought that he was a bit of a dark horse, but after this turnup, the horse is most definitely black. It saddens me. I thought we were close, and now it seems I barely knew him."

"Those poor children, sent away to boarding school when they'd never even been in this country before," said Catherine. "We've never discussed the matter, but I loathed boarding school. If it hadn't been for Dot, I daresay I would have run away."

"My boarding school was all right," said Harry. "But I missed the family. I doubt those two children have much of a family life with Elisabetta for a mother. She apparently works out of the country a lot, and I didn't like the looks of that nanny. She appeared as hard-nosed as Elisabetta."

"I have doubts about Mr. Milton's character, as well. He let the mask slip when Elisabetta threatened to tell the detective something he wanted kept quiet."

"Yes. I caught that. Also, Elisabetta didn't want the DI to see her passport. I imagine if she was married to my uncle, the name on it should be Haverford."

"You're right," said Catherine, tracing Harry's ear with a finger. "I didn't think of that. I almost feel sorry for her having to share the cottage with your Aunt Patricia and Mr. Milton, who obviously despises her."

"I think our Elisabetta can hold her own, but let's not worry about her tonight. I need your arms around me. I will miss Uncle Jon."

On that note, the newlyweds fell into bed and gave themselves over to a period of connubial bliss.

* * *

After breakfast the following morning, Patricia and Fox, Jonathan's valet, appeared at the manor. "I rang Mr. Brundage, Jonathan's solicitor, yesterday," said Harry's aunt. "I thought he might be trying to get hold of me. The reading of the will, you know. It's a good thing I did, because he told me to come here this morning by ten o'clock. He asked me where Fox could be found. I told him I would give him the message. So! Here we are."

"Splendid," said Harry's mother, giving Fox a hand to shake. "I think we'll assemble in the drawing room."

Mr. Franklin Brundage, the Haverford family solicitor, made his appearance precisely at 10:00 o'clock. Harry, Catherine, Patricia and Harry's parents were all awaiting him in the drawing room. "I don't have any secrets from my family," Sarah said. "We're all here to listen so I won't have to worry about forgetting anything."

Mr. Brundage said, "Ah, splendid!"

She introduced the solicitor to Harry and Catherine, who sat on one sofa, Patricia and Harold, who were in chairs flanking the fireplace, and Fox who stood behind Harold's chair as though he were waiting for someone to give him an errand.

Sarah said, "Mr. Fox, please come and join me on the sofa. Mr. Brundage, will you kindly take the chair just there." She indicated an armchair facing the group. "Now, I believe we're all ready to begin."

Mr. Brundage was clearly a gentleman of the old school. He wore immaculate morning clothes Catherine hadn't seen outside a wedding in her lifetime. His white side whiskers were past description. She had never seen the like, particularly on a bald man. As he was pulling papers out of a battered briefcase, Catherine leaned over to her husband and whispered, "He's straight out of Galsworthy."

Harry grinned.

"This is somewhat irregular; since one of the major legatees is not present," Mr. Brundage said. "But it was my client's wish that things be handled this way. It would be a very uncomfortable time for me to meet Mrs. Haverford for the first time at this reading."

Ah!" said Harry's father. "So, he was married!"

"Yes. He knew you would be surprised. At my urging, he had decided to tell you about Mrs. Haverford after young Harry's wedding. He had a good reason for keeping his wife at a distance, he said, but he never told me what it was. Now we shall never know. It is terribly sad and unfortunate that things worked out this way. He died too young.

"Now, if you will hold your questions until after the will has been read, I think you will find that it answers many of them."

The solicitor gave a preliminary cough and then started to read the will which was dated the previous October. It fell out that Patricia and Sarah had been left a Bronzino painting each. Catherine held back a gasp. The painter was the official portrait artist of the Medici family. Surely, these were the jewels of Haverford's collection!

Patricia looked confused and Harry's mother was stunned.

"Oh my!" Sarah Bascombe said.

Mr. Brundage broke off to say that he wasn't aware of their precise value at this date, but they would each be worth a small fortune. Mr. Brundage included their provenances in separate documents which he passed to each woman.

A lump sum of fifty thousand pounds was left to Elisabetta on the condition that she allowed the children to be brought up the way he specified in an attached document. It was to be paid out in lump sums year by year according to a schedule if she signed a waiver granting the Haverford trustees the power to make decisions on his children's behalf until they reached the age of twenty-one years. In the event that she did not choose to sign the waiver, she would receive five hundred pounds upon his death which amount Haverford believed to be sufficient given her own private wealth and large personal income.

Five hundred pounds was left to Mr. Archibald Fox in gratitude for saving his life during the late War and for his faithful service in all areas of the decedent's life thereafter.

The residual of his estate—primarily his paintings and his real estate—was to be left in trust to his two children until they reached the age of thirty-five. A yearly allowance and all school fees would be paid out of the trust and be determined by the trustees thereof. Said trustees would be Messrs. Franklin Brundage and George Baxter. An annual accounting of income and disbursements carried out by an independent third party was to be provided to the adult heirs. Reasonable fees for their services would be taken out of the trust.

An updated inventory of the paintings he owned was attached as well as a copy of the trust. In a surprise move, in addition to the five-hundred-pound bequest, he had left his restoration business and related equipment and materials to Mr. Fox. The man would be paid by the trustees to continue the restorations already in hand. Mr. Brundage said that Mr. Haverford had been training his man since 1922, and that Fox was well equipped to take over the restoration of the paintings. Fox would continue to receive his current salary and accommodations in return for his undertaking to manage the staff and upkeep of the townhouse. He would be the custodian of the collection which would belong to the trust. All sales would be managed by the trustees.

In the silence that followed, Catherine saw from the ferocious frown on Harry's Aunt Patricia's face, that she was not pleased. But, then she had undoubtedly counted on receiving half of the estate.

Catherine also didn't imagine for one moment that Elisabetta would be at all happy. Not only was she not receiving the majority of her husband's estate, but he would be reaching out from the grave to control her children's lives until they were grown. Catherine hoped she was nowhere around when the woman received that news. It made her uncomfortable to even think about it.

"Oh, heavens," said Sarah Bascombe. "What a surprise. I never expected my brother to leave me anything. How very generous of him."

"Have you ever met Mr. Baxter, the other trustee?" asked Catherine.

"Yes. He was at Harrow with Jonathan, so I have known him for donkey's years. He's an art dealer like Jonathan, so he's the perfect one to manage my brother's collection." Sarah wiped a tear. "I had no expectation to inherit anything."

"We knew nothing of his wife and children," said Aunt Patricia, her face grim. "I assumed his estate would come to us, Sarah, as you must have."

Catherine thought of the woman's representation of being too poor to spend the night at a Bed and Breakfast. She couldn't help saying to Harry's aunt, "You may not know that the Bronzino paintings are quite valuable. They are most probably the gems of his collection."

"Hmph," said Patricia. Catherine got the impression that she was holding her emotions very tightly in check. "Mr. Fox, I shall leave immediately after the conclusion of these proceedings, if you are coming with me to St. Ives."

When the murmuring had died down, Mr. Brundage called them to order. Patricia sat down again. "I have another document here. It was Mr. Haverford's request that he be buried in the family plot in Hampshire after an Anglican service at his childhood church there.

"He also has a request here that isn't tied to funds of any kind. The solicitor took out another document and passed it to Sarah Bascombe.

For a few moments, Sarah read it and tears began to slide down her cheeks. When she was finished, she fished for her handkerchief, wiping her cheeks and blowing her nose. "Those poor children," she said, her voice broken.

"Well, what is it, Sarah? I expect he's managed to find a way to give you more money," Aunt Patricia said.

"Jon was trying to ensure the children's emotional well-being, but, well, it is not possible to do such a thing. He says that if he dies while they are young, they will need guardians to provide nurturing and love during the time they are living in England. He asks that Harold and I fulfill the position of guardians, reaching out to them by letter and in person whenever we can. He requests that, if possible, we attend their Sport's Days, Drama productions, and Award's days.

"He also asks that we provide a home base for them during their Christmas Hols, and Easter vacation. He wants them to come to know and love Hampshire as he did growing up." She wiped her eyes again. "It's a rather emotional plea. Not typical of Jonathan. I think he must have loved his children very much. It seems to me that he is trying to keep them away from Elisabetta and her family's influence as much as possible."

"And how do you feel about that?" asked the solicitor. "That's a very large charge."

Sarah turned to her husband. "I would need the support of my family to do this. My heart tells me that I can and will do it, but I will need help." Harold put a reassuring hand on her shoulder.

Catherine was amazed at how this codicil to Jonathan's will

changed her feelings about the man. She could almost feel his desperation coming through his plea to his sister—"keep them safe, love them, and give them a place to go with their struggles." Catherine realized the man had been anxious to protect them from the influences that Elisabetta and her family might exert over them as they grew into adults.

Harry looked at her as though seeking affirmation. Catherine nodded. "Catherine and I can help," he said. "If you feel that your emotional well is running dry, we can take them sometimes. From the little I've spoken to them, I've formed the opinion that the children are very bright. It would be good to introduce them to Oxford and plant goals in their minds while they are young."

"Yes," said Sarah, squaring her shoulders as though a weight had been lifted from them. "I think that would be a very good thing."

"I'm happy to attend his football games and that sort of thing, as often as I can, and, of course, whatever events should arise for Adriana," said Harry.

"I wish I had been given a chance to know your uncle better," said Catherine. "He gave us a rather extravagant wedding gift. It showed thought, giving us a challenge which he knew we would enjoy."

"Yes," said Sarah with a genuine smile. "He discussed it with me. I told him it was right up your street."

Catherine smiled and told her father-in-law about their gift. "It was a lovely sketch purported to be from the workshop of Donatello. He wants us to become amateur art experts—studying the life and work of the artist, students of technique, medium, and reputation of Donatello. He said he had his own feelings about the identity of the artist. He left them in a sealed envelope that is with you, Mr. Brundage, or your successor to be opened in twenty years. Quite a challenge!"

Sarah laughed, her spirits obviously improved. "Oh, my. That sounds so very much like Jonathan." She sobered a bit. "I think it is a good thing that he left instructions about what to do with his remains. But that is another slight to Elisabetta. She wanted her husband buried in Italy after a Roman Catholic funeral mass."

Mr. Brundage said, "In any event, the funeral cannot take place until after the coroner's inquest. I understand that is to be held on Monday."

"Yes," said Sarah. "I received notice today that I am to appear to give testimony. You will have to appear also, won't you, Mr. Brundage?"

"I will."

"There is a bed and breakfast in St. Ives that is quite comfortable. I believe my husband and I will stay there tomorrow night so we will be on time for the inquest the next morning. I can give you the telephone number if you would like to ring them," Sarah said to the solicitor.

Catherine greatly admired her mother-in-law. Her concern for the solicitor when she was dealing with such difficult circumstances was nothing short of angelic. Her own mother had risen to the occasion as well.

What would they all learn at the inquest on Monday?

Chapter Four

The St. Ives courthouse was built from the same granite as Jonathan's cottage. Windows were few, giving a somewhat dim aspect to their courtroom. The coroner, in this case, a fairly young solicitor, was bald on top, with dark fringe around his head. His horn-rimmed spectacles were in the current style. He was also quite chatty. Catherine would not be surprised to see him play up to the twelve men and women who made up the jury.

The coroner began. "Ladies and gentlemen, my name is Tate and I am the coroner for St. Ives. We are gathered today pursuant to long-standing English law to determine how Jonathan Haverford, a resident of London, met an untimely death while apparently walking along our local seaside cliffs several days ago. Because of the gravity of the event, I have assembled a jury who will deliver their verdict concerning the cause of his death after all testimony is heard.

"We will be told by our esteemed Medical Examiner, Dr. Farnsworth, the condition of Mr. Haverford's body after it was found by a local fisherman. This will include the doctor's observations during his examinations of the deceased concerning the manner in which our visitor from London met his unfortunate demise. Also, we shall call witnesses to help you determine the circumstances which led to said demise, whether by accident or another."

Catherine had a small notebook on her knee where she was determined to take notes. Harry sat next to her with his arm along the bench back, just touching his mother's shoulder on the other side of Catherine. On the seat in front of her sat Elisabetta Haverford. Mr. Milton with his two friends down from London sat just behind Catherine.

First, they heard from the Medical Examiner. In response to questions by Mr. Tate, he explained in great detail how time and means of death had been determined. The victim appeared to have been knifed from behind with a narrow instrument, possibly a stiletto or a switchblade. The blade perforated the heart making death almost instantaneous. Thereafter, his body was rolled across the ground and over a high cliff, thereafter, landing on the seashore, which contained several large rocks, and a small cave not visible from the top.

"In your opinion," asked the coroner, "Could this knifing have been done by either a man *or* a woman?"

"Oh, yes," the M.E. said. "The wound was delivered with an upward thrust which could have been managed by a man or a woman. The body also had a variety of scrapes and bruises which appeared to have been suffered by Mr. Haverford during or after his fall from the cliff to the shore below. These injuries were post-mortem, showing that he was already dead when he fell."

Catherine clenched her teeth and drew her arms around her. *Gruesome.* Two of the jurors closed their eyes and another covered her mouth.

The coroner said, "Thank you, doctor. You may step down. The court now calls Mrs. Elisabetta Haverford, wife of the deceased."

The woman looked so changed from yesterday Catherine wouldn't have known her. She stood up and walked slowly and confidently toward the witness box. All the jurors' eyes were fixed on her. She kept her long shiny black hair loose and wore a fitted red silk dress with matching hat and high heels. The model fairly dripped furs. She gracefully ascended the steps to the witness box, then turned and faced the audience, lifting the veil that had covered her face.

A buzz of conversation arose among the observers and the coroner intervened. "There will be order in this court. Order! Bailiff, be prepared to remove any disorderly persons from this proceeding!"

The sizeable bailiff stood up with a stern expression on his face and the audience slowly quieted.

Elisabetta had large, deep brown eyes and her dress accentuated a perfect figure. She opened a small red purse, retrieved a tiny lace handkerchief and dabbed at her eyes without causing any damage to her makeup.

Harry leaned toward Catherine and whispered, "I had no idea she was such a *grande dame.*"

After the coroner had established that the model was Jonathan's wife and lived in Milan, Italy, he asked, "When did you arrive in Cornwall? Was your husband expecting you?"

Elisabetta responded in her accented English. "No. He was not. I did not come to see him. I came to get my children to take them back to Italy. I arrived on the afternoon of the 13th."

"Please tell the court what your children were doing in England, Mrs. Haverford."

The model raised her chin and looked across the courtroom. "My husband came to Milan when I was in Paris doing a shoot. He knew that I would not be there. It was last September. He took my children away and brought them here to England. He had, without telling me, enrolled them both in boarding school. Adriana is only eight years old. Not only were they away from me in a foreign country, they were away from one another for the first time in their lives. Giovanni is ten. Adriana is eight.

"My children and I write to one another. They tell me they hate the English schools. I knew they were in London for their break and would eventually go down to the sea after Jonathan's nephew's wedding. I came to get them to take them home to Italy.

I was not bringing them back to England. I did not care what Jonathan said."

"Please tell the court exactly what happened when you informed your husband of your purpose."

"He was, of course, very angry with me. This I had expected. Then he threatened to cut me off financially. This I had also expected, but I can manage very well without his money. I am a fashion model. I am in very much demand."

"For now," said Mr. Tate. "How much longer will you be in high demand?"

Elisabetta looked sharply at the coroner before turning back to the audience and responding.

"I take very good care of myself. I eat properly. I sleep properly. I stopped two photo sessions in Paris and Milan to travel to this country for my children. I am more in demand than ever before. I will be able to model for another twenty years, by which time my children shall be raised and on their own. I have thought of this, you see.

"You English! You think that because I am Italian and a model, I must be stupid. But in Italy, you must understand, it is the women in the families who have the brains. I am *il capo donna*. I have earned my own way since I was 16."

"What about your children? What do they want to do?"

"Adriana is terrified she will have to go back to school. She was miserable there. Giovanni is very, very intelligent. He began to like the school after the first month. But, still, he longs for Milano, for his friends."

Putting both hands on the rail, she leaned into it and looked straight at the coroner. "I will tell you something else. My husband left me a huge amount of money in his will if I allow my children to be raised 'in the English manner.' If I don't, I will get only one-tenth of the money. I choose the little amount and I choose my children."

"Did you know of this intent of your husband?"

"I did. He told me. He made a mistake. He thought I loved

money more than my children. English women are cold. They happily send their children away when they are Adriana's age. Jonathan didn't know how much I love my children. He thought money would make me leave them." She dabbed at her eyes with the handkerchief.

Catherine clutched her hands into fists in her lap. That had certainly been the scenario in her family. She and William, her brother, had both spent most of their lives away from their parents in school. She and Harry were not going to raise their children that way. Catherine felt an unexpected sympathy with Betta Haverford. Would a woman this passionate kill to raise her children by herself?

Sadly, Catherine thought she might. Though Catherine didn't have children of her own, she felt the model's sincerity. She also had no difficulty imagining Elisabetta killing her husband if he kept her children away from her and in English boarding schools. But where would she find a switchblade?

The coroner excused the model, who held everyone's attention as she returned to her seat and called Mr. Milton to the stand. He made a good impression with his navy pinstriped suit and Oxford school tie. The coroner asked him to tell the court about his acquaintance with the victim.

"Jonathan and I had known each other since we were eight. We both went to Harrow and later, Oxford. Since we finished university, we have remained close friends. We often met here in Cornwall where he has a cottage."

"What is your profession that allows you such freedom?"

"I breed and race thoroughbreds. My stable is in Kent. My off-season is wintertime. My mares are all bred and resting right now. We will become quite busy during the foaling in the spring."

The coroner nodded. He then settled himself back in his chair. "Tell us about this little gathering."

"We have two other friends we have come through school with—George Baxter and Viscount Lawrence Fawcett. Because the four of us are unmarried, we formed the tradition of getting together for the Christmas hols down here in St. Ives at Jonathan's cottage. We spend a few weeks here."

The coroner nodded. "Excellent. Now tell us what happened starting Friday, the thirteenth of the month."

"Very well. Friday during luncheon, Mrs. Haverford arrived, in full regalia with all her guns loaded, so to speak. I had no idea that Jon was married, much less that he was a father! She brought his children with her. They had just come down from school. They appeared to be quite fond of Jonathan, running to him before he knew what was happening, laughing and embracing him. His wife just stood there, observing. Her look was a bad combination of pain and annoyance."

"Was Mr. Haverford happy to see her?"

"Obviously not. She said something along the lines of 'I don't know why, but they seem to be fond of you'."

"All right. Just report the conversation, as well as you remember."

"He introduced her and the children to us. Lawrence and I were fairly bowled over." Mr. Milton frowned and pinched the bridge of his nose. "Before we knew where we were, he took her off to the study while she was remonstrating with him in Italian. To our further surprise, the children knew George, so, at his request, they began telling him all about school. I must say, from their mother's account, you'd think they would have hated it, but they were actually quite enthusiastic. Giovanni was a football star, and Adriana had a best friend whom she missed terribly. But she had missed Mummy and Fox while she was in school."

The coroner's eyebrows shot up. "Who or what is Fox?" he asked.

"Oh. He's Jon's man. His valet, cook, and general factotum. You haven't met Fox? He's a nanny when needed, as well. Man's a wonder. He was in the trenches with Jon. Jon saved his life and later Fox saved Jon's. That's him, there in the back row."

The coroner looked seriously displeased. "Stand, if you please, Mr. Fox."

Catherine looked over her shoulder at the tall, sandy-haired man with outsized ears that stood away from his head. He nodded at the coroner. She wondered how the police had missed him in their inquiries. No wonder the coroner was put out.

Mr. Tate said, "Please make yourself available when we adjourn these proceedings for lunch, Mr. Fox. You may be seated."

He turned to Mr. Milton once more. "You were telling us that Mr. Haverford had just gone with his wife into the study."

"Right. Well, Fawcett and I gave Baxter the third degree. We were at a loss to understand why Haverford had kept something as major as a wife and children from us. Baxter said Jon didn't want things to change among us. He liked his routine. Also, he was a bit embarrassed. He could be very Victorian, and well . . . to be quite frank, Elisabetta was not the sort of creature one married." Milton looked down at Elisabetta, frowning. He colored. Catherine could not see her expression as the model was sitting in front of her, but she did notice that Elisabetta sat up stiffly, her shoulders rigid.

After a moment, Mr. Milton said, "I wager that she had been his mistress for years. She entrapped him by letting herself fall pregnant with Giovanni. He wanted the child to have a father. So, he married her. But he had no intention of bringing her to England. Nor did she want to be brought. Soon she had Adriana. Jon was in Italy frequently and Baxter told us that Haverford had bought a nice flat in Milan where they all lived together when he was in the country."

Elisabetta rose, pointed her finger at Milton and said, "You make it sound as if Jonathan was ashamed of me. He wasn't. We were deeply in love for many years. But we disagreed about the children. That tore us apart."

The coroner thundered. "Sit down, if you please, Mrs. Haverford! I know this is difficult for you, but you must not interfere with the proceedings."

He turned back to Mr. Milton. "Briefly, then: what happened after the confrontation in the study?"

"Elisabetta joined me in the kitchen with the children. We were preparing dinner—Lobster Newburg. She didn't speak except to ask me what she could do to help. Jonathan came downstairs after about half an hour. He said goodbye and went off to the Tregowyn family dinner with his sister, Mrs. Buchanan. I had gone to bed for the night by the time he got home. I didn't see him again before he was killed." Milton folded his hands in his lap.

"What was your impression of Mrs. Haverford?" Mr. Tate asked.

"I was so shocked I could barely speak to her. As you can see for yourself, she is a splendid-looking woman. As she worked with me in the kitchen, her hands shook. I got the impression that she was barely containing a great deal of rage."

"When did you become aware that Mr. Haverford was missing?"

"The next afternoon when Mr. Harold Bascombe came to the cottage looking for his brother. He had missed the wedding. It didn't make sense. He was very fond of Harry Bascombe."

"What did you think had happened?" asked the coroner.

"I was flummoxed. Especially when Baxter rang Jon's townhouse. Fox said he had talked to him the night before, and Jon asked him to come down to St. Ives. We began searching then. He wasn't anywhere. We searched for miles up and down the cliffs and beaches. The beach where we later found him was empty at that time. We should have taken a boat in and looked more carefully, but we had no idea about the cave."

"You didn't report him missing to the police."

"It never occurred to us that he could be dead. George and Lawrence went back up to town. They had an idea he might have lost his memory. They were going to look for him there. I stayed with Mrs. Haverford. I felt someone should. The whole thing was deuced queer."

"Now that his body has been recovered, what do you think happened?"

"He must have been out on the cliffs and some desperate soul came along and tried to rob him. But that doesn't really make sense. Why would he kill Jonathan?"

"How were your relations with Mr. Haverford?" asked Mr. Tate.

Mr. Milton, who had been animated since Mrs. Haverford's interruption of his testimony, now sunk back into the chair. "Nothing new there. Things were just as usual."

"You will forgive me, Mr. Milton, but what was the usual?"

"The four of us are very used to one another. Winter is rather a bore, as far as I'm concerned. It helps to spend it with Fawcett, Baxter, and Haverford. We all have disastrous histories with women. Except for Haverford, it seems. None of us had family. Or so we thought. We spent a lot of time playing cards, billiards, or listening to Fawcett perform. He takes us through the works of various poets and novelists during the evenings. We are currently working our way through T.S. Eliot. He's brilliant, and our viscount gives a marvelous interp. We spent a lot of evenings rather the worse for drink, trying to make Eliothim out. It's jolly good fun."

The witness sobered. "We shall miss Haverford. He was the brightest star in our little firmament."

"Thank you very much Mr. Milton. You may step down. Ladies and gentlemen of the jury, we will take an hour break for luncheon. We will start this afternoon's proceedings promptly at 1:00.

Chapter Five

Catherine stood and turned to Harry. "Well! That was enlightening. I don't really know what to think about your uncle," she said in a low voice.

"Then, it's good you don't have the job of judging him," said Harry shortly.

Catherine felt as though she had been reprimanded. Retreating into herself, she realized that Harry was right. It wasn't her place to judge. "I'm sorry. What I really meant was that so far, I've seen him only through his wife's and his bosom friend's eyes. I find it difficult to make him out. Elisabetta's view and his friends' view are so different. And then I have my own developing view, which doesn't fit. Why don't we have some lunch and you can tell me about the man you knew. You're right, it isn't my place to judge him, but to find his murderer. I think it's important to see what other people think about him, though."

"You're right. I'm sorry I snapped at you," said her husband. "I'm angry about his death. Let's put this behind us for a bit. There's a pub right down on the water that dates back to 1312. I used to go there with my uncle. It's a bit on the rough side, but it doesn't play to the tourists. Not that there are any this time of year."

They left the courthouse and took a winding stone path down to the harbor's edge.

"It's much colder than I thought it would be," said Catherine. Harry put his arm around her waist. He was warmly dressed in an overcoat and scarf, whereas she wore only her winter tweeds. Fortunately, a warm cloche hat covered her head. She wore a lot of cloche hats these days as her hair was still growing in patches where she had injuries from their last close call.

The Sloop Inn was not fancy and had clearly withstood many a storm over the centuries, reminding Catherine forcefully as old places always did, of the brevity of her own three score and ten. It had probably been constructed of limestone, though it was hard to tell since it had weathered to a dirty brown. She wondered if the slate roof was modern. As they entered, most of the day's light was shut out. There were few windows and no electric light. Only a fireplace and oil lanterns lit the inside. Harry led the way to the bar.

"What's the catch of the day?" he asked.

"Crab," said the red-faced man whose age it was impossible to tell.

"We'll each have crab and chips then, with a draft of the house ale," said Harry. He led her to a table then and helped her to negotiate the bench seat. Sitting down next to her, he said, "What do you think?"

"About the Sloop Inn or the case?"

"The case. I can guess your thoughts about this place, but it is a true Cornish experience. You have to grant me that."

"Yes," said Catherine. "Well, now. I find myself regrettably in sympathy with Elisabetta. But I also wouldn't be surprised if she stabbed your uncle."

"I know what you mean. She's very elemental in her passions. I wouldn't be surprised to learn she was connected to the Mafia."

Catherine laughed. "Oh, Harry. You're type-casting. Just because she's Italian?"

"Probably. But like you, I'm rather drawn to her. I do see that my uncle may not have done right by her, taking her children like that."

"Boarding schools can be brutal, Harry. Mine was."

"Ah. That's why you have such strong character."

"What was yours like?" she inquired.

"Ah, not much like Harrow, I suspect. My mother made sure they didn't employ corporal punishment."

Two baskets containing whole crabs, crab crackers, and chips were placed on the paper-covered table. They were followed by tankards of ale.

Harry started to show Catherine how to crack open the crab, but she forestalled him.

"My dear young man," she said. "I am an experienced Cornishwoman. I've been cracking crabs since I could toddle."

"Maybe you should teach me, then. I aways make a mess of it."

Catherine said, "Well, since we've only an hour's lunch, I'll take pity on you." Taking his basket, she skillfully cracked open his crab in all the important spots and then did her own.

"I am humbled," said Harry. "You should take advantage of it. It doesn't happen often."

"All right then. I think I deserve my own motorcar."

He laughed. They ate their crab with single-minded concentration.

"All right. My uncle. A splendid man. There's a reason I chose him to stand up for me at our wedding. I always thought he was an honest and fine bloke. Rather a male version of my mother. He didn't have any preconceived idea of what I should be like. He seemed to enjoy the process of life. You know, the kind of person who gives his best to each day, no matter what the circumstances."

"What was life like for him and your mother growing up?"

My grandfather died when my mother was in her teenage years. She adored him. He was the reason she became a doctor. He had no preconceived ideas about how women should go about living their lives. He was remarkable that way. Mother didn't want to go away to school, so he let her learn medicine by accompanying him and listening to him explain the cases. My aunt Patricia was always a bit jealous of them. She was older and had wanted to go to boarding school when she was twelve, so Grandfather let her go. Aunt Patricia is brilliant but pursued by demons."

"What demons?" Catherine asked.

"Perfectionism. For herself and everyone around her."

"All right. Back to your Uncle Jonathan . . ." Catherine prompted.

"He saw that I was cut out for university. He took me on trips to the continent over my school holidays. Like him, I enjoyed a smattering of everything—art, of course, music, history, everything but literature. I discovered that on my own. Then I was consumed. He would read my assignments along with me while it was term time, and then we would discuss them through the holidays while we traveled. It was ideal. Every youngster should have that opportunity."

"And your father?"

"He is a businessman and a very good one. Our brains and interests are built differently. He's always treated me well, however. I'm far more my mother's son. Father and my sister Mary's husband get along like a house afire. James is a queer bird who hatched in a foreign place. Aunt Patricia and he are mates. His life is and always has been science."

Harry continued, "I'm beginning to see why Uncle Jonathan wanted his children to have an English education as opposed to the Italian alternative, but I still don't understand why his daughter had to begin at eight years' old in a boarding school. He loved Italy. Why was he so anxious for them to be raised in England?"

"Maybe it didn't have to do with the education itself, but rather the surroundings," said Catherine. "We have no idea what kind of mother Elisabetta is."

"The more I think about it, the more I feel you're right. I imagine it will come clear if we're patient," said Harry.

Their last scrap of crab had been eaten and the basket of rolls demolished. It was time to get back to the coroner's inquest.

On their way back up the hill to the courthouse, Harry told her of the legend of the unlucky portreeve who was having lunch with the St. Ives provost marshal back in 1549. The marshal had bade the portreeve, John Payne, to have a gallows built outside while they were eating lunch. Afterwards, they walked out to see the handy work. The Provost Marshal ordered Payne to mount the gallows. He was promptly hanged for being a 'busy rebel.'"

"That happened here in St. Ives?" she asked.

"Yes. And I've always suspected that the inn where they lunched was the Sloop Inn, though I have been wrong on occasion."

Catherine punched him playfully in the arm. "Very entertaining. I hope neither of us is hanged here, however. Now we go back to the hearing. It is worth noting that this may be the beginning of a process that will result in a modern hanging. Right here in 1935."

"Will they think us barbarians a century from now?" wondered Harry.

* * *

The first witness to be called that afternoon was Harry's uncle's man, Mr. Archibald Fox. He looked far from composed as he sat in the witness box. With ritual-like repetition, Fox's hands went from scratching his ear to straightening his tie to shooting his cuffs and fiddling with his cufflinks.

Mr. Tate asked, "Mr. Fox, how long have you been in the employ of Mr. Jonathan Haverford?"

"Since the War, sir," the valet replied.

"Did you accompany Mr. Haverford on his travels to Italy?"

"Oh, yes, sir. We spent a lot of time in Italy."

"When did his relationship with Mrs. Haverford commence?"

"Let me see . . . It was around 1922, sir. The year we came

upon our first Bronzino. She wasn't fashion modeling then. She was singing in a nightclub in Palermo."

"Ah. Yes. When did she commence modeling?"

When Mr. Fox swallowed, Catherine traced his Adam's apple going up and down. He also liked to chew the side of his lip. "Mr. Haverford arranged for her to be trained. She got her first modeling job in 1923, the year we moved from Sicily to the flat he bought in Milan. That way she could have access to the most prestigious modeling jobs with the clothing designers."

"In fact, it sounds as though Mr. Haverford was very generous."

"He was." The cufflink Fox was playing with fell to the floor. With a quick glance at the coroner, he bent and collected the errant jewelry.

The coroner continued, "And then, if you will excuse the indelicacy, she fell pregnant in 1925 or '26?"

"Yes. Master Giovanni, or Jon, was born in January, 1926. This year he will be 10."

"Mr. Haverford was a doting father?"

"Yes. Very much so. That is why he decided to do the thing properly. He married Mrs. Haverford that year. He also employed a nanny for the children. Francesca has been with us ten years now."

"Ah. Francesca, eh?" queried Tate. "No one has mentioned a nanny. What kind of policework do we have here? Is Nanny here in the courtroom?"

Fox bit his lip and his eyes scanned the room. "No, sir. I would have been surprised if she were. Who would watch the children if she were here?"

"Quite. Are you on good terms with the children? Could you possibly fill in for the nanny while she comes to court today?"

"Oh, yes sir! I am very fond of the children and have cared for them on many occasions in Milan."

"Good. Now then, who do you think killed Mr. Haverford?"

"The Mafia, sir."

The jury stirred, gasping collectively. Catherine caught her breath. Surely, he was joking!

Mr. Tate stared. There was a hubbub in the courtroom, particularly in the jury box . The coroner used rapped his knuckles on the table. "Silence!" He leaned closer to Fox. "The Mafia? On what grounds?"

"The weapon. The switchblade is one of the Mafia's preferred weapons."

"But, to my knowledge, Mr. Haverford had no dealings with the Mafia! Or am I mistaken?"

"Mrs. Haverford is the daughter of a Sicilian Mafia don, sir. The don might not have liked Mr. Haverford's plan to turn Master Jon into a proper English gentleman, sir."

More gasping from the jury.

Catherine and Harry exchanged looks. *The Mafia?* Truly? Harry was right? The coroner sighed. "Perhaps that may be a correct deduction, far-fetched though it sounds on first hearing. I don't recall any other death in the Duchy of Cornwall where a switchblade was involved. Did Mrs. Haverford have close relations with the Don?"

"Oh, yes, sir. I met him on several occasions in Italy. He seemed to be a very doting grandpapa. He always appeared with many toys and gifts, so many that he sometimes required the help of an . . . assistant who was quite a large fellow and never said anything. His assistant could carry any number of toys without any difficulty."

For the first time, the seemingly cold-hearted notion to take the children out of Italy to put them in English boarding school made emotional sense to Catherine. Of course, he would try to remove his children from a life dictated by the Mafia!

Fox was told to step down and accompany the detective to Caravaggio House to take over for the Nanny so she could come to court to testify.

Next interview was with Detective Inspector Ross. He was quite defensive about having failed to interview the valet and nanny, however his testimony did not contain anything new other than where the body was found. Catherine was a bit disappointed in him. It looked as though if anyone was going to be brought to book on this case it would not be by the police.

The next witness called was Viscount Lawrence Fawcett, of the Shropshire Fawcetts. Catherine was always interested in minor nobility. They were often scorned by those bearing greater titles and shamelessly toad-eaten by the merchant class who had everything but a title.

Lord Fawcett was so white-blond that it was difficult to see any hair against his scalp. According to Harry he was a money-making machine, he was so good at doling out investment advice that Fawcett could make money in any market. She wondered if the coroner had heard of him.

"My lord," the coroner addressed him, "How would you describe your relationship with the late Mr. Haverford?"

"I think I may say I am one of his closest friends. Apart from that, I am also his business advisor. I find the money he needs when he is investing in a new painting."

"That's certainly interesting. Just how often did he need your financial services?

"Not as often as he used to. He can finance his own acquisitions these days. Uh . . . he could."

"Did he have any debts to you at the time of his death?"

"No. His debts were paid in full with interest."

The coroner leaned forward to observe the witness closely. "Could you please advise the court of your observations and movements on the 13th and 14 of December?"

The Viscount folded his hands in his lap. "I don't suppose I can add too much to what Milton has said. We had just enjoyed a week's holiday at the cottage. We knew of his obligations with the Bascombe-Tregowyn wedding, but it didn't concern us. We had no idea we were going to be drawn into such a tragedy. The first surprise was that Haverford was married. Couldn't imagine it."

He paused and looked out over the courtroom until he saw Mrs. Haverford. He gave her the hint of a smile.

"The next shock was being introduced to the posterity! None of us, in our various marital adventures have produced any progeny. After I got over the shock and observed him with them, I realized he made a good father. I regret that he won't be able to carry on there."

"You are not married, I take it?" asked Tate.

"I don't see how that figures into the investigation," protested the Viscount.

"But you are not conducting this investigation. I am, on behalf of King George."

"Well then, for the sake of King George, my wife ran off last year with a Spanish Fascist. One of Franco's intimates, I understand. I am in the midst of a divorce. For all the good it will do her. Senor de la Rosa is Catholic. He won't marry a divorced woman."

"Thank you," said the coroner. "Can you enlighten us on the nature of relations
between the Haverfords?"

"I have no clue, really. I only saw them that once together. When they were quarreling about Jonathan having 'stolen the children.' I assumed their relationship was mostly about the children, at this point, although she is quite a beauty. As for this most recent encounter between them, it was just as Milton said. He tried to calm her, then without any public explanation, he took her back to the study. Jon must have left for the Tregowyn dinner through the back door. Unlike Milton, I waited up for him. He got in at half past twelve. He greeted me and then said, "Don't pelt me questions about Elisabetta right now, if you have a heart. I'm going to get a good sleep. Tomorrow will be difficult."

I said something like, 'You'd best come upstairs to the extra bed in my room. Your wife has taken the master suite.' Then I told him Fox had brought all his things upstairs to my room. He decided to sit down and have a brandy, after all. We just discussed his nephew's wedding and his fondest hope that the marriage his would be a success, as our marriages hadn't had much to recommend the institution.

At that point, I recognized that he was dashed unhappy about Elisabetta. He had hoped with the removal of the children to England, he would have to see her less. He said one would never take her for a concerned mother. Nanny and Fox had raised his children. Elisabetta put all of her energy into her modeling career. She was often gone weeks at a time. He was quite surprised she was kicking up such a fuss. Mother of the Year, she was not.

"Of course, that is before he told me about the Mafia. I suspect they would have been putting Elisabetta through the paces of being a good Italian Mafia mother raising the next generation of criminals. Do you know, I never thought of it before, but I wonder if Elisabetta isn't a bit frightened? According to Jonathan, this fierce mother dog she has exhibited earlier this morning, is not the normal role she acts. Jonathan was the more involved parent. Adriana and Giovanni seem to be pawns in their relationship. At least, as far as Elisabetta is concerned. As long as she has them, she has Jonathan's money."

At this Elisabetta stood again. This time her invective was in furious Italian. The coroner signaled for the bailiff to remove her from the courtroom. She was still railing at the viscount, the coroner, and the bailiff as she was being removed.

Catherine wished she could understand what she was saying. Since she didn't understand the model's language in words, she had been forced to listen to the tone and the emotion. The viscount was right. Her rant had started as outrage, but the more wound-up she got, Catherine thought she detected fear in the Italian's tone and demeanor.

"So you preceded the victim to bed? How long was it before he came up?" asked the coroner.

"He didn't come to bed 'til after I was asleep, and he was up and gone before I got up."

"You're sure the bed was slept in?" the coroner pressed.

The viscount considered. "Not completely sure. But his pajamas were gone, and the bed was mussed."

"Pardon me for asking," said the coroner with a smile. "What time did you awaken?"

"It was late, I confess. Probably after nine. I assumed he had left for the wedding. If I may ask, what was he wearing when he was found?"

"His walking kit," the coroner said in triumphant tones. "He would have had to get it from his bedroom. You have been most helpful, Viscount. You may step down."

Catherine immediately saw from the coroner's near glee that in order to get the walking kit, either at night or in the morning, Harry's uncle would have encountered his wife. Was she sleeping? Did she impulsively follow him out to have another go at changing his mind?

She could have mussed the bed and taken the clothes Jon had worn to the dinner at Tregowyn Manor away from the viscount's room. As a good Mafia daughter she carried a switchblade.

He called Mrs. Haverford's ladies maid. He seemed surprised to find that the police had actually thought to summon her. There was only one difficulty. She only spoke Italian. He asked if there were any in the courtroom who could speak the language. At first, only the nanny raised her gloved hand. However, Catherine thought that he must have discounted her because of her closeness to Elisabetta.

Finally, Viscount Fawcett stood and said he would "give it a go." A chair was placed as near as possible to the witness box.

The coroner opened a box sitting on the table in front of his bench. From it, he withdrew a tortoiseshell instrument. As he pushed the button on the side, a gleaming blade flicked out. Harry leaned down and whispered, "A very impressive switchblade."

The maid's complacent face changed into a mask of horror. Her eyes were large and she pressed her hand over her mouth.

The coroner put the knife back in the box. "I take it, you recognize this?" he asked.

A spate of rapid Italian fell from the woman at an hysterical volume. The viscount translated. "That is a horrible thing! It is the devil's tool. I will not name it!"

The coroner sighed. "Have you ever seen anything like this among your mistress's belongings?"

"My sainted Signora? No. And No. Never!" Her aged face closed as though by a drawstring.

"Is there anything you can tell us about the relationship between Signora and Signore Haverford?"

More Italian followed.

The translation was: "He adores her. The flowers, the jewelry, the presents . . . they are very happy together."

Catherine saw the moment when Tate gave up the interview as a bad job. He dismissed the maid and viscount and called the nanny.

The signorina was dressed in a simple fawn-colored sheath dress. Her reddish blonde hair was drawn back in a bun, as though she were a Victorian schoolmistress. She still wore her coat—a dull black affair that reached the ground. Even without the accoutrements of makeup and flattering dress, the woman was a beauty. Her English was as good as her employer's. The coroner showed her the instrument in the box.

When she spoke, the nanny could scarcely be heard and she kept her eyes on her lap. "I don't know what that is. I have never seen one before."

Chapter Six

"Thank you, Signorina. How long have you served as nanny in the Haverford household?"

Her voice grew softer if that was possible, "Ten years."

"But you also model?"

The woman merely nodded. Catherine found it very difficult to imagine this creature striding out on the catwalk. She seemed to shrink from being seen at all.

"Does modeling interfere with your work?"

She paused as though trying to form her answer. When she spoke, Catherine could not hear her.

"You must speak up, signorina. So the jury can hear you."

"To model is to work," she whispered. "To be a nanny—that is not work for me. I do it for love."

"In your opinion, was Mrs. Haverford close to her father?" the coroner asked.

"Oh, yes."

"Did they share like ambitions for Giovanni? Did Mrs. Haverford want her son to be the next don?"

"Yes. The boy will be a very important and powerful man one day," insisted the nanny.

Catherine suddenly grew ill. Jonathan's "kidnapping" of his own children was the act of a desperate man. Harry's parents were to counter the don by raising Jon to live an alternative life to the one he would have had in Sicily. How did young Jon feel about this?

The coroner put this line of questioning in train, but Francesca closed down. She obviously realized that Elisabetta's vision of her son's future gave her an excellent motive for killing his English father.

"Does Mrs. Haverford have a brother?" the coroner asked.

"He died in infancy," said the nanny. "Diphtheria."

So. Jon was the heir.

The coroner dismissed the nanny and recalled Elisabetta to the stand.

When she had seated herself, he asked, "Tell me, Mrs. Haverford. Is your father in England at present?"

The woman looked straight ahead, appearing to focus on the back wall of the room at a point above everyone's head.

"I do not know."

"Did he make the journey with you from Italy to England?"

"My father is very old-fashioned. He believed we needed an escort. The children had never flown before."

"So he came with you."

"Yes."

"Where is he now?"

The model wet her lips and repeated, "I do not know. I believe he had friends from home who were staying in England. He may have gone to visit them."

"I see. He has not been in touch with you, even though it was in all the papers when your husband was murdered?"

"My father does not speak or read English."

"Ah. All right, Mrs. Haverford. You are excused."

When the women had left the stand, the coroner stated that the inquest was concluded for that day and would reconvene at ten o'clock the following morning.

* * *

"Well, what do you think?" Harry asked Catherine as they left the courthouse and strode towards his motorcar. A few reporters tried to get Elisabetta to give them an interview. She dismissed them, her nose in the air, as though they smelled bad.

"I'm completely at sea," she said. "We don't know if he was killed at night or in the morning, so everyone is a suspect. I imagine Elisabetta's father is here in England. He is at the top of my list."

"At the top of the jury's list, too, I imagine. I wonder if he will make an appearance if his daughter is accused."

"Your guess is as good as mine. What a can of worms."

"Yes. I agree. Do you think your uncle would have gone walking late at night when he got home from our rehearsal dinner? Doesn't it make more sense that he would walk in the morning?" Catherine put her arm through her husband's as they strolled to the B & B.

"You know, my uncle loved the sea at any time of day. That's why he stayed here so much. He said it centered him."

"Was he troubled about something?" Catherine asked.

"I don't really know. He's always been that way. He used to discourse about Britain owing its wealth and stability to the sea—its provider and protector. He knew the navel battles in great detail and could discourse at length about the East India Company and its business acumen. But he never took me into his confidence about anything personal. To him, I was still a child, I think."

"It's incomprehensible to me that he never told your mother or anyone about his children. I must say, I can understand his putting them in boarding school now that we know about their grandfather the Mafia don," Catherine said, pulling her coat more tightly around her.

"Perhaps I should have asked about your lineage before we married," Harry said.

"Well, never mind. There are one or two Cornish smugglers who hated to pay import duties. Not to mention the line that goes back to the Conqueror," she replied looking down her nose at him.

They had reached the B & B. "It seems awfully early to return to the bed and breakfast, I think," said Catherine.

He put his arm about her and hugged her to his side. "I don't know about that . . ."

Catherine laughed. "Dinner first, darling. I need my energy replenished."

At that moment, Harry's father caught up with them. "We're going to The Grotto for dinner. We'd like you to join us."

Harry and Catherine agreed, and fifteen minutes later they had arrived at the fashionable fish eatery. Harry's Aunt Patricia accompanied them.

The aroma of fried fish greeted them, and they were seated at a table by the window. A heavy fog had descended outside, which, together with the winter's falling darkness, made the indoors seem cozy and warm. A free-standing fireplace stood in the center of the dining room. Catherine's mother-in-law asked to be seated nearby.

"I feel sure that Jon must have gone walking in weather like this and lost his footing," Patricia said.

"Let's talk of something else, dear," said Sarah Bascombe.

"Do you teach at the University in Edinburgh?" asked Catherine.

"I did," she answered curtly. Turning to her sister, she said, "Felix has left me."

"Oh! Pat," Sarah said. "I'm so sorry! When did this happen?"

"Right before the holidays, of course. Thank heavens I own our flat, free and clear. I don't know what I'm going to do for income. God rest his soul, but I was expecting more from Jon."

"You don't work at the clinic any longer?" asked Harry.

"No," his aunt said shortly. "I haven't for some time. New management. They didn't appreciate my suggestions."

"Oh! My dear! You must come to us, of course," said Sarah. "We just rattle around in that old place."

Catherine was slightly amused. The "old place" was a lovely Georgian manor house seated like a jewel in the Hampshire Downs. She thew a glance at her father-in-law who looked vexed. Catherine could sympathize with him not wanting to have his sister-in-law living under his nose. But how like Sarah to have offered!

"No, thank you, Sarah. I'm going to sell my Bronzino. It should bring a very good price, don't you think? When that money runs out, I will sell my flat and go to Wales or somewhere similarly inexpensive."

Catherine thought the woman brave to think of uprooting herself at her age. She had to admire her desire for independence.

Catherine and Harry had both ordered the Shrimp Scampi which turned out to be wholly delectable. The topic switched to Harry's sister, Mary who was not with them in Cornwall.

"How is Mary doing?" asked Harry. "Isn't she due about now?"

"Yes. Any day. And she's on complete bed rest. I'm watching her for pre-eclampsia. If it develops, we shall have to deliver her early. I feel very uneasy being so far away from her," said Sarah. "It was so hard on Mary to miss your wedding, darling."

Patricia issued a noise that sounded suspiciously like a snort. "And James? Has he filed for divorce yet?"

"He hasn't confided in us," Sarah said. "They are still living apart which suits both of them, I think."

"When will they release Uncle Jon's remains so we can take him back to Hampshire?" Harry wanted to know.

"Not until after the inquest," said his father. "I say, that wife of his is an Italian fire cracker. I worry about those children if they aren't to be educated here in England. Mafia! Imagine! It certainly never crossed my mind that we might have a connection in that direction. I wish there were some way we could find to keep little Jon and Adriana in this country."

"Not if their mother doesn't bite at the bribe in the will. I must say, as busy as she is going here and there for her work, it doesn't sound like she spends a large amount of time at home," said Harry.

"And the nanny doesn't look up to the job of providing guidance for them. I would feel much better if you and mother had custody of them."

"I don't fancy battling that woman for custody," said Harold. "But we could. The children are English according to the law."

I feel sorry for them," confessed Catherine. "They are so bright and intelligent."

"Well, my money's on her as a murderess. If the jury is doing its duty, it will remand Elisabetta into the custody of the Crown and she will be tried for murder," Harold said.

"She does seem to be the clear suspect," agreed Harry. "But it's too early to tell. I don't know Jon's friends well, but they deal with a lot of money between them. Something might be irregular, and Uncle Jon could have known." Now that he had finished his dinner, he went about lighting his pipe. "I have to say, I find it suspicious that two of them left for London when he was missing."

"Do you really?" said Catherine. "I thought I was the only one who noticed that."

Harry grinned, "Wither thou goest . . ."

She grasped his hand under the table.

Catherine's interest in the subject flagged as Patricia aired her opinions about the benefits of boarding school.

The topic passed from there to concern for the health of the King who was very ill with pleurisy.

"The Prince of Wales is entirely unsuited to be King if he puts That Woman before his duty!" exclaimed Patricia, speaking of Mrs. Wallis Simpson, the woman everyone loved to hate.

This statement elicited many comments and took up the rest of the dinner conversation.

Harry and Catherine said their good nights to everyone and proceeded back to the bed and breakfast on their own. It was still a novel feeling not having to say goodnight to Harry outside her door as well. Harry evidently felt the same, for as soon as the door closed, he pulled her to him and began to kiss her in a very satisfactory manner.

* * *

George Baxter was the inquest's first witness the next day. He was a pleasant looking man in an English sort of way. He had dark brown hair, well oiled, and arranged back from his forehead. There was nothing outstanding or unusual about his features, but he was well-dressed. Catherine looked forward to his testimony to try to make out the character of this man whom Jonathan Haverford had appointed executor and trustee of his estate. It was a further testament of his confidence that George was the only one of Jon's friends who knew of his marriage to Elisabetta.

The coroner asked him about this confidence first. "What did you think of your friend's decision to marry Miss Elisabetta?

"I felt it was the only thing for him to do if he wanted anything to do with his children. I knew Elisabetta, you see. I knew her to be . . . let us say not the kind of woman one would have wanted to be the mother of one's children though she certainly caught one's eye. Especially coming from the family she did. Jon talked to me about it extensively. It was my feeling that she had gotten pregnant with his first child in order to entrap him. He assured me that he was fond of the woman, but that even if it weren't for that, he would have married her, if only to legitimize the child and keep him or her away from the Mafia.

Catherine regarded Elisabetta who sat with her hands clenched in front of her, her eyes aflame. But to her credit she said nothing.

"He never considered moving the family to England?" asked the coroner.

"He did, briefly. But Elisabetta enjoyed her Italian high fashion model life. As you have heard, she considered the English a cold race. As one who also inhabits the art world, I can say she would have been a great hit among painters and sculptors, but perhaps not with older buyers."

"How much time each year did Mr. Haverford spend in Italy?"

"At least half the year. That's where he discovered and

purchased most of the art for his gallery. He spent more time the older his children got. He was entranced by his children."

The coroner leaned forward on his elbows and looked steadily at Mr. Baxter. "Tell the jurors about the evening and Saturday morning on the day Mr. Haverford went missing."

"I really don't have anything to add to Fawcett and Milton's account. It was just as they said. Elisabetta dramatically appeared. There were some angry words exchanged. English and Italian. He took her to his study, then left for his dinner engagement with the Tregowyns. The next morning, he must have gone for his walk early, for I was awake at eight and he was already gone. He often uses the back stairs when he comes and goes, and doesn't pass through the sitting room or the kitchen. We didn't see or hear him, but we assumed he had gone to the wedding." Baxter stopped abruptly. He gripped the railing in front of him. "It was an awful moment when Harold Bascombe came over in the afternoon and we found he'd never made it."

"What did you do, then?"

"I went to the room he shared with Fawcett to see for myself what state it was in. His clothes from the afternoon before were in the laundry. His evening clothes were over the chairback for Fox to press and tidy—whatever they required. It didn't look to me as though Jon had slept in his bed very long if at all. I concluded that something urgent may have arrived by the first post and he had driven back to London to take care of it. It is very odd, but it never occurred to me to look for his car."

This was a new twist. Catherine wondered why no one else had looked for the car.

"What kind of urgent matter would that be to take him away from a family wedding?"

George leaned back in his chair and pursed his lips as though weighing his thoughts. Finally, he said, "A valuable work of his had been stolen the previous week from his art gallery. Jon was extremely upset about it. For some reason, he suspected Betta, that is Mrs. Haverford, was behind it. I assumed that morning that the police had contacted him, and he had taken immediate action. He was very angry and upset about the theft. The sketch was the most valuable work in his collection."

This was news. Catherine and Harry exchanged a look. Harry shrugged. Apparently, he hadn't known either.

"Why didn't he remain in London, then? Why did he come down to Cornwall?"

"He was late in arriving. He told me the police assured him there was nothing he could do, and that they would let him know immediately if they got a line on it. High value art theft is handled by a special division of Scotland Yard.

"At any rate, if he got word of that sort, it would have put the wedding straight out of his head. Fawcett and Milton and I all slept in. Always happens—sea air."

"Wouldn't he have raised his man, Fox?"

"On reflection, I would have thought so, but you know I didn't think of that at the time. I was that sure he'd gone to London. I packed up and went after him. Once I was there, I couldn't find him. I thought perhaps the thieves had got hold of him. You can ask Scotland Yard. I made a hell of a stink. I probably don't need to say, I thought the Mafia was involved."

Catherine didn't even question her instincts—the man was lying. He was putting it all on. How could Mr. Baxter have forgotten to speak to Fox? And wouldn't Jon have changed clothes to go to London? Wouldn't the servants have seen him leave? And why wouldn't Baxter have checked on the Hispano-Suiza?

Why would he compose such a cork-brained story? She hoped the coroner would see through it, would ask some of the questions she had thought of.

But he didn't. Instead, the coroner went in a different direction. He questioned Mr. Baxter about the work that was stolen. Why did he think Elisabetta the culprit there?

"I think she was planning his murder. She wanted more of his estate than five hundred pounds. The work she may have stolen was an early da Vinci— no more than a sketch, but it was the gem of his collection—worth in the millions of pounds."

"And Scotland Yard? What do they think has happened?"

"They are zeroing in on the Mafia. The thought was that Elisabetta put them up to it. But at the point of Haverford's death, they had nothing. The police certainly didn't ring or write him."

"So, just to be clear Mr. Baxter: The last time you saw Mr. Haverford was when he took Mrs. Haverford back to his study to speak about boarding schools. From his study, he went up the back stairs to his room where he prepared for his evening engagement with the Tregowyns. He left from the back door, and you did not wait up for him, but retired before he came home.

"The next morning, you were up by eight o'clock a.m. but you did not see him. You remained on the property making a number of assumptions: Mr. Haverford had gone for an early walk, returned, dressed for the wedding, and left via the back door by ten o'clock to arrive on time for the festivities. He had not returned by the mid-afternoon when Mr. Bascombe came to the cottage from Lostwithiel, saying that Mr. Haverford had not turned up for the wedding.

"At that point, you did sums in your head, as it were, and came up with the notion that he had received early notice that morning that there was a lead on his stolen painting. You thought that, though the wedding was a meaningful occasion for the family, he left for London without taking a suitcase or ringing or writing anyone to let them know his intentions.

"That is quite a number of assumptions. Had you any reason to think he would act in this careless manner? Was it habitual for him to do so?"

Mr. Baxter drew himself up and stared hard at the coroner. "I am not in the habit of lying. Mr. Haverford was not in the habit of putting business before everything, but this was not business; it was a crime. I knew it was his greatest concern at the moment. It certainly never occurred to me that he had disappeared without a reason. It wouldn't occur to anyone who knew him that he would walk out in the normal way and be murdered! Was my construction anymore fanciful than that?"

The coroner looked hard at Mr. Baxter.

A real face-off. Catherine bit her lip.

"I ask the questions in this court. Mr. Baxter, who do you think killed Mr. Haverford?"

"The only one with a motive that I can see is his wife, Elisabetta Haverford. I also believe she stole the da Vinci, or had her minions do it for her. The Pinna family. I have made a study of them, Mr. Tate, and stolen art is one of their specialties."

Elisabetta rose and pointed at Mr. Baxter. "There is only one reason I can think of that you would make up such a fantasy! You have done all this yourself. You are the murderer and the thief!"

Chapter Seven

There was a hush over the room as her accusation rang out.

"You will be seated, Mrs. Haverford," the coroner said quietly. "As for you, Mr. Baxter, the police will take a statement from you after this court is adjourned. Do not attempt to leave without speaking with them. You may step down."

Catherine's brain was chasing one thing after another, and she longed for a private conversation with Harry and perhaps his mother. What did Sarah make of all of this?

Patricia Buchanan was called to the stand. Catherine had forgotten that Mr. Haverford's sister had been present that morning, as well.

"Mrs. Buchanan, am I correct in assuming that you have your own automobile and were not dependent on your brother for transportation to the wedding events?"

Patricia, who was dressed to the nines, but out of style by at least five years, said, "Yes. However, as I hadn't seen him in a while, we decided to travel down to the Rehearsal Dinner together in his car. And before you ask, no, he didn't speak of anything that was bothering him. We talked mostly of his children. I was very interested in them. They are very bright and obviously take after the Haverfords."

"What time did you return from the dinner at the Tregowyns?"

"It was very late. I hadn't met the bride, and so I took the opportunity of visiting with her and my nephew. She is a very interesting young lady. A published poet, you know. We probably arrived back at Caravaggio House near midnight."

"I presume you did not run into anyone else at that hour?"

"No. For a group of bachelors, Jon's friends went to bed shockingly early. They must have had rather a lot to drink."

"What time did you rise in the morning?"

"I am always up early. But Jon was up earlier. From my window, I saw him walking to the cliffs."

The coroner appeared first surprised and then angry. "And you told the police this?"

"I have not been questioned by the police."

He turned a hard stare upon Detective Inspector Ross. "That is unconscionable!"

"I did leave for Scotland straight from the wedding breakfast, so I had no idea there was a hue and cry for my brother. I did not know that he was to be the best man, and I spent my time at the wedding breakfast speaking with the bride's family. I was so happy for Harry. It is good to have a nephew so nicely settled. His brother has made a mess of his life. He's getting a divorce, you know."

"No! I don't know and I'm not the least interested!" the coroner had lost his temper, which didn't surprise Catherine at all. It appeared that Patricia loved setting the cat among the pigeons.

After taking a long draw from his water glass, the coroner finally continued. "So, now we know that Jonathan Haverford rose early on Saturday morning and took a walk, presumably along the cliffs. He almost certainly did not simply fall off the cliff as he had a stab wound. So someone met him there. That someone came prepared and killed him. Since you are such a font of untapped knowledge, Mrs. Buchanan, did you see anyone else out your bedroom window?"

"I did see a woman dressed in red trousers heading for the cliffs. She had a scarf over her head, but I assumed it to be my sister-in-law, Mrs. Haverford. A little later I saw the man I now know to be Mr. Baxter walking very quickly in the direction of the cliffs. I didn't see either of them return, but then I wasn't standing watching the window the whole time. I was packing my suitcase and getting dressed for the wedding. I left for Lostwithiel at ten o'clock."

"I never went to the cliffs that morning!" cried Elisabetta.

"The woman's making this up as she goes," Mr. Baxter said sotto voce.

"Thank you very much, Mrs. Buchanan, for a clear, intelligent testimony," said the coroner. "I'm afraid you must delay your return to Scotland. I would request that you make a statement to Detective Inspector Ross and wait while he has it typed up, so you can sign it." Catherine saw him turn to Mr. Baxter. "I would like your signed statement as well as the name of the people at Scotland Yard who you are working with on the stolen work of art."

"Detective Inspector, I assume, or do I ask too much, that you already have Mrs. Haverford's testimony?" the coroner asked.

"Yes, sir, we have it." Ross's underlip was more prominent than usual, adding to his truculent aspect.

"I don't think the jury requires any further evidence, so that concludes this hearing. Now, I will attempt to sum up for the sake of the jury."

There followed a surprising succinct summation by the coroner. Catherine noted it down in her little book as fast as she could write it.

In her mind, the suspects appeared to be Elisabetta Haverford and George Baxter.

Harry was duly impressed by her reasoning, but said, "I'm with you on Elisabetta, but I think George may have been telling the truth. He is a good fellow. I've known him all my life."

"Well, darn," said Catherine. "It does look beautiful on paper. I'm going to leave it there. I'm still convinced he was lying about something."

"And here he thinks so well of you."

Catherine blushed. "Sorry. I'm awful, aren't I? Way too full of myself. What happens next?"

"We amuse ourselves while the jury deliberates. It should be interesting to see what they decide."

"I wonder if they can deliver a verdict of either slash or."

Harry smiled at her and caressed her cheek. "Bloodthirsty, are we?"

"A little. Your uncle was a good man. What little I knew of him. His great sin was having a mistress and getting her with child. But plenty of men do that and it hardly ever gets them murdered."

"Remember we have a Mafia connection here. Now that was a big surprise to me."

"Me, too," Catherine said. "Do you think it's too early for lunch? I'm dashed hungry."

They went in search of sustenance, finding it in a tearoom down the street from the courthouse. Refreshed, they returned to the courtroom just as the jury was filing in.

When asked if they had reached a verdict, the foreman announced, "Unlawful killing of Jonathan Haverford by a person or persons unknown taking place on Saturday, the fourteenth of December, 1935."

"Very well, Mr. Foreman. The jury is excused and strongly requested not to discuss this case with members of the press. Thank you."

* * *

The doors to the courtroom were blocked by several enthusiastic members of the press carrying cameras and clutching stenographer's pads. "What is your opinion on the verdict?" they clamored. "Do you think the wife did it?" "Dr. Bascombe, will you and your wife be investigating this murder as you did the ones in Oxford?"

With succinct sentences of "No Comment" Catherine and

Harry were able to escape from the press to his parents' Bentley. They were soon joined by Harold and Sarah.

"I've got the keys to the Hispano-Suiza," Sarah said. "I see no reason why you shouldn't have it while we're waiting for probate."

"That would be helpful," said Harry. "Thank you very much. If I'd known we would be here in the area so long, I would have driven my Morris."

"I think I should like to get to know your Aunt Elisabetta a bit better," said Catherine to Harry. "Now that we have wheels, let's stay here at the bed and breakfast for the time being."

"Yes," said Harry. "Could you drop us at the cottage, then, and we'll get Uncle's car now. I want to get a line on Uncle's friends. Don't you think Uncle Jonathan would have spoken to them about this stolen painting? Yet, the only one who mentioned it was Baxter."

"Your uncle certainly placed lot of trust in him." Catherine said. "I know Uncle Jon must have found him trustworthy, and even taking your opinion into account, Baxter seemed a bit evasive to me. And nervous. And there is Aunt Patricia's statement about him. Tell me about her. Were you surprised by her statement?"

"Surprised by *what* she said, yes. But not surprised that she said it. She is as different from mother as two siblings can me."

"Now then, Harry," said his mother. "We've had very different lives and different challenges,"

"You always think the best of everyone," said Harry. "Whereas Aunt Patricia always thinks the worst and is eager to share her opinion. It seems to me she's gotten more like that. Probably something to do with her husband leaving her."

They had reached Jonathan Haverford's garage behind his cottage. Harry thanked his mother again and said good-bye. "See you sometime tomorrow."

Harry was in his element behind the wheel of his uncle's luxury vehicle. "What we need is a straightaway so I can test her speed," he said.

"I somehow don't think that's what your mother had in mind when she lent you the car, darling," said Catherine. "Let's be nice and reliable, and return to the bed and breakfast."

Once inside the cozy inn, Catherine was glad of the fire which had been laid in their room. Harry got it going while she added another jumper under her tweeds. "This damp cold isn't good for you, Harry. You need to add another layer. Don't you have a sweater vest?"

"Listen to you coming over all wifely. I didn't imagine we would be staying St. Ives so long. You'll just have to canoodle with me."

"Before dinner?" asked Catherine.

"It's only to prevent me from catching a chill and one of the great advantages of the married state," Harry said with an innocent face. "Didn't you know?"

Catherine laughed and sat on Harry's lap. She wasn't inclined to give up her inquiries yet, however. "Tell me this my darling Satyr: Would you be more inclined to believe your mother's or your aunt's assessment of character?"

"My mother's. But that's only because I agree with her. Shall we ask Mr. George Baxter to dine with us?"

"Absolutely," said Catherine.

But George Baxter declined their invitation, delivered by telephone, in favor of his own to them. "Old Rodrigo has been stewing Bouillabaisse for two days. It's his specialty. You don't want to miss it! In fact, come over to the cottage now. We're having cocktail hour."

Harry agreed, then asked, "Is the widow dining with you?"

"After her testimony, of course not. She and the nanny have taken the children and made themselves scarce, though we did offer to feed them."

* * *

All three of Uncle Jonathan's friends were a bit high-flown as the drinks went down easily at Caravaggio House.

"We're having a delayed wake for Jon," explained Baxter. "What'll it be?" he asked.

Catherine asked only for tonic with lime, but Harry had a short whiskey. Caravaggio House looked mellow and welcoming by the light of several gas lanterns and the huge fire at the hearth. All the men were dressed formally, so Harry was glad that he had, too. It was a measure of respect for his uncle. Catherine wore her black velvet dinner dress, and Mr. Baxter complimented her saying she was a "brilliant ornament for their sad group."

"To Uncle Jonathan," Harry said, raising his glass.

"A great man, hear, hear," said Viscount Fawcett.

"Best of the best," said George Baxter.

"A man of taste for the ages," Roderick Milton added.

They all drank. Catherine felt a bit out of place, being not only female, but the only one present who didn't know Jonathan Haverford except from the brief pre-wedding parties.

As though feeling this, Harry leaned toward her and said, "Uncle Jon drew me aside at dinner the other night," her husband told her. "He wondered how I'd ever convinced you to marry me. Said you were a dashed fine woman."

Catherine teared up, surprising herself. "How kind. You know, he told me in one of our conversations that he had bought my book of poetry. He made some very cogent comments about it."

"And then, there was his present," said Harry. He turned to the others. "Uncle Jon gave us a sketch from the workshop of Donatello as a wedding gift. He expects us to work to discover if it was actually the work of Donatello. An art mystery."

"You know, it's reached our ears that you two here are something in the detective line," said the viscount. "Will you be investigating this murder?"

"Without a doubt," said Harry in his heartiest voice. "I invite you to divulge all your misgivings and suspicions to my lovely wife. Don't lie because she's the brains behind our operation."

"Surely we're all agreed that the murder must have been committed by *his* wife," said Baxter. "How he came to marry her is one of the great mysteries of the Western world."

"Actually, not," said the viscount. "She was pregnant, remember? Also a stunner and very Italian. Perhaps the climate and the chianti fogged his senses."

Catherine felt uncomfortable but she didn't exactly know why. Surely, she agreed with them? But her experience had taught her that even the most innocent-seeming person had secrets. Her mind flew back to her first meeting with Elisabetta here in this room. Hadn't she implied that she knew Mr. Milton's secrets though this was the first time she had met him? And hadn't he called her "a little tart?" What had all that been about? She wondered if Harry knew.

"You know, it doesn't feel right, our sitting here like a scene from an Agatha Christie mystery. This is *Jon* we're talking about," said the viscount with some heat. "He's not just missing. He's dead."

There was a moment's silence. "You're right," said Harry. "We're making the whole business a 'thing' so it doesn't seem so real. I saw his body after the postmortem. To me, at least, it should seem damnably real."

"We're all in shock, still," said Catherine. "You're right, my lord. We haven't really taken his death on board. It's too soon. But if we wait until we can *feel* it, that means we are leaving it to that incompetent policeman who must come up with answers *now*. I was just as surprised as the coroner, I think. The detective inspector's lapses were unconscionable."

"I think we all overwhelmed him a bit," said Harry. "No matter that he's been involved in a 'few murders in Plymouth,' I doubt they had to do with a viscount and priceless paintings."

"Not to mention a temperamental Italian beauty who knocks his socks off," said Catherine. "As they say in Hollywood."

George started to laugh, but he stopped quickly when no one joined him.

"Let's start with the money," said the viscount. "That's my bailiwick. Were there any surprises in the will?"

Harry answered. "It would have been much more of a surprise if we hadn't already met my uncle's secret family. Most of it concerned them. He left a lump sum to his man, Fox, plus the restoration business. The paintings themselves, his real estate and cash were left to the children in a trust to be administered by George and Mr. Brundage, the solicitor. The widow was left two choices. She could come in for a large amount of cash to be administered to her over the years provided she signed a waiver, giving the trustees the authority to make all choices pertaining to the children and how they were raised, i.e. boarding school, university, etc. If she doesn't sign the waiver, she receives only ten percent of that amount and nothing further.

"Oh, and two rather valuable paintings were left to my mother and aunt."

"Where *is* your aunt?" asked Mr. Milton, looking around him cautiously as though she might be hiding behind the chairs.

"My mother finally prevailed upon her to stay with them," said Catherine. "All the suspects are to remain in the vicinity of St. Ives according to the police."

"Yes, they rang me this morning to make certain of that," said George Baxter. "The signora and her retinue have taken over the master suite here unless she's left the country. The children are sleeping in one of the upstairs' bedrooms. It's rather an awkward arrangement. The woman can't look at me without wishing for my painful demise. I almost searched her room to make certain she didn't have a switchblade handy. But it's my duty to stay here and see that she doesn't run off with any souvenirs. There are some valuable paintings here in the cottage. That small portrait hanging by the fireplace would fetch at least ten thousand pounds from the right buyer."

"Is she maintaining her stance regarding giving up her inheritance so she can keep the children with her?" asked Catherine.

"Thankfully, she hasn't said anything to me since the inquest. I really don't know what her plans are," said George.

"They're so young!" said Catherine. "It makes me shiver to think of their future with the Mafia lurking. I'm sorry, Harry, but this has all the elements of a Dickens' plot."

"Heaven save us, you're right," said her husband.

"I'm counting on the mater to intervene," said Harry.

"If she didn't know about the will, Elisabetta had a huge motive for wishing Haverford dead," said Milton, lighting a pipe. "She may be an artist's dream, but I took against the woman on sight. I knew she was trouble."

Catherine surveyed the group of friends. Had one of them killed Uncle Jonathan? What possible motive could they have had? They all seemed to be successful men, polished and involved in lives they enjoyed. They had been Jonathan's friends for decades.

George Baxter with his art business, Roderick Milton with his horses and his cooking, and Viscount Fawcett with his investment consulting—oh, and his poetry recitals. She supposed she and Harry needed to look at them all more closely, but she hoped she wouldn't find anything nasty under the rocks. They were all so amiable.

Harry said, "Did I hear something about Bouillabaisse? My wife gets fretful when she's hungry. I wouldn't want her to tag any of you for murder due to lack of nourishment."

Mr. Milton rose. "We don't run to a dining room here, so the kitchen is all set. Let's eat, by all means."

Catherine wondered what and when Elisabetta and her crew ate. None had put in an appearance at all.

Chapter Eight

"So darling," said Harry much later when they had returned to their cozy room. "What are we going to do for New Year's Eve tomorrow?

"Mother's not doing anything special because of Father's health. What do you have in mind?"

"Well, there's always the Sloop Inn. We could ring in the New Year surrounded by honest, hardworking fisherman. I imagine they'd have a tale or two."

She threw a pillow at him.

"Come here, devil woman," he said.

She did. There was no more talk about New Year's Eve.

* * *

They were awakened very early by the proprietor of the Bed and Breakfast.

"Mrs. Bascombe," she said through the door. "I'm sorry to wake you, but there's an urgent telephone call for you."

Urgent? She climbed out of bed. The radiators were not even on yet. The fire was just a memory. "Thank you. I'll be right down." A dressing gown would have to do. Hers was wool and fortunately warm.

The phone call was from some kind of noisy place. Her mother came on the line. "Catherine, I'm calling from Bodmin hospital. Your father took a turn. The fact is . . . he's had another attack. This one doesn't look good. Oh, Catherine," there was a sob, "Please come as soon as you can."

"I will, Mother. I'm sorry I'm not there already. Hold steady. I'll drive like the wind, I promise."

Catherine raced up the stairs and woke her husband. Their hostess had warm rolls ready wrapped in a tea towel and coffee in a thermos.

"Bad news?" she asked.

"Yes. My father is in hospital in Bodmin. I'm sorry. Please send the bill to Tregowyn Manor, Lostwithiel. Thank you. You've been so kind. I'll return the thermos."

The road was deserted this early. In fact, it was scarcely light out.

"Darling, ease off a bit. There's a bad curve coming up," Harry pleaded. Catherine had insisted upon driving.

"Mother was very shaken. She's not known for making a fuss. I'm afraid we won't make it."

"It's just that we were in the hospital not all that long ago. I'm not in favor of an encore."

"I'm sorry, Harry." She slowed down for a bad curve and blind corner. The sun was barely up by the time they reached Bodmin.

They found her mother waiting for them in the lobby. Harry's mother was with her. "He's in the emergency room, still. They won't let me in there," she said. "What if he dies? Oh, Catherine, I have been such a bad wife to him. His parents were right to disinherit him when he married me."

"No, they weren't," soothed Catherine, shocked to her core by the words her mother was speaking. Whereas her mother had neglected Wills and Catherine, she had always attended to her father. "You've been a wonderful wife. Tell me what happened that made you decide to bring him." She drew her pacing mother down beside her on the waiting room sofa.

Sarah said, "I'll go see what I can find out."

Harry sat on her mother's other side.

Her mother said, "He woke up in the night with pain in his chest and down his arm. Of course, the last thing he wanted to do was to move. Your father refused to come to the hospital in his dressing gown even though he was doubled over in pain. Stebbins helped me dress him. It was a nightmare!

"Then I had to wake Sarah and ask if she could drive us. She has been a brick. I've never been so scared."

Harry asked, "Mother's driving was that bad?"

"No, but my husband had another attack. I thought he was going to die right there in the auto! And I felt less than worthless because I had no clue what to do. I should have had some training or something after his first attack."

Harry's mother joined them. "Dear, I just spoke to the nurse in charge. They've got him stabilized. They're putting him on a small ward with the most critical patients. You can see him, but only for a few minutes."

"Oh, thank you, Sarah. I can't imagine how I could have managed without you!"

"You would have managed fine. A crisis obviously brings out the best in you. Most people would have fallen apart completely."

"Give him my love, Mother," said Catherine.

"I will, dear," her mother said. "Hopefully you can see him and tell him, yourself."

But it was not to be. Her mother reached him just as he was having another and what turned out to be a final heart attack.

* * *

Catherine sat on the hard leather couch in the waiting room outside the small ward where her father had died. Harry was next to her, holding her cold hand which refused to warm up. Sarah Bascombe had both arms around Catherine's mother and was speaking softly to her.

Other than shock, Catherine didn't know what her feelings were. Her father hadn't had much of a life this past year after his last attack. But that year had given her time to grow as close as she could to the rather forbidding man she had at times feared and sometimes almost forgot. Now she realized he'd had no model to follow. His own parents had been distant, forbidding, and severe in their judgments. They had cut him out of their will, leaving everything that wasn't entailed to Catherine. They had never forgiven her father for marrying Catherine's mother who wasn't from the aristocracy. There had been an express provision in Catherine's trust that administered her money forbidding her to give any of it to her parents for any reason. The money had allowed Catherine to live independently from her parents. Until last year when a combination of factors had thrown them together, she had never felt close to her parents since the age of eight when they had sent her to boarding school.

Her father's first heart attack had softened him toward her and toward Harry who was the son of a prosperous wool merchant and that rare thing—a female doctor. The Baron Tregowyn had tried in his own way to reach out to her and had been partially successful. He knew what it was like for a child to be shunned for marrying below their station. Catherine and her father just didn't have much in common or any traditions to build on. Their relationship had slowly evolved over the last year to a place where she now felt affection for her parents, and they seemed to feel that way as well.

One thing she was certain of. She needed to be a support to her mother. Her brother Will was the entailed heir, and he was a long way off in Kenya. The baroness would be alone in the big manor house. Harry's parents had just gifted Catherine and Harry with a comfortable house in Oxford. There would be room for her mother, but weren't there dire warnings out there about mothers-in-law living with newly wedded couples? She must talk it over with Harry.

There was a Tregowyn townhouse in London which Catherine and Will used freely. Perhaps her mother would rather live there?

Well, there was plenty of time to decide this. The main thing surely must be not to leave her alone in Cornwall in the middle of the winter.

Harry asked, "How do you feel, darling? I can almost hear the wheels spinning in your head."

"I'm just thinking about what's to become of Mother. But there's plenty of time to worry about that."

"Whatever we do, we'll do it as a team," said Harry. "I'll be whatever help I can, Catherine."

Just then her mother and Sarah returned from the hospital office where the baroness had been closeted with the doctor filling in forms and making out the death certificate. Harry rose diplomatically.

"I'll just go ring the pater," he said.

Catherine embraced her mother who, now that the worst had happened, was surprisingly dry-eyed. "I'm so sorry," Catherine said. "I know you will miss him horribly."

"He hasn't been himself this last year. In many ways, this is a blessed release for him, and I need not worry about him anymore."

"I suppose that's the way we must look at it," said Catherine. "Shall you feel up to organizing the funeral, or would you like me to do it?"

"It will give me something to do. The chapel is looking at its best after your wedding, so all that really has to be done is to write the obituary, order the flowers, choose a casket, and leave the rest to the vicar. You're still on your honeymoon. When does term start?"

"In two weeks. There will be a reception for Harry and me in Hampshire next week."

"Ah, yes. We must have the funeral soon. I don't imagine it will be large. So many people in the neighborhood have passed on already."

* * *

Catherine was to remember New Year's Eve of 1935 for two things—first, her father died, and second, Elisabetta Haverford was arrested. The grief-stricken Haverford children and their nanny were invited to live with the senior Bascombes. But then they learned that they needed to remain in Cornwall until the legal system had run its course and things were decided about the children's mother.

Catherine's mother showed a heart of gold by opening up a wing of the manor which hadn't been used for years for their use until legal matters were concluded. Patricia and the senior Bascombes would stay there with them. The baroness called in several charladies she knew from the district and had them clear the rooms, sweep the floors, and change the linens. Fires were built in all the rooms to burn off the damp.

Sarah Bascombe was overcome by the baroness's generosity. While Catherine pitched in to help the chars in the east wing, Harry went back to St. Ives to bring Nanny and her charges to Tregowyn Manor. He also intended to find out from the friends in Jonathan's cottage what was transpiring with Elisabetta's arrest.

"Scotland Yard has finally been called in," said Harry over the telephone to Catherine that afternoon. "After the dressing down the local constabulary received during the Coroner's Inquest and the fact that now that they're dealing with the daughter of a notable Mafioso, the locals were finally convinced that they were playing out of their league.

If Mussolini has carried out his plans, Don Pinno will be considerably strapped for cash and influence. He is going to want to get his hands on his daughter's British pounds. I would guess he or his minions will be certain to show up here, if they're not already waiting in the wings. Mr. Brundage was good enough to ring Baxter and warn him since he is a fellow trustee. He saw the headlines this morning before any of us did. Scotland Yard arrested Elisabetta late last night. Baxter had rung the coroner when he thought she was getting ready to flee."

"Crikey," said Catherine. "It's a good thing you took the Bentley. Will it hold the nanny, the children, and all their paraphernalia? And what's happening with Fox?"

"He feels he must stay in St. Ives for the time being and hold a watching brief. He thinks that's what Jonathan would have had him do. He's packing up all the artwork to send back to London. How's your mother holding up?"

"I think all this company is actually good for her. She's in the attic looking over all my old dolls and things, trying to see what's fit to be rescued for Adriana.

"But, Harry, I was thinking. Will the children be British citizens since your Uncle Jon was their father?"

"Yes. And they are entitled to the protection of British law. And don't forget both their guardians are British."

"That's the worry. Do you think the Don will try to take them away?"

"I admit that's a legitimate worry. I expect that's why Scotland Yard is acting quickly. But save your questions. We're ready to go."

Chapter Nine

Since they were arriving by train, it wouldn't be long before the police from Scotland Yard would arrive at the Manor. Catherine had sent a hasty telegram to her brother, Wills, in Kenya. Sarah and Catherine's mother were in the east wing settling the Haverford family in their new quarters at Tregowyn Manor. Harry was helping Catherine compose an obituary for the *Times*. Harry's father was with them in the sitting room reading the various newspaper accounts of Elisabetta Haverford's arrest. It seemed she was being arrested for theft, not for the murder of her husband.

"Theft?" Harry questioned. "This grows more complicated by the minute. Did they say what was stolen?"

"A painting turned up in their search of her luggage. Not the da Vinci. It's another one."

It was at that moment that the police arrived, and everyone gathered in the drawing room. The Detective Inspector introduced himself as Detective Inspector Duncan and his partner as Detective Constable Sullivan. They were a strange-looking pair with the senior looking like a prize fighter with his cauliflower ear and his junior companion resembling a morose leprechaun. Catherine had expected them to look more gentlemanly like other police she had known. After they introduced themselves, she said, "I am Catherine Tregowyn Bascombe. This is my husband, Dr.

Harold Bascombe, Jr. and his father, Mr. Harold Bascombe. The murdered man was my husband's uncle." She invited everyone to sit down.

"We'd like you to fill us in a bit about the victim's family," the DI said.

"We didn't even know he was married," said Harry's father. "Elisabetta and the children were a complete surprise to us."

Harry put them in the picture, telling the policemen about their wedding, the subsequent disappearance of his uncle, and the discovery of his murdered body upon their return from their honeymoon. "I always felt quite close to my uncle. The fact that he had a family was a complete shock."

"Why do you suppose he kept them a secret?" DI Duncan asked.

Harry shook his head. "I wish we knew. I never would have thought him to be the secretive sort. I'd have said he was an open book."

"Mr. Bascombe?" the DI asked Harry's father.

"I think it was pure, old-fashioned shame. He'd gotten the woman pregnant. We're not fancy or anything, but she wasn't our type of person. You probably know she was a fashion model with connections to the Mafia. Raised in Sicily."

"Was he certain the children were his?" the policeman asked.

"If he had any doubts, they disappeared as his oldest grew up. Little Jon looks exactly like Jonathan," Harold said.

"How much time did he spend with them?" Duncan asked.

"His principal residence was London. He took three to four long trips a year to Italy on business. I expect he lived with them on these occasions. He was an art dealer and restorer. Very successful," Harry's father said.

"We have seen his London townhouse," said DS Sullivan, nodding.

"And the wife comes in for the lot?" Duncan asked.

Catherine intervened, "Far from it, but then, she learned that only after his death." Catherine disclosed the details of the will.

"He had virtually taken them away from her." She went on to explain the boarding school situation. "I'm sure he didn't want his doting criminal papa-in-law to do the raising of his children."

"That is understandable. Any thoughts about how far Don Giuseppe would go to get his hands on those fifty thousand pounds? Did Papa even know about his daughter's inheritance?" asked the DI.

"I don't know. Elisabetta indicated at the inquest that she knew," said Catherine. "I don't know if she told her father. She doesn't seem the type that would let any man push her around," said Catherine, "But I must admit the family dynamics of the Mafia are completely outside my understanding. We have an inkling that Don Giuseppe may be here already. He could even have committed the murder."

"So I understand. You have to remember, there is a loyalty to centuries worth of tradition there," said DI Duncan. "Do you know if she had a brother?"

"No," said Harry. "There was one, but he died. Am I right in supposing the don would expect Little Jon to take his place in the clan?"

"Yes, I believe so," said the DI. "He is probably in hiding with someone who has family connections. I was put on this case because there are several Mafiosi living in London. They're like a Government-in-Exile, waiting for Mussolini to fall from power. They are praying for a war. I have had some dealings with them. But so far they have been careful to keep their dirty doings outside of Britain so we can't deport them. They are passionate and proud of their heritage. I think Don Giuseppe would consider it his life's work to enlarge his daughter's inheritance in trust for her son. He would use it to engage in all sorts of illegal activities that would turn a huge profit. All this could only be done if Mussolini is gone, however. You have to look at it from the Mafia point of view. Their families have been running things in Sicily for centuries. Mussolini is one man. He has a small life span compared to the Mafia's," said DI Duncan.

"I don't know Elisabetta's feelings about all this," said Catherine, all at once feeling weary. Her emotions had been severely taxed by her father's death. Her head was buzzing with fatigue.

The DI said, "Among her things, the local police found a painting which she stole from her husband's collection. She was very defensive about it, claiming he owed her something for having raised his children. We are actually holding her for theft, but we are in the process of building a case for murder."

"Who identified the painting?" asked Harry.

"Mr. Fox, his man."

"He would know," Harry said, nodding his head. "The nanny is upstairs if you wish to talk to her about it. She and the children are staying here."

"Yes. We would like to talk to the nanny. I know it's unusual, but since you are familiar with the household, perhaps you and your wife would sit in.

Harry nodded. His father rose, saying he would go see how the family was settling in, and send the nanny down to the drawing room.

Francesca Sassari was the complete opposite of Elisabetta. She preferred to stand, she said in a small voice. She tucked a strand of hair behind her ear and Catherine noticed that she had chewed her unpolished fingernails down to the quick.

The detectives introduced themselves.

"How long have you been employed by the Haverford family?" asked Duncan. Catherine noticed that he had softened his voice.

Francesca wet her lips and then moved them over her teeth as though she were refreshing her lipstick. "Since Giovanni was born. Ten years," she said.

"When was the last time you saw Mr. Haverford?" the DI asked.

"The evening before he . . . was killed."

"Did you converse?"

"J . . . just the usual sort of thing. He told the children he would be out that night, but that he would see them in the morning. Afterwards, he had to leave to go to a wedding." She wet her lips again. "He wanted to know if there was enough of the things they liked to eat. When they said, 'No,' he passed me a bit of cash and told me the local market was open until eight o'clock.

"It sounds like he was a considerate employer. Where did you meet Mr. Haverford?"

"At home. In . . . Sicily. Mussolini had just put my father in jail on false charges. We needed the money the nanny job offered. I wanted to be a fashion model. Signore Haverford paid me to work for him and to get training from his wife."

At this memory, her shyness disappeared. With tears in her eyes, Francesca said, "I was so grateful! I felt like he was sent to me by the Virgin. The only bad thing was that we had to move far away to Milan. But that was best for me and my career."

"He does sound like an answer to prayer," said the DI. "Now tell me, why did that idiot Mussolini put your father in jail?"

"It was some manufactured charge. Mussolini put my father and others in jail so he could take their land and money and give it to others who supported him. It is a sad time for Sicily. So many people have been jailed or shot." She gave a shiver. "I will never forget. He is a very bad man." Catherine was amazed at Francesca's openness about her feelings.

"In your position in the household, you have the chance to see much of the comings and goings. Do you remember if the children went down to the cliffs the next morning to meet their father?"

"Adriana went, but I think Elisabetta caught up with her. Giovanni was playing checkers with Mr. Baxter. He is a very nice man, Mr. Baxter. He likes our children."

Our children. From the slight nod of the head, Catherine could tell the detective had caught the words. Francesca felt herself to be part of the family.

"What will you do now if the children are going to be in boarding school?"

She gave a sigh. "Signora Haverford says she will have the children in Milano. Now that Mr. Haverford has died, there is no reason for them to live in England."

The DI didn't correct her misconception, but just said, "Thank you very much, Miss Sassari. We appreciate your cooperation."

The woman looked around her and suddenly blurted. "She strikes them."

"Pardon me?" said the DI. "Who strikes them?"

"The signora."

Catherine was stunned.

"I know it's not the English way, so I thought you should know. The signora doesn't like her children. It is very sad now that their father is dead."

"But if she doesn't like them, why is she fighting so hard to keep them in Italy?"

"It is their Nonno. Don Giuseppe Pinna. They are his grand-children and in Sicily that is important. Giovanni will be the Don Giovanni Haverford Pinna when his nonno dies. Family is very important in Sicily. This Mussolini, the Fascist, he will not last. The Pinna family has been in Sicily since the 1300s. Many have attacked us, but we survive and they are gone. There have been Mafiosi in Sicily since the 1300's." She snapped her fingers. "The fascist will be gone. My family and other families will see to it. We have the long view. It is very important."

Catherine could see that the DI had managed to uncover a well spring. She began to wonder about Don Giuseppe. He would be scorned if they were taken away from him. Was the murder of Harry's uncle a power play? Seen in the "long view", the don must have a strong antipathy towards the whole idea of his only grandson becoming an English gentleman.

But this business of Elisabetta hitting her children did not sit well with Catherine at all. The Mafioso must not be allowed to steal little Jon away from his civilized English heritage.

How would the courts see this case? Would they uphold the wishes of the father as given in Jonathan's will?

Harry took her hand in his. She looked up at him. He mouthed, "It will be all right."

How? She wondered. Elisabetta could opt for the small inheritance and take the children back to Italy. *But will she?* For one thing, there was this business of the art theft.

"In your opinion, Miss Sassari, what do you think Mrs. Haverford will do?" asked the DI."

"The desires of her father will weigh like bricks on the Signora."

Catherine found that her fists were clenched, and her stomach was tight with anxiety.

"Thank you, Miss Sassari. You have painted a good picture for us. You may go. But you must stay in touch with us, here in England. Your testimony is very important. Do you think you could send down the young Master Haverford?"

The nanny's eyes flashed with alarm.

"Don't worry. I will be very gentle with him."

Once the nanny had gone, Catherine said, "Phew! That was a different view on this situation."

"Yes," said Detective Inspector Duncan. "She wasn't afraid to be frank once she realized it was the family we wanted to talk about. I don't get the feeling she thinks a lot of Mrs. Haverford."

"She seemed to have a lot of respect for Jonathan, though," said Harry.

A few moments later, young Haverford entered the room. His eyes darted around and rested upon its occupants of the room. Harry said, "Jon, this is Detective Inspector Duncan and his Detective Sullivan. There's no need to be nervous. They just have a few questions. Come and sit by me."

Jon came forward and shook the hands of the policemen. "Have a seat," the younger detective said. "I have a son right about your age. Ten?"

Jon nodded and sat on the edge of the sofa next to Harry. "Why did you arrest my mother?" he asked.

"The charge brought against your mother is the theft of an artwork." said the policeman.

"But she was his wife. Wasn't the painting just as much hers as his? That's what she told us."

"The art in your father's houses belongs to a trust that your father established. At the moment, you and your sister are the beneficiaries of that trust. So you own it."

"We own the painting?" It took a moment for Jon to take this in. Then he said, "But she took it before he died!"

"Well, she may not have been aware that at that time she was not a beneficiary under the trust. Until his death, your father was the sole owner. It has to do with tax law, which I know nothing about. Have you and your sister a solicitor?"

The boy looked at Harry in puzzlement. Harry told the boy, "Mr. Brundage is his trustee and a solicitor. Will he need another one?"

"It might be a good thing for him to have a guardian ad litem. I'm just going to ask you some questions about the murder of your father. Background, mostly. You're not being accused of anything and won't be in any trouble because of your answers."

"Oh. I guess that's all right, but I want my mama out of jail. My sister cries all the time for her. If what you say is true, my sister and I own the paintings now. We will give it to her."

"That is something for you to discuss with your solicitor. Now, another question," said the sergeant. "Did your mother and father get along well?"

"They used to. But my mother says she gets very tired of being alone. She sometimes has other men friends. This made my father angry."

"How did your father act when he was angry?"

"He got more English. He wouldn't speak to her. That made her even more angry and she started shouting at him. But he never shouted back. That made my sister cry."

"Your nanny has told us that your mother hits you. Is this true?"

Jon looked away and then down at his hands. Huffing a short, explosive sign, he said,

"Sometimes. When I make her angry. But never when my father was around. I can tell you, I was very happy to go to boarding school. Will she be allowed to take us home?"

"That is not for us to say, Giovanni," said DC Sullivan. "There will have to be a hearing in court. Your solicitor and your mother's solicitor will decide what is the best thing. I know it is hard to wait, but that is how we do things in England. You are an English citizen since your father was English. Your solicitor, who is called a guardian ad litem, will bring the case to the judge. Your mother's solicitor will bring her case to the judge.

"Jon. Please call me Jon. What is a guardian ad litem?"

"He is a solicitor who would represent only your interests. If you don't want to live with your mother, it would be his job to try to work that out for you. I think that in the circumstances you describe it would be a help to you. Who is the other trustee?" DC Sullivan asked.

Catherine said, "He's Jon's father's best friend, George Baxter. Perhaps Jon could ask him what he recommends."

"That is a good idea," said DC Sullivan. "Now then, you are free to go, Jon. I wish you the best of luck." Both policemen shook hands formally with the young boy. "We would like to speak with your sister now. Could you bring her to us?"

"My mother could have killed him, you know. She could have just gotten angry and pushed him over the cliff. She is very strong."

Catherine was appalled at his calm suggestion. What had his mother done to give him such feelings about her? She wanted to scoop the boy up and somehow make him feel his world was safe.

Had Jonathan understood how his son felt about his mother? No wonder he had sent Jon and Adriana to boarding school. What would happen now? Would she really take only a hundredth of a percent of the money Jonathan left her to keep her children with her in Italy? Or had that been a ploy to appear a good mother in the eyes of the jury?

"Is that what you think happened?" asked the DI.

"I don't know. I didn't see her. But it could have," said Jon.

"It is very important that you keep these thoughts to yourself until you get a solicitor," said the elder policeman. "We don't want you putting yourself in danger."

Harry said. "Don't worry, Jon. We are in the process of finding a guardian ad litem for you."

For a moment, it looked like the boy was going to let go and cry. But, he wiped his eyes with his hands and squared his shoulders. "I'll bring my sister down," he said.

* * *

Adriana came into the room carrying one of Catherine's old stuffed animals, a stuffed lamb she had named Sally. The police rose at her entrance and introduced themselves. The girl wandered toward Catherine and squirmed in between her and Harry on the sofa.

"This is Sally," the girl informed the room.

The DC smiled. "Good afternoon, Sally. Is it all right if we ask your friend Adriana some questions?

"What about?" answered Adriana/Sally.

"About her father," said the detective.

"Don't make her cry!" the lamb said belligerently.

"We don't want her to cry either. I will be gentle with her, I promise," said DC Sullivan.

"All right," said Adriana and her lamb.

"Adriana, I really like your name."

"It means Daughter of the Sea."

"Lovely! Now, tell me a little bit about your father."

"We like to play games. I'm getting too big now, but he likes me to get on his back and he gallops like a horse. Mama says I'm too old."

DC Sullivan asked, "Was this on the day your father disappeared?

"Yes," said Adriana. "He went out the door and that's the last time I saw him."

Catherine handed the girl her handkerchief and pulled her close stroking her back.

The DC was very quiet. Catherine was thankful that Scotland Yard had someone who was apparently at ease with children.

"Is that the end of the story?" Catherine asked.

"It wasn't a story, it was real!" Adriana belted out. "I was really bad."

"How were you bad?" Catherine asked.

Stretching up, the girl whispered in her ear, "I wet my bed that night." Catherine hugged her and whispered, "That happens sometimes when we're scared. I think you were very brave. If you remember anything else later, tell me or the policemen, all right?"

Adriana nodded and sniffed.

"Shall we go upstairs and find your Aunt Sarah? I'll bet you anything it's almost time for tea. And you know what? This was my house when I was a little girl, and I loved having tea in the nursery. It is so nice and cozy. Do you want your cousin Harry to carry you?"

"Can he do piggy back?"

Cousin Harry replied, "I sure do. I'm a wonderful piggy. Come over here then and climb on my back."

Harry went galloping off with his little cousin perched on his back, gripping his hair in her fists. "Your mane is very short."

Harry's reply was lost as they exited the room.

"Well!" said Catherine. "That was unexpected."

Whether Adriana's mother killed Jonathan or not, Catherine couldn't help thinking that she was a poisonous person. Both children harbored fears that their mother murdered their father. It seemed, however, that children were very good at keeping things in different cupboards. Was it because there were so many things in their world they didn't understand that they were used to putting them in a part of their brain where they didn't consciously think of them? The other thing they did was to keep ugly things in another place. Children were very good at living in the moment. Catherine remembered very well living in a pretend world where she was the princess in Restormel Castle, the circular ruins of which lay close to her home. Of course, her parents didn't know their daughter was a powerful princess, who went about them in disguise.

Catherine was grateful for Sarah Bascombe's broad experience with healing. She would bet that she had Adriana in her arms at that very moment.

Chapter Ten

The next person to be interviewed was Harry's Aunt Patricia. Harry and Catherine were not invited to stay for that interview, unfortunately. Catherine went to check on her mother who was embroidering upstairs in her boudoir.

"How are you coming on?" she asked.

"I don't know. I feared your father's death for so long and tried to imagine what I would do. Now that it's happened, I can't really take it in." Her mother suddenly hunched over in her rocking chair and threw down her project. Catherine handed her a handkerchief as her mother commenced sobbing.

"I cabled Will, but who knows how long it will take for him to get it," Catherine said. I sent it in care of his company." Her brother was working hard in Kenya to develop potable water sources to villages where typhoid and other water-born illnesses had been a constant danger for years. Unfortunately, he was often out in the bush for weeks.

"It will be strange once everyone leaves," her mother said. "It's nice to have the house full of Harry's family."

"Everyone really appreciates a comfortable place to stay. I'm glad it isn't overwhelming you."

"No," her mother replied. "And Harry's father has been a tremendous help with the flowers for the funeral. I would love to see his garden one day. He speaks about it with great enthusiasm. Then the Women's Institute and the vicar are taking care of everything else. Thank you for doing the obituary. It was lovely."

"Do you think you might move to the London flat for a while? Once everything settles?"

"It depends on Will. I'll remain here with him if he's going to come home to stay. It's really a tragedy he and your father never got on."

"I shouldn't say speak ill of the dead, I suppose," said Catherine. "But Father was never an easy person to love. The most one could hope for was that there wouldn't be out and out disagreements."

"I meant what I said about not being a good wife to him, Catherine. Someday I will tell you more about it, but now is not the time. I'm too strapped with guilt. I need to seek the vicar's counsel, I think. I should have done it years ago."

Catherine's chest hurt as she witnessed her mother's sorrow. She took her parent's hand and said, "You know, our family seems positively idyllic compared to what Jon and Adriana are used to. I think both of them suspect their mother of murdering their father."

"But that's dreadful for a child to even think such a thing!" her mother said. "Poor mites."

"Yes. It's been more difficult than you or I can imagine, I think," Catherine said. "But, back to you. When Harry and I are settled in our new house, you are welcome to come and stay at Oxford for a bit."

"Thank you, dear. But you are newlyweds. I wouldn't do that to you. I have quite a number of old friends who've moved to London, or who spend a good part of the year there. I may go there as you suggest. With your father's ill health the last year, we haven't been social. I need to catch up with everyone."

* * *

In the future when Catherine looked back on this short few days in her life, what she most remembered was all the intense conversations that took place in Tregowyn Manor. Harry and Catherine took a walk that afternoon, braving the elements to get some fresh air and a little bit of time together.

"All of this talk of the difficulties in Jon and Adriana's family and then again this afternoon about my mother's regrets over our family has set me thinking," Catherine told Harry.

"Imagine that!" teased Harry, putting his arm across her shoulders as they walked in the past the archeological dig of a Saxon church which had recently yielded Roman artifacts. "One of the things I love about you is that you're never boring. You're constantly revising your thoughts as though you were living in one of your poems. I just hope you won't revise me out of your life one day!"

"Not a chance, Dr. Harry," she said, playfully punching his side. "But I hope you are realizing and are ever grateful for your family. There are some things that if you miss them in childhood, you can't really make up for in your adult life. You can improve upon them in your marriage, but you can't live over your childhood."

"You have me curious. I do hope you'll explain," he said, giving her temple a fond kiss as they walked. There was a heavy frost on the lawn and the sky was overcast, promising rain or light snow this evening. They walked by the remains of the old tin mine, now boarded securely against vandals. Their destination was the inn which served a splendid high tea.

"I remember I tried to explain about the frozen part in my emotions," said Catherine, almost positive he would have forgotten the conversation.

"Yes. You said you explored it with your poetry."

"Yes. It's the part of my childhood and adolescence which should have been fulfilled by family life and experiences I never had, particularly after Wills went to school when I was left home alone with the housekeeper."

"Yes, you said you filled the loneliness with fantasy and solitary games among the castle ruins."

"Yes. I had a strict protocol I followed from the time I woke up in the morning until I went to bed at night. I was deep in my secret life, secret self. It was wonderfully satisfying to me, but it became frozen over when I moved into adulthood. It's part of my life that I have never shared, even with Rafe. Thoughts, discoveries, games, dreams."

Catherine stopped for a few moments. She had never gotten this far in explaining these most private thoughts. "There are certain colors which bring that part of life to mind. Vibrant colors—magenta, teal, burnt umber. Also, the music of Vivaldi."

Spying a smooth round stone at her feet, she bent over and picked it up. After examining it for a second, she threw it as far as she could.

"I guess I'm still a little skittish about it. I'm having difficulty explaining how vivid it was," said Catherine.

He stopped and turned her, so she faced him. "You're doing very well."

"When we were at the altar," she said in a low, tentative voice, "it was as though I had stepped back into one of those dreams, only this time I wasn't alone. You were an essential part of them. You are the missing piece. I love you, Harry. In a way I don't really know if you or I can completely understand."

"I will do my best to live up to those dreams, darling, if at all possible."

"We are continuing them. We're not going back to those days, but forward to a new adventure. I've let you in, Harry, and that's terribly important."

"This is no dream, Catherine. This is reality."

"I know that. I mean how much more real can you get? It's just that I've opened up and I'm thawing inside."

"You're no longer solitary."

"Right. I just wonder about Adriana and Jon. Do they have a dream life? Or was it beaten out of them?"

"I think Adriana does. I'm not sure about Jonathan."

"I hope they can make England part of it. And our family."

They had reached the inn and had a lovely tea.

* * *

The evening of that day that had been full of police inquiries was spent in the company of Catherine and Harry's parents, in front of the fire in the drawing room. They discussed their concerns about Jonathan's children.

"I'm glad you contacted the solicitor about representing Jon and Adriana," Harry's mother said to her husband. "I am anxious to fulfill the role Jon wanted me to take, but I don't know where we stand. If their grandfather shows up, will he be able to take them away and back to Italy?"

"That is one of many questions for the lawyers," said Harry. "The kindest thing may be to take the children home to Hampshire for the remainder of the school holiday. Since Scotland Yard have taken over the case, I don't imagine we need to remain in Cornwall."

"We have excellent legal counsel," said Harold. "But they are in London. They informed me that any custody hearings need not take place here. They would actually prefer London. They have arranged for a Mr. Guthrie to act as the guardian ad litem for the children. He is to come down here tomorrow from London. He will interview the children and Sarah and me."

"That's wonderful! You will be already for the custody hearing. You know, I wonder how the children feel about their nonno," said Catherine. "I picture him as large and loud, bearing gifts, and intentions to take them back to Italy and away from their schools."

"That may appeal to them more than the more academic life Jonathan wished for them," said Harry's father.

"They are so susceptible right now," said Catherine. "I wonder what they want?"

"They need stability at this point," said Sarah Bascombe. "And non-threatening surroundings. They seemed to like boarding school. Probably the routine appeals to them."

When they said good night to the parents, Harry and Catherine ascended to the Blue Room which her mother had readied for them.

Catherine collapsed in a chair. "What a day. On top of everything else my poor mother is tormented by something to do with my father that is making her feel terribly guilty. She mentioned an appointment to discuss whatever it is with the vicar."

"Come to bed, darling," Harry said. "Let's try not to drown in all this. Aunt Pat came to me tonight with her financial concerns, so we've got more than enough reasons to get this business settled. But let's tackle things tomorrow."

* * *

Catherine rang George Baxter the following morning. She was relieved to find that he was still at Caravaggio House.

"We've got a solicitor coming down today to take on the children's affairs. Since you're their trustee, I think maybe you should be here. When are you planning to go back to London?"

"I was going to go up today. Brundage wants to go over Haverford's affairs with me, but we don't have a firm appointment."

"Why don't you come for luncheon first? Mr. Guthrie, the solicitor, will be here this afternoon. He's taking the train."

They settled matters, then Catherine went to inform her mother that there would be another for lunch. Her mother was sitting in her boudoir with red puffy eyes, and Catherine wasn't even sure her parent heard her.

"I'll speak directly to Cook," Catherine said. "What can I do for you today? You look as though you didn't sleep last night."

"I'm going riding this morning," her mother said rousing herself. "The cold air will revive me. I need to take myself in hand."

"Would you like company?"

"No, dear, but thank you. I need to be alone just now."

Worried, Catherine went to the kitchen and conferred with the cook. Harry and his Aunt Pat were waiting for her in the sitting room.

"Everything set?" her husband asked as she sat next to him before the fire. Catherine had felt chills all morning. She hoped Wills would finally put central heating in this ancient manor.

"It's getting there," said Catherine. She told him about George Baxter coming in the afternoon. He put a hand on her knee.

"Mrs. Tregowyn-Bascombe is on the job," he said. "Disruptions will soon cease."

Aunt Patricia sat in the chair next to Catherine. "I understand that this George Baxter is an art dealer. He's coming for lunch, I take it. Do you think I should ask him if he can sell my Bronzino?"

"I would, if I were you," said Catherine.

Luncheon was a mixed affair with George holding forth on the painting that Elisabetta had stolen, Aunt Patricia vying for his attention, Catherine's mother partaking only of the soup, and Harry's parents speaking of their decision to go down to Hampshire the next day before Catherine's father's funeral, taking the children and their nanny.

Catherine's head was spinning. She hoped she could keep track of everyone. The last thing her poor head needed was the children's new solicitor, Mr. Guthrie, to show up directly following the meal. For all the lonely days she'd had as a child, one would think that all this family around her would be just what the doctor ordered, but Catherine suddenly knew she couldn't sit through the situation with the children's guardian ad litem and hear everything all over again. Sarah, Harry, Harold, and George were certainly adequate to the task of discussing the children's past and future. She needed some space by herself for a time. It did no good to chastise herself.

"Harry, darling," she said when luncheon was over. "I think I might like to go for a ride while you are with Mr. Guthrie. I know it is monstrously selfish of me, but I need to get some perspective. I'm that close to wringing my mother's neck if I hear any more of her whining. And I'm not the best person to decide about the children's future. My life was very different from theirs. I'm sure you'll do fine without me."

"I'm getting a bit tired of endlessly rehashing the circumstances, too," said Harry. "I'd offer to go with you, but I can tell you need to be alone for a while. I'll play Douglas Fairbanks and hold down the fort."

"Umm," she said. "The strong, silent Harry. That will be something to see. Everyone in Hollywood said you were his double."

"Scat, you wretch," he said, spanking her behind.

Catherine escaped to the stables and sought out her mare, Biscuit. She gave the horse an apple to keep her busy while she saddled her. Once she was astride and riding out of the stable, Catherine felt her heart lift. She hadn't realized how heavy it was.

It was those children. Her heart absolutely ached for them. She was trying very hard to be a competent adult, but her memories were suddenly too present. Maybe if she acted on them, she could face the worst and replace those memories with her present-day happiness.

She realized that Biscuit assumed they were headed for Restormel Castle, where all her good memories of childhood lay. That was probably as good a destination as any. She put on the imaginary mantle of Princess Catherine du Bois—beloved daughter of King Hamilton du Bois who reigned over all of Cornwall from his throne at the spherical Restormel Castle. He was off fighting the Crusades, leaving her in charge of the kingdom.

Catherine wondered if it hadn't been for Princess Catherine whether the Poet Catherine Tregowyn would ever have existed. In those years when escape during the summers to her magic kingdom was one of the few pleasures she had in life, her heart had been wide open. She was full of longing—so ready to love and be loved. Her feelings had been intense and uncomfortable until she had begun her diary, which she knew still rested in her saddle bag.

She had written it all out in story form. Those childhood dreams took the form of fairy tales. Reading them was torture, for they were so raw and naïve. Yet she had taken images and ideas from them for use in her poetry, which featured a theme of unrequited love more often than not.

Would she even be able to write, now that she was so filled up to the brim with love for Harry and his love for her? She laughed. Professor Harry's condescending review of her first book had even fueled her second book.

Catherine had been allowing her steed to have her head. They were within the circular granite walls of the castle now. There was even a bit of green grass here for Biscuit to munch. She realized only now that she hadn't dressed sufficiently warmly. She wore only a heavy cape over her riding habit and the wind had picked up and blew at her back. Snow was on its way if she was not mistaken.

She nudged Biscuit into a canter, and they rode out of the castle on their way to the old tin mine, which her stories had dressed as a prison. Out of nowhere a hare unwisely ran in front of Biscuit and the horse, who had been close to galloping, came to an abrupt halt, throwing Catherine down off her back. Landing on a particularly hard piece of ground, Catherine felt excruciating pain in her right ankle. This was the present and she was not any kind of a princess, but a mortal woman with adult problems and concerns. She had neither legendary powers nor kingdom. Immersion in childhood fantasies was certainly not what was called for in this situation.

"Dash it, Biscuit. You've gone and broken my ankle, I think. Confound it!" Her horse snorted, pawed the ground, and then took off, presumably for the stables. Her ankle hurt like blazes. Plus, she was jolly cold and faced with a three-mile walk over the hills. All she could do was crawl! That would teach her to fantasize!

Well, she had best get on with it. She was crawling into the northern wind now, and she could feel the first flakes of snow on her face. Catherine cursed herself for her inconvenient rebellion and wished herself just about anywhere but here. It didn't take long for the rocky soil near the mine to tear at her fine riding gloves, though they were leather. The gloves held together, but were so thin, she felt the pebbles dig at the palms of her hands and knees. Mostly, however, her ankle was in so much pain that she just wanted to curl up and preserve her body heat. Blackness rimmed the edges of her view.

She grew furious with herself. How had she ended up in this situation when she was so needed by her mother, mother-in-law, little Jon and Adriana? Not to mention, Harry? These mental castigations drove her across the ground for upwards of an hour. She could no longer feel her limbs. Her hands were frozen. The cold was winning.

She wouldn't let it! She was on the verge of despair when she heard her name being called. It sounded like her groom.

"Miss Tregowyn? Are you all right? Can you hear me? Miss Tregowyn!"

She gathered herself together and gave a shout. "Here! Rogers! I'm here! On the ground! I'm injured!"

"I hear you! Shout again so I have your direction!"

It was probably only five or ten minutes before he rode up on Biscuit, but it seemed to be eons. Just the idea of rescue had brought feeling to her arms and legs and they were tingling like Billy-o.

"There you are! This useless horse! I'm that sorry, Miss Tregowyn. She hasn't helped at all. I'm glad I found you. What is wrong, then? You must be nearly frozen through."

"It's my ankle," she said.

The groom, Carruthers, dismounted and surveyed the situation. "First job: get you warm. Here." He handed her a flask. It contained brandy she found out, but she took a sip anyway. She felt the liquid burn all the way down to her stomach. It was such a welcome sensation, she took another sip and handed it back to

Carruthers. "Now then," she said. "I think you had better help me up."

Standing behind her, he gripped her under her arms and slowly she stood with his help. Biscuit stood next to her, and she could feel the horses warmth. She laid her frozen face against Biscuit's neck.

"Can you mount, miss?" the groom asked.

"It's my left ankle, so I can try." Inserting her good foot in the stirrup, and ignoring the pain she was able to mount with Carruthers steadying her from behind. It wasn't an elegant move, but her stiff body finally was atop the temperamental horse. "Get up behind me, Carruthers. You can't walk back in this weather."

The groom obeyed, and, using her stiff knees, she signaled the horse to canter. Her frozen behind bounced up and down in the saddle, as she held the reins in hands that were lacerated from crawling on the pebbly ground.

She had never been so happy to see the stable. She found Harry there, just saddling up to come and look for her.

"You're here then. Did you injure yourself? What happened, Carruthers?"

"He rescued me," Catherine said. "Blasted horse shied at a hare and threw me. I landed on my ankle."

"The devil!" Coming over to Biscuit, he helped her to dismount. "You're wet clear through!"

"I need I hot bath. I've been crawling for ages. Wretched horse. Bless you, Carruthers. Thank you for coming after me."

* * *

Her mother-in-law examined her ankle once Catherine was out of her wet things and lying on a sofa in a lesser-used sitting room.

"Darling, I know it feels jolly awful, but it's just a bad sprain. I'll wrap it, and you'll have to stay off of it. Do you have any crutches?"

"Somewhere. Mother will know. Thank you, Sarah."

"I have something for the pain, but it's best to take it before bed, because it will make you sleep. Here are some aspirin for the time being."

Crutches were located, and Catherine joined everyone for tea in the drawing room. It seemed like she had lived a lifetime between luncheon and teatime. The tea was warm and soothing, the aspirin helped marginally. George had left, but Catherine's mother had invited Mr. Guthrie to stay the night as the snowstorm had turned treacherous.

The children and their nanny had joined everyone else for tea, and it was into this family group that Stebbins arrived to announce Don Giuseppe Pinna.

Catherine had expected a larger man, so her first impression of the don was that he was short, though muscular. He reminded her of a wrestler.

Adriana cried with joy and went to her grandfather, hugging him. He bent down and lifted her up to kiss her on both cheeks. "Ah! Adriana mia!"

Out of the corner of her eye, Catherine noticed that the nanny had perked up visibly.

"Buongiorno, Don Giuseppe!" the woman said.

"Buongiorno, Francesa!"

They communicated in Italian for a few moments, and Jon leaped to his feet. "No, no!"

Adriana grinned happily and ran out of the room. Catherine could hear her mounting the stairs.

Jon turned to his Uncle Harold in alarm. "He thinks he's come to take us home to Italy! He told us to go get our coats and hats! There is a taxi waiting to take us to the train station!"

Mr. Guthrie said to the nanny, "You must tell him that the courts will decide guardianship. The hearing is to be held on Monday. If he takes the children now, contrary to the wishes of their father, he is subject to arrest and confinement."

The nanny's face fell. She looked at Don Giuseppe with tears in her eyes but didn't speak.

Jon had no such compunction. His sister had arrived downstairs with her coat and hat, carrying her stuffed animal. Her brother burst into a font of Italian, during which the don's face grew dark and angry. He spouted what sounded like a threat.

At this the nanny went to him and put a soothing hand on his arm. She spoke softly in Italian.

Jon nodded at his uncle and aunt. His grandfather spoke to Adriana in a gentle voice, then turned on his heel and left the room. Moments later, they heard the front door slam.

Catherine took a deep breath. Phew! That had been close. What if Mr. Guthrie had not been there?

Her mother-in-law went to Adriana and embraced her, speaking soothing words. The little girl broke free and left the room. Everyone listened in silence as she clattered up the stairs.

"Oh, dear," said Sarah. "This is going to be difficult. I didn't realize her feelings for him."

Jon spoke up. "She isn't old enough to understand. At school, I learned about the Mafia. I know that our grandfather is not a good man."

His nanny spoke to him in sharp Italian. Jon responded, "I am too old for a nanny. Plus, you are part of the old ways. Adriana and I are English now. We have a family here. We do not need mama and nonno. I will go up and find Adriana. I can explain things to her in a way that she will understand."

Jon's intentions took Catherine's breath away. The children were close. His idea was probably the best one. Catherine had wondered how they were going to make Adriana understand about her grandfather without breaking her trust in them. But John was right. He could do it better than anyone.

Meanwhile, the nanny, holding her handkerchief to her eyes, excused herself and left the room. Catherine realized that she must have been in touch with Don Giuseppe by telephone. How else would he have known where to find them?

Dinner was a somber meal. Food was sent up to the children in the nursery. Catherine had the fleeting thought that they were losing the illusions of childhood quickly today. Perhaps those realizations were the reason for her own odd foray back to her childhood coping strategies this afternoon.

After dinner, Harry helped her up the stairs. She was ready to lie down for the night. Harry had also said good evening to the party of people left in the drawing room. He intended to keep Catherine company, and for this she was grateful.

He helped her remove her habit and put on her nightgown and dressing gown. Assuming his velvet smoking jacket, her husband tended to their fire and sat in the armchair filling his pipe.

"So, how do you think your mother is going to do at the funeral tomorrow? She's had far too much going on around her to have made much progress in her grieving," he said. "She's not in good trim just now."

"I don't understand her," Catherine said. "She is torturing herself with the idea that she neglected my father. But she didn't! All my life she's stuck by his side, and they traveled together all over. They even went to New York! It wasn't my father who was neglected. It was Wills and me!"

"Catherine, you know you can be with someone physically and not emotionally. That's probably what she's talking about."

She knew she was pouting. It was not attractive. "Do you think your mother can give me that pain medicine now? I'm hurting, and it's making me fractious and unpleasant."

"I'm sure she can." Leaning over her, he kissed her forehead. "Do you feel warm enough?"

"Yes, I'm nicely toasty and very glad to be alive. I don't deserve to be. I was unforgivably stupid going out like that with just a cape over my habit."

"That's what your guardian angel is for, darling." Leaning down he kissed her again on the lips.

Chapter Eleven

When he came back to the room and had given her the draught his mother had prepared, Harry said "This isn't exactly the start to our marriage I envisioned. I feel I should apologize for Uncle Jonathan."

"Well, my father dying wasn't part of the program, either. Those are both pretty big emotional blows to try to get on with. It helps to have someone to share these things, I think. But by far the biggest thing is that it would be truly tragic if those children were placed in the care of Don Giuseppe. I'm glad we are able to help with that part at least."

"Do you think Elisabetta killed my uncle?" he asked.

"I think it's possible. She comes from a family and culture where things are evidently solved by intimidation and violence. Besides, who else is there? None of the others at the cottage had any dispute with him."

Harry said, "And we haven't even begun to discover who stole the Da Vinci sketch from his townhouse. It's terrifically valuable. Elisabetta wasn't even in this country when it was taken. If Uncle Jon learned who took it, and if it was someone with a great deal to lose, the thief would have a motive to shut Uncle Jon's mouth permanently."

"In Agatha Christie, it's always the one you don't suspect,"

Catherine said, then immediately apologized. "I know. This isn't a game, it's real life."

Harry resettled himself with his pipe.

"I suppose we should look into his three friends. See if any of them want for money. Fox may know," she said.

"Where is Fox, anyway?"

"I believe he was going to see Caravaggio House closed up after everyone left."

Catherine began to get very sleepy quite quickly. Harry helped her lie flat in the bed and arranged her pillows.

"Sleep well, my love," he whispered.

* * *

Harry had to wake her up in the morning in order to get ready for the funeral.

"How is the ankle?" he asked as she moved tentatively with her crutches.

"Much improved. Now I just feel silly."

"Everyone takes a spill sometimes. It was the horse's fault anyway. Are you prepared for the funeral?"

"I'm almost a new woman this morning!" she said. "We need to speak to Fox," said Catherine softly as they walked down the stairs. "We need to find out if Jonathan knew about the boyfriends Adriana told us about. That could be important information for the hearing."

"Yes, you're right. Fox is the only one in England who would likely know if Jonathan knew about them," said Harry. "What made you think of that?"

"I told you. I'm a new woman this morning. Have you seen Adriana today?"

"No, but I just spoke to my mother. She found her in tears last night. Adriana didn't know who she belonged to and who would love her if she didn't have her nonno. They had a long talk, and my mother is hopeful that she is beginning to let go of him, but it's going to be a long process unless he shows his ruthlessness somehow."

"Your mother is probably right. And we can't exactly wish that for her. Poor child. Her world is certainly shaken up right now. Losing her father was only the beginning. Does Jon understand about his nonno and the Mafia?"

"Yes. He told me that his father explained who and what his nonno was and cautioned him not to be taken in by him."

She felt heartsore herself, just imagining the eight-year-old's grief. Then, she thought of her own loss. Maybe she was feeling it more than she knew. "Has anyone seen my mother?"

They got downstairs just in time to say goodbye to Harry's parents, the children, and their nanny.

"We'll try to see you sometime on the Sunday," said Catherine. Harry's family was planning on coming up to London to their service flat on Sunday to prepare for the hearing the next day.

Catherine shook hands with Jon, kissed Adriana on both cheeks, and hugged Harry's mother. Harry's father gave her a kiss on the forehead, "Don't overdo with those crutches," he said.

"Harry will keep me in line," she said.

After they waved the Bentley off from the front steps, Catherine said, "The funeral visitors will start coming in an hour. I need to get a cup of tea and then do something with my hair. Perhaps I'll just wear my little black hat with the peek-a-boo veil."

"I love that hat," said Harry. "It's devilishly attractive."

She swatted him. "Why don't you see if Fox is still at Caravaggio House? If he is, try to make an appointment with him in London."

While she drank her tea, Catherine had a look at the newspaper. She was surprised to see that Elisabetta had been released from jail. Where would she go? The newspaper said that the police had decided to let her go as her lawyer determined that she "couldn't steal that which was part of marital property." Hmm. Lawyer. That was interesting. Catherine certainly didn't agree that the painting was part of marital property. It was part of Jonathan's business.

Harry came in. "Fox is driving up to London today. Apparently, he got the Hispano Suiza as it was registered to the business. He says he will see us at 10:00 o'clock tomorrow morning. Does that suit you?"

"Splendid," said Catherine. "I say, did you see this?" She showed him the article in the newspaper.

"I did. Sounds like she got herself a good lawyer. I hope Father's lawyer is as good as he thinks he is. We'll probably see that fellow in court on Monday."

"Have you seen Mother?" she asked.

"She didn't eat much this morning. I tried to encourage her, but she said she would eat after the funeral. She is upstairs getting dressed, I imagine."

"Her emotional state is so tangled right now. I hope this funeral will help her, rather than hurt. I think she needs to come up to London and put this place behind her for a few months."

Harry frowned, "How will that affect you?"

Catherine shrugged. "I don't know. But I do think it's the right thing for her." She stood, balancing on one foot until Harry handed her the crutches. "I'll go speak to her now, before I get dressed."

Her mother was sitting at her dressing table looking at herself in the mirror. Catherine decided that she would try being brisk.

"Mother, I've been thinking. I think if anything happened to Harry, I would need Dot. Is there anyone in your London life before Father that was your Dot?"

Her parent was quiet, biting her lip as she gave the question some thought. "There is dear Madge. Tutworthy. Lady Madge Tutworthy. You probably never met her, but she was my Dot. She lives in London now, I think. Her husband died last year. She has a daughter about your age who's been studying in America."

"Well, I think you must be quit of this place for a while. I'll only be in the townhouse for two weeks, then it's off to Oxford. Why don't you come up there? The sooner the better. I really do think it's the only thing."

Her mother leaned forward and began to do her face as she looked intently into her mirror. "You are right, darling. Absolutely right. I'm just on a carousel of grief right now. It's positively useless. Madge will see me through. And she understands what I'm dealing with. Things I wouldn't tell another soul. Yes. You are absolutely right. I shall ring her straightaway."

Catherine felt a huge load lift. Thanking Providence, she went through to the hall and downstairs to her own bedroom. Harry was dressing in his mourning kit. Catherine put on her makeup first, and then Harry helped her get into her black silk shantung suit and little black hat.

"This wants a gardenia on the lapel," said Harry. "Do you have any in the conservatory?"

"I have no idea," she said. "What a clever idea. I do look a bit like they've already said the last rites."

"Darling, after yesterday, I'm happy to have you alive at all. A flower will cheer you!"

"Don't go just yet. I want to tell you something. Sit down," she said.

"You sound deuced serious. What is it, old thing?"

"I'm a terrible wife. I've completely overlooked the fact that you are grieving as well. I've been so wrapped up in my mother and the children . . . and myself. I forgot. It was horrible and completely thoughtless of me. And now I've gone and invited my mother to London."

Harry stood and walked to the window, his back to her. "It's best for me to keep busy, Cath. That's how I cope."

"But that's not really coping," she said. "However, I can't say I really know what I'm talking about. What I feel for my father is nothing like what you felt for your Uncle Jonathan. He was a big part of your life. Almost a second father."

Harry said nothing. She wished she could leap up from her bench and go put her arms around him. Blast! Had she said the wrong thing?

"From this point on, I am emotionally available to you, I

promise. As soon as Father's funeral is over, we leave for London. We have each other all to ourselves."

"It could be worse," Harry said. "My sorrow, I mean. It could be for my mother or father." His back to her, he reached in his back pocket and took out a handkerchief. After blowing his nose, he turned to face her. "The best thing you can do for me is just what you're doing. Trying to find his killer. Taking care of his children."

Crutches be damned! Catherine stood from her table and limped to Harry. When he saw what she was doing, he met her halfway and they embraced. He kissed her thoroughly.

"Let this be a promise. To be redeemed tonight," she said.

"I love you, Catherine," her husband said.

"And I you," she said. "Now you need to wipe off that lipstick!"

"Hullo? What's this?" said Harry. He held an envelope in his hands that had rested on Catherine's pillow. That's mother's handwriting, but it's to 'Catherine.'"

Catherine hobbled to the bedside, took the envelope, and opened it.

Dearest Catherine,

I meant to talk to you in person, but there simply hasn't been time. I wanted to make you aware of a little conversation I had with your mother. Perhaps it will help you to understand her a little better in regard to her grief.

"She mentioned some kind of secret that prevented her from being the kind of wife she should have been to your father."

Catherine flashed back to the attic one afternoon last year when she was down from Oxford for an archeological dig. She had come across some love letters in her mother's hand to someone called Neil. They had stunned her. She could only read enough to realize what they were before stuffing back into their dusty box.

Was that what was causing her mother's nervous exhaustion and regret? She read on.

> *"There was another man in her life. Not physically. I don't believe she ever even saw him after her marriage. But she was still emotionally involved with him. I think she may feel she never gave your father the love that should have been his.*
>
> *"Your mother thinks it's her fault that he was remote. She blames herself for the distance you and your brother felt from him."*

Catherine pinched the bridge of her nose. No wonder her mother was so distraught.

> *"He was actually quite proud of both of you,"* Sarah wrote. *"I know this is hard to believe, but your mother says he was afraid of being rejected if he showed his feelings. That is quite typical of men of his generation. But your mother claims that is her doing."*

Catherine swallowed hard as she felt the sting of tears.

> *"This all came down on her after your father died. She can't make it up to him now. That ship has sailed, so she is steeped in guilt and regret.*
>
> *"I tried to be a good listener. I've got one of those faces. People tell me things.*
>
> *Love, Sarah."*

Wordlessly, Catherine handed the letter to Harry. She couldn't speak.

When Harry had done, he said, "Mother is something, isn't she? How nice that you have this in time for the funeral."

"Yes," Catherine croaked. "It makes all the difference. Thank you for gifting me your mother. She's truly a wonder. How she and your Aunt Patricia can be sisters is beyond me." Catherine looked up at Harry, her eyes round. "I'm terrible. I've lost track of your aunt. What has become of her?"

Harry laughed "She drove her car to the train station and took the train back to Scotland. She will be back for Uncle's funeral and will get her car then. She had some business matter to take care of at home."

Chapter Twelve

The funeral for Catherine's father was meant to be lovely and soothing, but sitting next to her sobbing mother, Catherine could find no peace in it. "Live Your Life So You Need Have No Regrets," was the subject of the short sermon.

She was glad that Sarah had warned her about her mother's *mea culpa* misgivings. Otherwise, Catherine might have made her mother feel worse. As it was, she was able to kiss and hug her mother goodbye after spending an hour and a half in the manor's drawing room receiving condolences following the burial. Her mother would be secure in the bosom of the Women's Institute which was filled with decades-old friends. She dropped a word in the ear of the Vicar about her mother's need for counsel, and then went to hug her mother again.

"I'll see you in London, Mother. Soon. At the townhouse," she said.

"I don't exactly know when I'll be able to get away," her mother said fretfully.

"Talk to the Vicar and your solicitor. Wills won't be here for a while yet. Let the solicitor earn his fees and let large decisions await Wills' arrival."

"I don't know if I'm ready for London," her mother confided.

"London will be ready for you. It won't be good for you to

sit around in an empty house and wring your hands. You need a change. You know Father wouldn't want you fussing over him. Now, go talk to your friends. They are longing to be of help." She squeezed her mother's hand and stepped back so Harry could give his mother-in-law a kiss on the cheek.

"See you in London," he said.

* * *

Harry talked to Catherine about memories of his uncle in the train on the way up to London. "He was such a prudent man in the normal way of things. He built up his gallery more rapidly than anyone would have expected and became the man to see for anyone interested in acquiring fine Italian art. I understand that competitors with more years of experience were quite put out when Uncle Jon stole all their best customers."

"It's really difficult for me to see how he allowed himself to become involved with a woman like Elisabetta," Harry said.

Catherine laughed. "Is it really? I have a hard time believing you are that naïve."

He replied, "Hah! Of course it was Elisabetta who did the choosing."

"Never underestimate a woman's power and guile, my dear. Perhaps she got him thoroughly drunk," said Catherine. "Maybe even slipped a little something in his glass that encouraged him to be imprudent. Then she completely seduced him. It needn't have been more than that one night. He never stood a chance."

"You're right, of course," Harry said reluctantly. "He must have cursed the gods when he found out she was pregnant. And, of course, Don Giuseppe would have insisted on marriage if Jon had waivered. Especially when she had a boy. His heir!"

"Well, he did try to make the best of a bad job, getting her out of Sicily and helping set her up as a fashion model in Milan," said Catherine. "I don't remember if you were there or not, but she claims Florence as a birthplace. Her father is proving useful to her just now, I imagine. But that doesn't mean she didn't want to distance herself from Papa in the beginning."

"He might have proved exceptionally useful in fencing that painting she stole. That, to me, shows she thought she was going to be cut off if she and Jonathan came to fisticuffs over the boarding school issue," Catherine said, pulling her coat more snugly around her. "I say, it's hideously cold."

"You're a bit of hothouse orchid, darling. Can't abide ordinary temperatures after Spain and Cornwall. Not to mention motoring around in a Bentley and a Hispano-Suiza."

"I guess not. Right now, I wish I were a hardy dandelion."

* * *

The Tregowyn town house brought back pleasant memories of the early days of

hers and Harry's courtship. She had been living in London then, volunteering as an East End Boys' School teacher and writing poetry. Harry was the one who had most encouraged her to accept the offer from Somerville Women's College as an English tutor. She had written much of her first book of poetry in the townhouse. But she enjoyed her job, and especially loved living in Oxford. When the next term started in a few days, she and Harry would be living in comfortable house equidistant between her college and Harry's—their wedding gift from Harry's parents. But now, before the term began, they needed to concentrate on finding Uncle Jon's killer. And that was certainly looking to be Elisabetta at this point.

Catherine's maid, Cherry, greeted them with her usual good cheer, and Catherine was very glad to see her.

"You're ever so brown!" cooed Cherry. "But I'm so sorry to hear about your uncle, Professor Bascombe!" The maid had already offered her condolences to her mistress over the telephone the day before. "Whatever is wrong with your leg, miss . . . uh, ma'am?"

"I took a spill. Nothing to worry about," said Catherine.

"Thank you, Cherry," said Harry, giving her his hat and coat.

"There's soup and rolls ready for you," she said, to Catherine's relief. They kept no cook at the London residence and though Cherry was only too willing to try her hand at cooking simple meals, she wasn't very successful at anything beyond soup from a tin and the odd shirred egg. Just thinking of her maid's attempts at cooking made Catherine blanch.

"That sounds lovely," she said. "We'll eat in a moment. Thank you for airing the place out. And flowers. How thoughtful."

The London town house was quite somber with its charcoal painted walls. Using the generous inheritance from her paternal grandparents, Catherine had smartened it up with white leather furniture and modern carpets.

"Well, darling," Harry said later over their soup and bakery croissants, "Where do you propose we begin our inquiries?"

"I think we ought to start with George Baxter." Putting down her roll, she enumerated her points. "I know your uncle trusted him and thought highly of him, but I had the distinct feeling at several junctures during his testimony at the inquest that he was lying. Have I mentioned that?"

"You might have, once or twice," said Harry.

"Sorry. Well, I have a very knowledgeable man of business I inherited from my grandfather. His name is Mr. Tomlinson and I am going to see what he can find out by putting his ear to the ground. Perhaps George has had reverses on the exchange or has lost a bit too much on the horses."

Harry raised his eyebrows. "So you think Baxter's a more likely suspect than Elisabetta?"

"Well, Patricia did see him walk down to the cliff that morning," Catherine said. "No one's ever questioned him about it that we know of. Was Jonathan there? Or did George not see him? I was rather surprised that the coroner didn't quiz him on that point. The presence of a fiery Italian model cast Baxter into the deep shade."

Harry tapped the table with his index finger. "To be fair, darling, Elisabetta's behavior was a bit blatant. I think she probably blinded the coroner as well as the jury with her suitability as a suspect."

Catherine carefully folded her napkin and laid it beside her plate. "You're right, of course. She certainly didn't do herself any favors. It's clear she's accustomed to getting away with things because of her beauty, but in this case, it rather worked against her. No one else seemed half as guilty as she did."

"Well, Baxter does bear looking into, I suppose. But I rather think he's a man's man. What appears suspicious to you, may just be his everyday behavior. Horse racing, gambling on the 'change—these are the pursuits the seasoned rich use to stave off boredom."

"Thank goodness, you aren't classed among the 'seasoned' rich. I should hate that." She leaned forward and with a teasing glint in her eye, asked, "Do you know why he isn't married?"

"Actually, he's a widower. However, the marriage was of short duration. She caught a cold on their honeymoon which developed into inflammation of the lungs. She died in Monte Carlo," Harry said. A moment later, he added, "His wife had inherited pots of money which went to him."

"Hmm. Could he have gotten through it all? I wonder how good he is as an art dealer?" Catherine mused.

"He must be good, or Jonathan never would have made him trustee over his collection. That's a weighty responsibility requiring careful decisions. But I wonder . . . why did he lie at the inquest?"

Catherine cudgeled her temples with her fists. "I wish I could remember what he said that gave me that impression! There were so many witnesses—so many stories to keep straight. I think we must make a chart."

When they had left the table and were settled in the drawing room. Catherine took a piece of her stationery and began her chart. She started with Elisabetta, progressed through the Don, on to George, listing alibis and motives.

"I wondered at the time why the judge never questioned him

about whether he saw my uncle at the cliffs that morning," said Harry. "It was like George had him cowed somehow."

"That's it!" Catherine said, pouncing on her husband's words. "George was lying when he explained why he'd gone to London instead of staying to look for Jonathan. I don't know why. But he was."

"You're right. It didn't feel like he was on solid ground there. I wonder why the coroner didn't press him." Harry frowned.

"Baxter had the coroner cowed. I told you. But he won't cow us. We must make an opportunity to press him ourselves. He said something ridiculous when we tried to talk to him about it before, as I recall." Catherine was standing now, hands gripping the back of her chair.

"Darling, you can't fly at him like Themis, the Goddess of Justice, and demand a proper testimony! You are far too worked up. We must be subtle. We could have the merry band of men over for drinks. But not for a day or two. They must not think we are quizzing them."

"But we will be. Let's put my man of business onto Mr. George Baxter before we do anything else."

* * *

Harry insisted that they relax and try to put things into the proper perspective. He poured himself a whiskey and tended to the fire. Then he reminded Catherine she must ring Dot.

Her dear friend lived in London where she worked at an advertising agency.

"Darling!" Dot greeted her. "Are you very brown?"

"I am, but I'm fading fast!" She inquired after Dot's job and her fledgling business she operated on the side.

After getting caught up, Dot said, "So things are pretty much the same here. Now I must hear about Spain!"

"It was grand," Catherine said. "I brought you something.

Can you meet Harry and me for lunch tomorrow? One o'clock at the Savoy?"

"Sounds lovely!" her friend agreed. "I'll see if Max can come down from Oxford to meet us."

"How is the boyfriend?"

"Carrying on. He's been spending quite a bit of time in London over the break."

"Splendid! I'm anxious to see you both."

They rang off, and Catherine went to inform Harry of their plans for the next day. "We'll go to the Savoy when we've finished speaking to Fox."

"And now, my darling," said Harry, "We need to reset our priorities. Have you forgotten we are on our honeymoon? For the first time since Friday night, we are alone, barring Cherry, of course."

"Darling," Catherine laughed. "You do exaggerate. The Blue Room was perfectly private for our purposes."

"We weren't in our own castle, however. There were knights about. I am always wary of another's knights."

She bashed him on the head with a throw pillow. "You have forgotten the B & B!"

Then she sobered. "We have had a murder and my father's passing, you know."

"Forgive me, Catherine." Harry stood and stirred the fire. "I didn't mean to make light. How are you feeling about your father's death? You have seemed much more worried about your mother."

She sighed. "I am hoping that my father is at rest. As you know, he didn't have a happy life. He could never satisfy his parents, and I think he felt that keenly. My mother told me long ago that they had picked his bride for him when he was thirteen—a perfect match to carry on ancestral glory. They couldn't forgive his defiance at marrying my mother."

"I knew they disinherited him, but I didn't know the reason," said Harry. He did a tattoo rhythm on the mantle. "Rum. Not so good for your mother, either."

"She's having a hard time laying him to rest," Catherine said with another sigh. "She feels she wasn't a good enough wife to him to make up for all he suffered at his parents' hands. I'm hoping when she comes up to London that will divert her. She will be in mourning, so no parties. But she can visit her London friends, at least."

For the first time, Catherine wondered if the man with whom her mother had corresponded was still alive. If so, she predicted there could be emotional complications. How would she feel about her mother being reunited with the man she had secretly loved all those years? She couldn't bring herself to tell Harry about it.

"You're looking melancholy, Cath. I'm so sorry I've been so insensitive."

"Your uncle was murdered. There's an excuse if you need one."

"But I haven't properly mourned him, either. A marriage, a honeymoon, a murder, an inquest, two new young cousins, and another death. I'm afraid there may have been too much going on for my poor brain. I haven't taken it in."

Catherine stood up and joined him at the hearth. She kissed his cheek and stroked his hair. "Darling, we can't, either one of us, be blamed if we want to go back to a week ago. Life intervened far too quickly for my brain, as well. I do love you so. And in spite of everything, you are starting to melt my frozen separateness."

He took her in his arms then, and for the rest of the night they allowed all their other concerns to recede in importance. And the ice melted a little bit more.

Chapter Thirteen

Jonathan Haverford's London townhouse, which also contained his gallery, was situated in Notting Hill. Fox met them at the door, and Catherine was happy to see him.

After inviting them in, he said, "Let me give you a tour of the major's gallery to start with."

The downstairs had been converted into several large rooms off a central hall. The rooms were painted a dramatic terra cotta red, and Catherine counted twenty paintings framed in heavy gold frames. All were portraits of subjects dressed in stiff Renaissance-era clothing.

"He owned all of these?" she asked in awe.

"Most of them. Several belong to patrons who trust our security system here more than their own. They have purchased the paintings as investments, and their main concern is not having them disappear as they continue to accrue value. Typically, they don't live year-round in London, so rather than leaving them in a vacant house, they bring them to us while they're gone. I would have said that we have excellent security before it was breached somehow."

"What about the paintings that were stolen? The one Elisabetta took and the one that disappeared before that?" asked Harry.

"Fortunately, both of them belonged to the major." Fox named a value for the paintings which was beyond what Catherine had supposed. "I knew the second work was missing when I made my rounds before going to Cornwall. I suspected Mrs. Haverford. It was I who suggested the police search her belongings. She had thrown out the frame, and the canvas was rolled up there in her luggage.

"Shall we go through to his office? It's this way," Fox led them through to a smaller room that looked out over a boxwood hedge, enclosing a dormant garden.

Fox seated Catherine on a wing-backed chair close to the fire. Harry sat on the companion chair, Fox on a leather sofa facing them. He ran his hands down the creases in his trousers.

"I'm sorry I didn't get a chance to give you my condolences on your father's death," he said. "It must have been a blow coming in the middle of all the confusion surrounding the murder, the inquest, and the plight of those poor children. What is to be done?"

Catherine thanked him for his thoughts and explained that, with their mother in jail, the children had gone to their aunt and uncle in Hampshire. "Their future will be decided by the courts," she said, kneading her fingers together. "But their present circumstances are good. Dr. Bascombe—that is to say my husband's parents—are very kind."

Fox's face darkened. "Now that I am no longer employed by the family, I can say that their mother was not kind. Her nanny is worse than useless. I certainly hope they will not end up with those people or Don Giuseppe will take over their lives. The major was their only hope for a secure future away from their criminal connections."

"We certainly hope the court will see it that way. Would you mind very much being a witness if it should come to trial?" asked Harry.

Fox's eyebrows drew together, and his lips pinched. He clenched his fists. "Hopefully it will not come to that, with the missus being incarcerated."

"I understand that you would rather not oppose the Mafia," said Catherine. "Harry and I have solved several murder cases in the past. We are working hard to try to find the murderer of his uncle. What can you tell us, Mr. Fox?"

Fox ran a hand over the back of his head. Then he straightened his tie. "The master was preparing to change his will, leaving all his money to the children and keeping them away from Mrs. Haverford. According to the children, there were other men in her life." He looked at Catherine briefly, then his eyes darted away to the fireplace. "She didn't even try to hide what she was doing from her children. Young Jon was old enough to know it wasn't right.

"Her relationship with her children was not a happy one. There were many good reasons for the major to bring them to England and put them in boarding school."

"I understand," replied Catherine. Sitting back in her chair, she tried to imagine how difficult things must have been for Harry's uncle. Elisabetta seemed a selfish woman with few saving graces. But did that make her a murderer?

Harry asked, "What can you tell us about the theft of the first work—the da Vinci? Is there anyone you or my uncle suspected?"

"No. We couldn't account for it. Our security is excellent. We have a responsible man on duty at night. All the doors and windows have first-rate locks." Fox's hands fisted and unfisted. "However, it was taken while the master and I were out of town. We had gone to a house party in Lincolnshire, held by one of his friends from Oxford days. Cook doesn't come in when we're gone, and the maids have a day off instead of a half-day."

"Has it occurred to you that the theft and the murder might be connected?" asked Harry. "Perhaps Mr. Haverford was beginning to suspect someone and tipped his hand."

Fox sprang to his feet. "I have asked myself that question a thousand times. I am afraid that might be so. I feel responsible for not protecting him. But I have no idea who that might be." He paced the room. Catherine didn't know when she had seen a man so nervous. His manner was extremely unsettling. She stood.

"We'll be going, then. But if you think of anything else, or if something else happens, please ring us." Catherine took a calling card from her purse with her London number on it. "Thank you for seeing us, Mr. Fox."

Harry rose, too, and Fox led them to the front door. A car backfired nearby causing the valet to start and look about wildly. He closed the door quickly.

When they had successfully hailed a cab and were seated inside, Catherine said, "I don't know how your uncle lived with a man so unsettling. Was he with him long?"

Catherine told the driver to take them to the Savoy.

"Yes. Years. And Fox has always been that way, although he usually hides it better than he did today. I blame the War."

* * *

There was much rejoicing when Catherine and Dot were reunited. It felt like months instead of days since they'd seen each other. Always the fashion plate, her redheaded friend was dressed in a teal suit with a fur boa around her neck.

"Darling," said Dot, smelling scrumptious, as she kissed Catherine's cheek. "So sorry to hear about your father. How are you coping?"

"Later," Catherine whispered.

Harry clapped Max on the back while shaking his hand. The American was now one of his doctoral candidates, but a great friend from before that. Max had hosted them in California at his college the year before. He was the only one Catherine knew who could wear cowboy boots to the Savoy and not look ridiculous.

"I was sorry to hear about your uncle, Harry. I imagine the two of you are assisting the police?"

"Scotland Yard, this time," said Harry.

The maître d' showed them to a table, and they ordered drinks.

"Well, no sooner do you arrive back in Britain, than you find another mystery at your door," said Dot. "Tell us about your uncle, Harry. Were you close? I am sorry."

Catherine's husband said, "He was a thoroughly good chap, though it turns out his judgement was a bit flawed when it comes to women."

"To say the least," added Catherine.

As their drinks were served, Harry began telling their friends about his uncle, Elisabetta, his two cousins, and the mafioso grandfather.

Dot and Max were immediately drawn into the story. "The children sound like rather good value," said Dot. "But this must be a terrible time for them. However are they managing?"

"It is difficult," Catherine said. "Jon hasn't fully taken it on board yet, I don't think. Poor Adriana has spent a good deal of her time crying. Partly because she now knows her grandfather isn't the fun-loving man she's always thought him but is up to no good. I don't think for a moment that we've heard the end of Don Giuseppe."

While they enjoyed their drinks and looked over the menu of the day, Catherine felt something inside her unknot. There was no other friend in her life quite like Dot. They had known each other since starting boarding school together when they were eight. Not only was she possessed of unfailingly good sense, Dot was also tremendous fun. The world always seemed manageable when Dot was near, no matter what chaos reigned in other places.

"Well," said Max. "I can't imagine that this gal, Elisabetta, will stay in jail long. I don't know much about the Mafia, but I imagine they know the basics. Her father will get a lawyer who knows what he is doing and get her sprung sooner than later."

"Yes," said Harry. "My poor parents. They have really been put in a bind. There's a very good chance my new aunt is a murderer even if she isn't technically a thief."

On that note, they all ordered their luncheon. Catherine was starved, having had only a day-old croissant for breakfast. She ordered linguini with clams which was a particular favorite of hers.

When Harry and Max began discussing Max's dissertation, Dot said to Catherine, "Now tell me. How can you possibly be holding up?" She buttered a roll with precise movements. "Being hit with all this and then your father's death on top of it must feel the floor has disappeared from beneath your feet."

"You're right in some respects, but you have to remember that we weren't as close as you are to your father. My father's death was very sad. His relatives didn't even attend the funeral, and he had no close friends. I don't think there was ever anyone that understood him very well. It made him cross most of the time. My mother is feeling tremendously guilty for not having been a better wife. Her feelings are actually the hardest thing to bear right now. She's coming up to London to stay and she needs buoying up. I'm hoping her old friends here will be a help to her. She doesn't listen to me much." Catherine helped herself to one of the rolls for which the Savoy was justly famous. "Now, you tell me. How is the business coming along?"

Dot knew when Catherine didn't want to discuss things below the surface, so she gamely cooperated with this gambit. They discussed Dot's bath products business which she was launching in the States and Britain. Catherine admired her drive and daring.

"I have never seen Harry looking so well," Dot said *sotto voce*. "In spite of everything, I will hazard a guess that your love life is thriving."

Catherine blushed and straightened her silverware. "Yes, there is that. It seems to help steady me and keep things in proportion. How is everything with Max?"

"Going strong. We're traveling to the States—New York City and Chicago—on a business trip during the next break. He's funding it. I'm considering bringing him on as a partner. He's been a tremendous help with finding markets for me in the U.S. Every now and again I stop and laugh at the idea of an American cowboy selling feminine bath products!"

Catherine laughed. "That's lovely. I know you're going to have a spiffing summer. Now, do you feel like meeting some of the players in our little drama?" asked Catherine on the spur of the moment. "We're having Jonathan's friends over for drinks this Saturday night."

"A detecting opportunity? I thought you were sure the Italian wife was the culprit."

"I'm not completely satisfied. A man called George Baxter is one of Jonathan's trustees, and I've taken a dislike to him. I don't think it's a good thing that he has control over the children's money. Harry thinks I'm barmy, but I think he's too trusting with his uncle's school friends. You know with that 'we're all lads together' attitude."

"You're talking to the only female account executive in a male-dominated business, darling. I understand lads perfectly, and we'd be glad to come. What time?"

"I've only just thought about it. How about 6:30? We can go out for Indian food after."

"Sounds lovely. What exactly do you expect this man Baxter has done? Could he actually be the murderer?"

"Well, I suppose that is a possibility, but I rather have something else in mind."

Catherine sighed with delight as her soup was placed before her. She told Dot about the stolen sketch.

"There were two paintings stolen?" Dot asked.

"Yes. But the one Elisabetta took has been recovered."

"Rum," said Dot. "Why do you suspect this Baxter person?"

"He strikes me as a gambler. And he drinks too much. He just doesn't seem trustworthy to me. I'm certain he lied at the inquest. I'm anxious for you to give me your impressions of him."

"Well, I will put on my signature scent and my best frock and try to vamp the man. I promise, he will divulge all!"

"Dot, dear, he's as old as your father," Catherine said, laughing at the picture her friend conjured up.

"If he's not dead, I'll get something from him," replied Dot.

By the end of luncheon, Catherine was seeing the world a little more clearly and was thoroughly relaxed.

* * *

Catherine had to be in the right mood to enjoy the bustle of London. On Friday afternoon, she was full of purpose as she and Harry took a taxi down into the City to see her man of business. She watched the people come and go and tried for a moment to comprehend that each of them had concerns and plans. The nearer they came to the City—the business heart of London—the more purposeful the pedestrians seemed to be. They walked more briskly, their focus on the grand plans they were making in their heads.

Catherine always wondered whether Mr. Tomlinson was born looking like a man of business. He was long and lean with a receding hairline that gave him an impressive forehead. His resting face looked automatically skeptical, but for all that, he was actually quite kind to Catherine. He had complete management of the trust that her grandmother had endowed upon her, but he came in jolly handy for other things, too. He had negotiated her contract with Somerville, managed the London flat when she and Will were out of town, and gave her a monthly accounting of her investments in terms she could understand.

Things had been a bit dicey during the last few years with the depression, but Tomlinson had somehow managed to keep her funds out of the banks that had failed and invested soundly in businesses that were not gutted by export losses. At the moment, she knew he was investing in real estate which was increasing in value as developers extended the suburbs of London to the south. That building activity was helping the whole country climb out of the depression, and Catherine was very happy to have such a foresightful money manager.

He stood as she entered his neat office, the walls of which were hung with antique etchings of Regency-era vehicles. The only papers on his desk were those contained in the Tregowyn file.

Today, she introduced Harry. "Mr. Tomlinson, this is my husband, Dr. Harry Bascombe. Harry, meet my own private wizard, Mr. Tomlinson."

"Congratulations on your nuptials. I am pleased to make your acquaintance, Dr. Bascombe." They shook hands firmly.

"Point number one," said Catherine, I shall be keeping my maiden name, I think; since I don't want to change a million documents. My books are out under the name Catherine Tregowyn, and then there are my students. Harry doesn't mind, do you darling?"

"Of course not," he said, sounding a bit over-hearty. *Did* he mind? She hadn't even thought to ask him. How unfeeling of her! Well, they wouldn't discuss it in front of Tomlinson who seemed happy with her decision.

"Noted. I'll send you a letter confirming your decision. What else can I do for you?" he asked.

"Have you seen the stories about the murder of the art dealer Jonathan Haverford?"

"I say, don't tell me you're involved in another murder." He frowned heavily. "I can't think what your grandmother would say." Mr. Tomlinson gave a sigh. "I hope you are not going to ask me to help. Mr. Haverford wasn't anyone close to you, was he?"

"My uncle, actually," said Harry. "My mother's brother. But with one thing and another we hadn't seen each other in a couple of years. He was supposed to be my best man, but he didn't show up at the wedding. Turned out he'd been murdered that morning."

"I've read the details, actually," said Tomlinson, steepling his fingers in front of him.

"Well," said Catherine. "His wife could very well have killed him, but we'd like to look at three of his friends to see if any of them have the kind of problems a murder might solve. We have their names for you."

Mr. Tomlinson took up his pen and a fresh sheet of paper. "I'm ready."

"Okay. The first is Mr. George Baxter," said Catherine, kneading her hands in her lap. Harry reached over and put a hand on top of hers. She looked up at him and her hands stilled.

"He is one of two trustees of Jonathan Haverford's fortune which includes a number of Renaissance paintings," said Harry. "Baxter was the only one who knew Jonathan was married. He's an art dealer, just like Uncle Jon, only less successful." Catherine was glad of Harry's support, though she knew he didn't think any queries would bear fruit.

"Baxter's wife left him a fortune," Catherine said. "Someone stole a DaVinci sketch from Uncle Jonathan last year. November, I think. It's worth a million pounds at least. I didn't take to Baxter. He lied at the inquest on Jonathan's murder, and I wouldn't be at all surprised to find out that he is the thief."

Mr. Tomlinson nodded. "Proceed," he said.

She felt she must explain herself. "That isn't as whimsical as it might sound. The fellow drinks too much. He's not the sober type I would have chosen as a trustee, but apparently Uncle Jonathan has known him since he was eight."

Tomlinson surprised her by saying, "So they grew up together while enduring canings and frozen dormitories. Many a friendship has been born thus."

"Precisely," said Catherine. "The other two are also friends from school—Viscount Fawcett and Roderick Milton, a thoroughbred horse breeder in Gloucestershire."

"Ah, Milton. Yes, I know his man of business. And I've heard of the viscount, of course. He's a very shrewd investor. Perhaps a bit too shrewd on occasion."

Catherine became aware that Harry was looking at Mr. Tomlinson with keen eyes. "You think he's had a few tips from the inside?" her husband asked.

"Always possible, always possible," murmured the man, as he looked through a stack of newspapers on his credenza. "Now.

Yes. Here it is." Mr. Tomlinson pulled a *Times* from the neat stack behind him. "I recall that theft from your uncle's collection. And it was written up in the newspaper again as a side note when he was murdered. Is Baxter short of money? I thought you said he inherited a fortune."

Catherine waved his words away. "Fortunes can be lost. But I have every confidence that you will be able to find out if Mr. Baxter is short of money."

"Yes. Unfortunately, news of that always comes out. Not immediately, but eventually. What about Milton? Do you have any doubts about his situation that might lead to his killing your uncle, Dr. Bascombe?"

"None. In fact, he's the only friend of the group who stayed to look for Uncle once he was discovered missing. The viscount and Baxter both made for London immediately. Baxter had some lame excuse, but Fawcett didn't even offer one."

"Hmm. Odd, that."

"Jolly odd!" said Catherine. "Fairweather friends."

The man of business folded the newspaper and added it to the Tregowyn file. "I will do my best to make some very discreet inquiries and find anything that may appear out of place or inter-esting in light of the stolen sketch and the murder. You may safely leave the task to me. Best that you stay out of it, Miss Tregowyn. It could be dangerous, you know."

Catherine and Harry stood and shook his hand. "Thank you so much, Mr. Tomlinson. As usual, I rely on you."

Chapter Fourteen

They returned to the townhouse, to find that Catherine's mother had arrived. Trunks of her clothing were being settled into her room by her chauffeur.

"Oh! Catherine! I hope you don't regret this. I am going to be very much around."

"Just as it should be. I hope you don't mind if we're in and out," Catherine said, kissing her mother's cheek.

Cherry entered the room and said, "Pardon me, Mrs. Bascombe. You have a telephone message. It's from Dr. Bascombe down in Hampshire. She wishes you to ring her. She says it's urgent."

"Thank you, Cherry," said Catherine, reflecting that it was strange to hear Cherry call her Mrs. Bascombe.

When the trunk call to Hampshire went through, Catherine was cheered to hear her mother-in-law's voice. "Is everything all right?" Catherine asked.

"Yes. The children are settling in nicely. The animals are a big help, it turns out. Harold is teaching both of them to ride, and there are the puppies, as well."

"That's lovely," said Catherine, feeling a weight slip off her shoulders she didn't even realize she was carrying.

"I just learned that the hearing is Monday afternoon. That is when we find out if the children are to be with us or with their mother."

"I understand that Elisabetta has been released. She has a lawyer," Catherine said.

"The man from Scotland Yard told us. The judge in Cornwall finally decided that she wasn't guilty of theft since she was married to Jonathan. I still don't understand what all was involved in his decision. I wouldn't have thought the painting was marital property, but what do I know?"

"So is the hearing to be here in London?"

"Yes. At one o'clock in the afternoon. We'll be coming up on Sunday to stay at the flat. I'm very nervous about this, Catherine," Sarah Bascombe continued. "I know Jonathan wanted us to have the children. What will become of them if they go to their mother and grandfather?"

"We must hold good thoughts," said Catherine, wishing she had more concrete help to offer. "My mother is here, and she's brought her cook. Would you like to come to Sunday dinner along with the children?"

"Oh, yes! That would be lovely. What time?"

They settled on one o'clock and Sarah rang off. Catherine went to tell her mother.

* * *

At five o'clock in the afternoon while Catherine was in the middle of getting her mother settled, there came a frantic telephone call from Fox.

His voice was low and furtive as though he wanted to make certain he wasn't overheard. "There is a lady here," he hissed. "She says she knows where the DaVinci sketch is. I know I should call the police, but I'm wondering, do I need a lawyer? What if the seller tries to put blame on me and says that I sold the sketch? What if they combine to accuse me? I've been worried about this.

I am nobody, but I have the feeling the man who stole the sketch is someone important. Like Mr. Baxter."

Catherine's thoughts flew. She realized what Fox was worried about and after half a moment's thought, she realized he was probably right to worry.

"Harry and I will be there as soon as we can get a cab. Don't let her get away!"

When she explained the situation to Harry, he agreed they needed to go to Notting Hill with all speed. Cherry had rung for a taxi, and it was there when they arrived downstairs.

"Poor Fox is in agony. He is certain he is going to be blamed. Did you ever think he might have stolen it?" asked Catherine.

"It never crossed my mind, but servants are always vulnerable in a situation like this. They are terrified of the police," said Harry as the taxi inched its way through the Friday afternoon traffic. "I never expected the sketch to surface again."

Fox answered the door before they even rang the bell. "Thank you for coming. Follow me. We're in the office."

The lady whom Fox introduced as Lady Jane Mowbray stood when they entered. She looked to be in her fifties with a roman nose and high cheekbones. She was dressed in tweeds and pearls with her shoulders and arms appearing unusually muscular for a lady, as though she trained horses. "Lady Jane, will do," the woman said. "That is who I was before I was married, and I continue to be."

Harry introduced Catherine and himself. "The sketch you are inquiring about was stolen from my uncle, Jonathan Haverford."

"Yes, that is why I came here. It was in the newspaper. But the name rings a bell. Is it possible that he's the fellow who was found dead in Cornwall?" Lady Jane asked.

"Yes. Why don't we all sit down," suggested Catherine. "Mr. Fox has such a nice fire going."

Harry said, "You are correct. My uncle was murdered. We don't know if it has anything to do with this sketch or not."

Turning to his uncle's valet, Harry said, "Fox, do you have a photograph of the da Vinci?"

The former servant seemed relieved to have a task. "Yes, Dr. Bascombe. It's in the file."

There was a moment of silence while Fox looked through the file drawer of his employer's desk. He took out an 8 x 10 glossy photo and handed it to Harry who said, "Can you tell us if this is the sketch you saw, Lady Jane?"

The lady studied it carefully. "Yes. This is it."

Catherine asked, "Where did you find it, my lady?"

"We have a beach cottage in Devon. Well, we call it a cottage, but it is rather large. Eight bedrooms. I am recently divorced from my husband, but we still share that property. I wanted to bring some of my sculptures up to Town. I am an artist. I had left some of my pieces there in the cottage, and of course, they are very special to me. I didn't want them to be picked over by Henry's new wife."

Catherine remembered reading news of the high-profile divorce in the newspapers.

A tear appeared in the corner of Lady Jane's eye, but she had a handkerchief ready. She continued after a moment. "The drawing was all rolled up, but it was stored in the locked cupboard with my pieces. I couldn't imagine what it could be, so I looked.

"I must say, it was a shock. I read *The News of the World* you see, and there was a piece about the theft, including a photograph in the Sunday paper. You don't see a da Vinci every day. Even if it is a sketch."

"I take it you haven't questioned your husband about it?"

"No! Oh my goodness, no. I left it where it was and came straight to this gallery. I've had such horrible thoughts! What if Henry stole it? And what if he killed Mr. Haverford? I didn't know it when I married him, but he is a very unscrupulous man."

As though he were speaking to a small child, Harry calmed her, "Whoever stole this sketch had to have a lot of inside information about the gallery. I think it far more likely that he bought it from the thief."

"Whatever am I going to do?" Lady Jane broke into tears.

Harry said, "The best thing to do is to speak with Scotland Yard. They are pursuing inquiries about this sketch. They will handle it from there. If you wish, they don't even need to mention your name."

"Oh, yes!" she said. "That would be the best thing, by far."

"Then if you'll excuse me," Harry said. "I'll put in a call to the man in charge."

Harry was gone for some time. Catherine engaged the lady in conversation. "Lady Jane, tell me about yourself. Do you live in London?"

"Not in the wintertime. I find it far too dreary. I usually spend the winter in Spain or the Canaries, but with the divorce this year, I've been staying with friends in Cornwall."

"Oh!" said Catherine. "I'm Cornish. We just came up to London on Wednesday. I've been getting married there. Lostwithiel. Tregowyn Manor."

The lady's face pinkened and she came alive. "Well, isn't that a coincidence! I've been staying on Bodmin Moor with my friends, the Castleberrys. We've been to Lostwithiel to see the castle ruins. They are rather spectacular. I understand there's a Roman dig there, but it was shut down for the season."

"Yes. It's quite interesting," said Catherine, glad she could offer a bit of cheer.

Harry returned to the room. "Detective Inspector Duncan will be arriving shortly," he said. "He has been looking into my uncle's murder and I thought I'd best call him in case there is any connection between the crimes."

"Oh, dear." Lady Jane began tearing at her handkerchief. "Henry is going to be terribly cross."

Perhaps after you tell DI Ross your story and hand off the sketch to him you can go on back to Bodmin Moor. You'll have to speak at the trial, though, I'm afraid."

Her eyes grew round. "Will Henry be arrested?"

"It depends upon whether he knew it was stolen. But I would say he certainly must have," Harry said. "There has been a great deal of publicity about the theft."

"Bodmin Moor is too close. I think I ought to leave for the Canaries," Lady Jane said. She began scratching at a spot on her arm that was already red and inflamed from such attention.

"You realize, you will be needed to testify at your husband's trial. You will have to leave your address," said Harry. "And at the moment, you are needed to tell your story to Scotland Yard."

Lady Jane bit her lip. "Yes. Yes. Oh my."

"I'll sit with you while you talk to them," Catherine offered.

"You're very kind," said Lady Mowbray.

"The fact that you brought this right in as soon as you found it will impress them favorably," said Harry.

The police arrived shortly, and Fox brought them through to the sitting room. The office had become a bit crowded. Harry greeted them and introduced Lady Jane Mowbray.

"Thank you for coming forward, my lady," said DI Duncan. DS Sullivan nodded. "Perhaps you won't mind repeating your story?"

Lady Jane obliged.

"Now then," said the Scotland Yard man, "We must make haste to go to Devon to retrieve the sketch. Are you prepared to do so?"

"Oh, yes. I suppose I must. Dear me. Oh yes," the lady said. "I suppose you think I should be shocked, but the truth is, he's bought stolen paintings before. Mrs. Bascombe, would you mind very much coming with us? I should feel so much more comfortable if you did."

Catherine looked at Harry who nodded. "Certainly, if you wish it," she said.

The drive to the cottage was long and awkward. Catherine never felt at her finest around these policemen, but suddenly Lady Jane seemed to have no qualms. They might be going off to a garden party. She spoke fondly of her friends in Bodmin, of her love of Spain. which Catherine echoed, and carried on about her disgust with the Fascist, General Franco. "Mark my words, he won't get out of this without a war."

Lady Jane inquired about her family and offered condolences on the death of Catherine's father. However, the conversation disintegrated from there into a catalog of all her former husband's faults and the disgraceful way he had treated her.

At last, she seemed to wind down and fell into a doze for which Catherine was grateful.

Though it was near midnight when they arrived at the "cottage" the first thing they saw was a large Rolls Royce parked in the circular drive.

"Good job we got right down here. We're just in time, it appears," said DI Duncan.

Chapter Fifteen

Lady Jane walked straight to the door and opened it without ceremony. It would seem that being with the police gave her courage. The party followed behind her. Into the entry hall strode a tall, handsome man in his fifties who looked like very much like a film star. He immediately lost his temper.

"Jane! This is my weekend for the cottage. What are you doing here? Who are all these people?"

"Excuse the bother," said the detective inspector. "Allow us to introduce ourselves. I am DI Duncan from Scotland Yard. This is Detective Sullivan."

"Henry, I've come for my sculptures." Saying nothing further, she led her followers back to the large conservatory which Catherine imagined looked over the sea during daylight hours.

"Wait!" cried her former husband. "What are you doing? You can't go in there!"

"I told you, Henry. I've come for my sculptures." Opening a large cupboard in the wall she exclaimed in mock surprise, "Oh! What have we here?" She pulled out a long tube which Mowbray immediately grabbed.

"What do you think you're doing?" he cried.

"Restoring a stolen da Vinci to the police. Did I neglect to introduce you? Allow me. Detective Inspector, this is my ex-husband, Henry Mowbray. He purchased the artwork."

Catherine enjoyed seeing Mr. Mowbray lose all his color as he stood clutching the sketch.

DI Duncan stepped forward and held out a hand for the stolen article. "Thank you, Mr. Mowbray." Handing one end of it to his sergeant, the policeman unrolled it. It was indeed the stolen da Vinci sketch. Most of the chalky colors had faded, but the charcoal strokes were still visible. She could still smell the chemical fixative that had been used, but Catherine realized that the rough handling of the sketch would damage it permanently in no time.

"It must be treated very delicately," she warned. "It is only a charcoal sketch."

Giving the painting to Sullivan who began to roll it up slowly, Duncan then removed handcuffs from his pocket. Losing no time, he cuffed their host and said, "Mr. Henry Mowbray, I arrest you for receiving stolen goods worth an amount in excess of a million pounds." He then gave him the usual warning.

Catherine enjoyed the whole thing immensely, only wishing Harry were there.

"But I didn't steal it! I bought it! I paid the earth for it!" Mowbray protested, his face now beet red.

The DI remained cool. "From whom did you buy it, Mr. Mowbray?"

The accused said, "From Mr. Jonathan Haverford! I have the provenance!"

Sullivan added his voice to the fray, "You didn't find it odd that he reported it stolen to the police? And that the matter has appeared in the *Times* among other places?"

"I have been out of the country. I just returned!" averred Mowbray.

"Perhaps you would tell us what Mr. Haverford looks like?"

"Why should I do that? Why don't you just ask him if he sold me the sketch?"

"I am sorry to inform you, Mr. Mowbray, but Mr. Haverford has been murdered."

The man said nothing, but, eyes round with shock, he looked at his former wife and then the others members of the party, as though waiting for the policeman to be contradicted. "Murdered?" he asked finally.

"You shall be questioned in connection with that, as well," Ross said.

"All I did was buy a sketch!" he hollered.

A startlingly beautiful young woman entered the conservatory. "Henry?" she asked. "Who are all these people? What sketch?"

"We are just leaving, ma'am," Duncan said. Catherine thought this was probably the most satisfactory moment of his career.

"Goodbye, Henry," said his former wife." Turning to Catherine, she said, "We can spend what is left of the night here. I have no desire to travel back to London tonight. This was exhausting."

The beautiful young woman was standing, greatly confused, in the conservatory as Catherine and Lady Jane followed the policemen out. "You will want to leave, Darla, dear," the older woman said. "I shall be staying the weekend. I'll have Simpson pack your things and call a taxi to pick you up." Turning to Catherine, she said, "Simpson can find you a nightdress, I am certain. You may have the flower room."

Catherine appreciated the scene fully, and she went to the assigned bedroom chuckling. Lady Jane had invited her to place a trunk call to Harry, but she didn't want to disturb him at 1:00 in the morning. Spending one night without him shouldn't have been a hardship, but it was. Not only did she miss his warm presence in bed, but Catherine longed to discuss this recent turn of events.

How could Mr. Mowbray have bought the sketch from Jonathan Haverford? He was either lying or an imposter had taken Jon's place. So, either the sale took place outside the gallery, or it happened when both Jonathan and Fox were gone.

She didn't buy the idea that Mowbray didn't know it was

stolen. Surely a theft of such magnitude would have been reported all over Europe in the arts press.

Catherine only got to this point in her reasoning when her thoughts took the bizarre turn that presaged sleep.

* * *

The next day she took the train back to London, after saying farewell to the ebullient Lady Jane. Catherine, though glad to be traveling alone, fretted the entire way to Town, wondering what was going on without her. What did Mowbray do when confronted with a photograph of the real Jonathan Haverford? Could George Baxter have been the man from whom he had bought the sketch? If so, wouldn't Mowbray have been told he had to keep his possession of the da Vinci absolutely secret? In that case, he had to have known it was stolen. She would have to buy all the latest newspapers when she arrived in London.

What was Harry doing today? Had he remembered to invite his friends for drinks that evening? Where had Tomlinson's excavations into George's financial doings led?

It wasn't until she was halfway to London that she remembered Elisabetta. She was out of jail. Where had the woman gone? Presumably, she was with her father. Would she turn up at Harry's parents' home, demanding the children? Monday's custody hearing couldn't come soon enough. Had Mr. Guthrie agreed to appear in court on Monday as the children's guardian ad litem?

Was Elisabetta guilty of murdering her husband? Or was it the man who had stolen and sold the da Vinci?

She felt as though her questions had brought her into such a state of confusion that she was nearly mad. Unable to even eat the lunch she purchased in the dining car, she chastised herself. She had to bring order to the chaos in her head somehow. If the police had not yet made an arrest, there was certainly a possibility that she would face the thief of the da Vinci and possibly the murderer of Jonathan that evening in London. Had Harry come to the same conclusion?

Having been alerted by Lady Jane, Harry knew which train Catherine was on and was there to meet it.

"My darling, I've missed you frightfully," were his first words as he seized her on the platform and kissed her. She put her arms around him and held him close, inhaling the welcome fragrance of his cologne and hair pomade.

"We have so much to discuss!" she greeted him when she had caught her breath. "Oh, darling, you did remember to ring Jonathan's friends, didn't you? About tonight? 6:30 for drinks?"

"I did," he said, eyes sparkling. "No one has been detained by the police, as yet. I am longing for you to tell me all! What did the cad of a husband say? From whom did he buy the sketch?"

She told him.

"The deuce!" Harry said. "That's a proper stunner! I wonder if he'll tell how much he paid for it."

When they arrived at the townhouse, Catherine went to bathe immediately. She felt as though there must be train cinders in her hair after the long journey.

When Cherry was drying her mistress's hair, brushing it before the bedroom fire, Harry entered their room unexpectedly.

"You'll never guess," he said.

"What's happened now?" Catherine asked.

"No one knows where Elisabetta has got to. Scotland Yard just rang. She walked out of the St. Ives jail to Don Giuseppe's waiting arms, and no one knows where she is. DI Duncan is calling my parents and the Hampshire police."

"Did she know about the custody hearing on Monday?"

"The St. Ives' police didn't know about the hearing."

"Does anyone know where her father was staying? What about the lawyer?"

"Apparently, he was provided by the don. A Londoner. I expect he helped persuade the St. Ives constabulary to release her. He's not saying where she is either."

"She must be the murderer," said Catherine. "Why else would she disappear?"

Cherry was finished drying her hair and now applied the heated tongs.

"My thoughts exactly," said Harry. "This case has grown into an octopus. Is it really two cases: a burglary and a murder, or one big case?"

Catherine put her fingers to her temples. "Crikey! I am going mad."

"Not right this minute, ma'am," said Cherry. "We need to get your hair arranged first."

Catherine made a face. "Has anyone told Fox that we recovered the da Vinci?"

"I'll ring him right now," said Harry. "Poor fellow."

By the time Harry had returned, Catherine was dressed in her black cocktail frock and Cherry was applying her make up. "I want to be done with dressing," she had told her maid when Cherry had protested that it was only 3:30 in the afternoon.

"The police had already been by with Mowbray to see if he could identify Fox as the imposter," said Harry. "Poor Fox. He was even more nervous than usual, but he was cleared immediately, of course. Looked absolutely nothing like Mowbray's description. Apparently, they were taking Mowbray back to the station to work with a sketch artist now that Fox had been cleared. They will call on Fox again to see if he can identify the sketch artist's work. Apparently, the da Vinci was paid for with cash, so there's no help from the banks."

Harry added, "Fox told them that George Baxter had access to the gallery, which I didn't know. It seems that Baxter sometimes checked on things when Jonathan and Fox were abroad."

After Catherine was finished with her grooming, she visited Cook in the kitchen to make certain the canapes were in hand. She had already spoken to her about Sunday dinner with the Bascombe clan, so that was also organized. It appeared, they were having roast beef and Yorkshire pud tomorrow. Suddenly, Catherine was ravenous. She stole an apple and some cheese from under Cook's nose.

"Still up to your tricks I see, miss. I mean, madam."

Catherine and Harry settled in the sitting room where her mother was trying to embroider. This surprised Catherine as her mother was really not the needlework type of person. She seemed to have taken it up since Father's death.

"Are you doing penance or something, Mother, with the needle and thread?"

"I'm trying to embroider a yoke for a dress for Adriana. I haven't done anything like this since I was working on my trousseau."

"Are you going to be all right in London without your horses?"

"Hopefully, I will have some friends to go about with."

"Is there anyone you would like to invite for drinks tonight? Harry did tell you we're having a small party, didn't he? Jonathan's friends, Dot, and her boyfriend are all coming."

"Yes. I have asked my friend, Madge to attend. She was recently widowed as well."

They discussed the strange developments in the case for a while, and then her mother fell back into her *mea culpa* again. "If only I had shown a little more interest in his pursuits," she said. "I was always going riding, traveling with friends, or off to the Women's Institute and he was alone. I was so busy trying to keep myself occupied so I wouldn't feel my broken heart that I never thought of his. I mean he must have loved me a lot to have given up his inheritance."

"Poor Father. I don't think he had ever been truly happy," said Catherine. "He didn't know how to show affection, never having received much growing up. I expect you would have had to dig pretty deep before you found his feelings for you. And you were fighting your own feelings."

"I'm sorry I was such a poor mother. I know I was never there. I hope you will be better than I was."

"Mother, we can't go back. All we can do is go forward from here. I am happy, and I think Wills is reasonably happy. No permanent harm was done to either of us."

Chapter Sixteen

Catherine was very pleased to finally lay aside the cane she had been using before their drinks party. She hoped never to need one again. Harry hid it in the deepest reaches of the wardrobe.

To Catherine and Harry's disappointment, all three of Jonathan's friends showed up for drinks that evening, so no arrest had taken place among them. Her mother's school friend, Madge Tutworthy, came up with them in the lift and was introduced to all. Catherine had not seen her for many years, so she was delighted to introduce the tall, buxom woman to Harry. Lady Tutworthy was thrilled, and Harry's cocktail party bonhomie won her over immediately. After speaking of Spain and Harry and Catherine's honeymoon, the group began talking about the royal family--the poor health of the king and the scandalous behavior of the Prince of Wales.

Dot and Max arrived next, and drinks and canapes began to circulate. Harry entertained everyone with a Brit's take on Hollywood. Max provided the American point of view with appropriate regional accents.

This left Catherine time to chat with Dot. She told her in confidence about her errand to Devon the night before. She whispered, "My money is on George Baxter as the thief."

"The one with dark hair who talks so loudly?" asked Dot in an answering whisper.

"Yes. He lied at the inquest, I'm positive."

"You've never worked with Scotland Yard before. What are they like?"

"Very professional. I wish you could have seen them arrest that louse, Mowbray, last night." She gave Dot a *sotto voce* account of Lady Jane and her antics.

Roderick Milton made his way over to them. "Can't have two such ravishing women keeping all to themselves," he said. "What are you whispering about?"

Catherine responded easily, "Girl talk. Now that I'm married, we don't have as much time as we used to."

"Ah! Girl talk! That most fascinating of all conversations for a male to overhear. Continue, please! I'm all ears."

"Not on your life," said Catherine. It always startled her when an Americanism popped out of her mouth. "Dot, Mr. Milton raises thoroughbreds. How many more weeks of freedom do you have before they start to foal?"

"The early ones come at the beginning of March. The weather makes it a bit dicey, so I like to be there."

People were on their second drinks when Cherry surprised them by leading Detective Inspector Duncan and his sergeant into the drawing room. Conversation stopped immediately except for George Baxter's exclamation, "I say! What is this?"

"I am sorry to disturb your evening, but I'm afraid I'm here to serve a warrant for an arrest," said the DI. "Lord Fawcett, could you come with me please?"

The viscount looked startled. "I didn't kill Jonathan Haverford!"

"That's as may be. Right now, I'm arresting you for stealing the da Vinci sketch from the deceased, Jonathan Haverford, and selling it to Mr. Henry Mowbray for a million pounds."

The viscount put down his drink and stood taller. "I don't know what Mowbray has told you, but I was acting as agent for Haverford."

"That is patently untrue," scoffed Harry "If so, why did he report it missing?"

"He was in need of money. He wanted to claim it on his insurance," the viscount said, his voice cool, his color high.

"If you colluded with him to defraud an insurance company, that's another crime, but it doesn't explain your fancy dress," said the DI. "Save your fairy stories for the jury. Now, are you going to come quietly, or do I have to cuff you?"

Fawcett's eyes darted around the room as he looked for deliverance. He broke into a lunge for the entrance to the room, but Harry grabbed him by the arm. "So it was you who killed my uncle!"

The viscount bared his teeth in a snarl. "No. Now unhand me, you little toad!"

Catherine felt as though she had been punched in the solar plexus. For a moment she couldn't breathe she was so angry. All the blood rushed to her head.

"Hold on, darling," said Dot, gripping her arm. "Let the police take care of it." A pair of officers restrained the viscount, and everyone was silent as the cuffs went on his wrists. The usual warning was given him. Catherine's eyes flew to her mother whose mouth was pinched. Her friend was steadying her, as Dot was steadying Catherine.

Could Viscount Fawcett have really killed Harry's uncle? He's absolutely the last person I would have suspected—so calm and aloof and seemingly wealthy.

She realized the viscount was the one of Jonathan's three friends she knew the least. During their brief encounters, he had always maintained an air of self-containment, rarely talking about himself. How could Uncle Jonathan not have realized his friend was full of vice?

The police hauled Lord Fawcett out the door as they left. Cherry had remained in the room and her eyes were like saucers. "Oh, ma'am," she said. "I never thought . . ."

Catherine said, "No one blames you, Cherry. The man brought it on himself. Now, I think we need some more canapes."

The room was completely silent, and Harry had the whiskey decanter by the neck. "I think we all need another drink with the canapes."

"Fawcett!" sputtered George Baxter. "I don't know when I've been more surprised!"

Roderick Milton's face was white with shock. Catherine called to her husband, "I think Mr. Milton would like another whiskey, Harry."

"I had no idea he was short of money," Mr. Milton said. "He was just the same as always."

"He took the prize of Uncle's collection," said Harry. "I don't blame you for being shocked. We have a scorned wife to thank for the recovery."

"Are they sure it was Fawcett?" asked Baxter. "I can't believe it. We've all known each other for years."

"Money does strange things to people," said Harry. "So does the lack of it."

"What can you tell us about how they came to decide Fawcett did it?" asked Milton.

Harry turned the floor over to Catherine, who told about Fox's telephone call and their subsequent meeting with the scorned wife of Henry Mowbray. She went on to describe the arrest in Devon. "Lady Jane says he's bought stolen pictures before, which must be how the viscount knew to approach him. Apparently, Mowbray has more money than sense."

"He couldn't resist a da Vinci," said Baxter. "You know, looking back, there was a day I couldn't lay my hands on my keys to Jon's house. Fawcett must have 'borrowed' them to make a wax impression of the key to the gallery. I found the keys later in a place I had looked at least twice before. I thought it was strange. Fawcett had been over for cards the night before, but I had no reason to suspect him."

Milton was still in shock, "I can't believe it of him. Really, Bax. We've known him since before the flood."

"What is this sketch he stole?" asked Lady Tutworthy. "Are you speaking of the Havford who was just found murdered?"

Harry spoke. "I'm sorry you had to witness that. Yes, Jonathan Haverford was my uncle. He has a lovely collection of Renaissance pieces he's found in out of the way places in Italy. He restored them and occasionally sold one. But he would never have sold the da Vinci. It was a charcoal sketch of one of the apostles for da Vinci's painting of The Last Supper—the prize of Uncle Jonathan' collection. And Lord Fawcett has been his friend since boarding school. I'm almost glad my uncle is not alive to discover this betrayal."

"Yes," said Baxter. "There is that."

* * *

When everyone had finally gone, Catherine was in no mood to go out for Indian food. Her mother said Cook had made a chicken cassoulet for her and Lady Tutworthy's dinner. It would easily stretch to six, and there were plenty of rolls. It wouldn't be hard for the cook to make some extra veg.

So, they had dinner at home. Harry brought Max and Lady Tutworthy into the picture concerning the murder and the details of the theft.

"Well," said the baroness, "This should let that Italian wife out of the running for murderer. Perhaps Jonathan confronted the viscount about the theft and got stabbed as a result."

"I can see that," said Lady Tutworthy. "He seems a very rude man. Nose in the air. And he's only a viscount, not the King of England. I must say, I didn't take to him at all."

"He could be quite charming," said Catherine. "But obviously he has a dark side."

Harry said, "He is an investment manager, you know. He could have lost a lot of money and who knows how many clients during this depression."

Max added, "No one was really prepared for their stocks to be suddenly worthless. He probably had a lot of investors who blamed him for their losses. And he could have lost his own money as well."

"Things are not the same for most of us," said Catherine's mother. "Our son, Will, pulled his father and me out of quite a big hole. He has quite a few patents to his name. I think worry about finances contributed to my husband's death."

Catherine was surprised her mother spoke of something as private as money. It is something she never would have done when her husband was alive. But maybe Madge Tutworthy was the kind of friend that Dot was. Perhaps her mother could tell her anything without worrying that it would end up in the gossip pages.

At the conclusion of their meal, they took coffee in the drawing room. Catherine learned that Lady Tutworthy was the widow of a barrister who had died ten years ago.

When Lady Tutworthy learned that Max was from a ranch in Colorado, she exclaimed, "How in the heavens did a cowboy end up studying Nineteenth Century English Literature at Oxford?"

"My parents speculate that I must have been switched at birth in the hospital," said Max with a laugh. "Truly, though, I am fascinated by the Industrial Revolution and the changes it made in the most entrenched society on earth. This is all reflected in the literature. America is so different. Our upper crust has a much shorter history and involves untamed land."

"It is different," said the baroness's friend. "But I find the difference endlessly refreshing. My husband and I spent a month doing a whirlwind train tour of the States."

"What a smashing idea!" said Catherine, pouring herself a cup of coffee. "What place did you find most interesting?"

"I enjoyed New Orleans. It was completely different than anything I was accustomed to. Such a mish mash of cultures. And I loved their jazz. We planned our trip so we were there for Mardi Gras. What an experience that was! Americans sure know how to put on a party."

"You have seen more of the country than I have," said Max. "I've always heard that going to New Orleans for Mardi Gras is taking your life in your hands."

"We stayed on our balcony and watched all the goings on from above."

"It does sound like a unique experience. A nice change from murder," said Harry as he filled his pipe.

Dot laughed. "If you and Catherine took a train tour like that, it would end up being like Agatha Christie's *Murder on the Orient Express*."

Catherine made a face. "Well, at least this murder looks to be solved. The only problem we have left is making certain Harry's parents get custody of his little cousins. I don't know where Elisabetta and her father have vanished to."

"Maybe now that an arrest has been made, she will appear," said Catherine's mother.

"Now, I feel you must tell me about this Elisabetta . . ." said Lady Tutworthy.

The rest of the evening was spent trying to explain the flamboyant Elisabetta and her presence in their lives to those who had never met her.

* * *

"It is lovely to be in London again," said Catherine's mother as they sat in the drawing room the next day waiting for the Bascombes to arrive with Jonathan's children.

"I liked Lady Tutworthy very much," said Catherine, arranging hot house irises in a white vase. "She's lively. That's just what you need right now."

"She reminds me of who I am underneath all the baroness requisites. We got up to so much mischief when we were young!"

"I fully plan to quiz the woman and find out all your guilty secrets!" teased Catherine. "I won't tell anyone but Dot. Not even Harry."

Cherry entered with their guests, and Catherine left off her flower arranging to go kiss her mother-in-law's cheek. "Sarah, how are you?"

Harry's mother didn't look to be in top form. There were shadows under her eyes and her posture was a bit limp. "Catherine, dear, it is so good to see you."

Clinging to Sarah's skirt was Adriana who had begun sucking her thumb again. The poor child's life had been shattered in the past two weeks. Jon was more upbeat very happy to see his cousin Harry. Soon they were discussing motorcars and airplanes. How much confusion must be hidden under his happy-go-lucky exterior?

"Mater, did you read the *News of the World* this morning?" Harry asked.

"No. I'm afraid I was rather too busy," she said.

"Pater?" Harry asked his father.

"You know I don't read that sensationalist rag," Harold said. "What did I miss?"

"One of Uncle Jonathan's bosom friends, Viscount Fawcett, was arrested right here yesterday for stealing and selling Uncle's da Vinci sketch," Harry replied, giving his father a one-armed hug.

Sarah's eyes grew large. "Did he commit the murder?"

"We don't know yet. Fox put us on to Fawcett." Harry told the story of Fox's recognition of the man beneath the disguise. "It was high drama when the police came. The last person I would have suspected was the viscount. He tried to bluff his way out by saying Jonathan had recruited him to institute insurance fraud. As soon as he did that, my sympathy evaporated. I knew he was guilty."

"Well! That's certainly a bit of good news," said Sarah. "Hopefully, this will be over soon!",

Cherry took everyone's coats and hats. "Dinner will be ready in twenty minutes," she said.

"Would anyone like a drink?" asked Harry

The children asked for orange squash, Sarah wanted tonic with lime, and Harold took a short whiskey along with Harry.

The children made for the dominoes which Catherine had set out on the table along with two large children's puzzles.

Dinner was lively with Harry and Catherine telling the story of the plucky Lady Jane and the discovery of the sketch her ex-husband had purchased from the thief.

"I remember the viscount from when we were staying in St. Ives," said Jon. "He wasn't fond of children; I can tell you that. Not like Mr. Milton. He was wizard. He taught us to play Gin Rummy."

"What about Mr. Baxter?" Catherine asked, curious.

"He tells good stories. He's been to Africa. He shot an elephant."

"I'm not sure that puts him on the list of my favorite people. Why would anyone shoot those wonderful beasts?" asked Sarah. "I will never understand why men think it's so manly to shoot things."

"I'm with you, Sarah," said Catherine.

"I think it's wizard," contradicted Jon. "When I grow up, I'm going to be a big game hunter."

At this juncture, there was a happy interruption as Wills, Catherine's brother, walked into the dining room.

Chapter Seventeen

"Did I hear someone talking about big game hunting?" he said. "Hello Mother, Catherine."

"William!" the baroness exclaimed, jumping up from her place at the table. She embraced her son. "It's so wonderful to see you. You must have taken an airplane!"

"I did. Rafe flew me in his plane. I would have been here sooner, but we received the news when we were way in country, and it took a while to hike out."

While Harry asked where they had been working in Kenya, Catherine took a moment to recover from Wills' news. Rafe! Her boyfriend from the time she was ten until Harry's advent in her life. She was not anxious to see him. At all. Their relationship had not ended well, to say the least. Thank heavens he had not shown up with Wills. But that didn't mean he wouldn't show up on his own at any time.

She stood up and hugged her brother. His physique had broadened at the chest and shoulders, and he sported a suntan and well-trimmed beard. "I'm so glad you could get home. Let me introduce you to my new family."

She presented Wills to Sarah and Harold. Harry exchanged cheerful greetings with him.

"And who are these charming characters?" Wills asked of Jon and Adriana.

Harry explained, "They're my new cousins. My uncle Jonathan's children. Jon and Adriana. Explanations later."

Wills nodded and went to shake each of the children's hands. "Hello! I'm Wills and I'm pleased to meet you! Jon, I promise we can talk about Africa later." He stooped down to Adriana's level. "Do you know what? I'm famished. Roast beef and Yorkshire pud. How I've missed it! And I get to eat with a lovely little girl like you, Adriana!"

At that moment, Cherry arrived with extra silverware, a napkin, and a plate and set the empty place between Jon and Catherine. Harry pulled up an extra chair from the side of the room. Catherine noticed that Adriana's thumb was back in her mouth, and she was cuddled up as close to Sarah as the two arm-chairs would allow.

"As you heard, we were talking about Africa when you came in." Harry said when Wills was seated. "Well-timed. Children, Wills, lives and works in Africa, digging wells and purifying water for the people to drink."

"Don't they have water in Africa?" asked Adriana shyly.

"Yes, they do, Adriana, but some of the water makes the children and their parents sick because the water isn't nice and clean like yours is." Wills further explained about the plumbing problems he dealt with in a way that everyone, including Adriana could understand.

"That is a tremendous thing you are doing," said Sarah. "How are you funding it?"

Wills told her about his contributors and his ongoing quest for more.

"That is something we should like to contribute to," said Harold Bascombe. "Do you have anything I could read to learn more about your work?"

"I'll make certain you get a detailed description of our projects and plans. Thank you," said Wills.

After dinner, they adjourned to the drawing room. Wills entertained them with harrowing and humorous stories. Jon asked him about all the beasts. Catherine worked on a puzzle of London with Adriana, but all the while she was thinking of Rafe and what ill-begotten plans he might be making to intrude into her life. Harry did not like him one single bit, and his feelings were reciprocated by Rafe who had punched Harry in the face during their first meeting.

Though Catherine enjoyed herself, she was not sorry to see Harry's parents and the children leave, as she craved time alone with Wills. She kissed Sarah good night.

"See you in court tomorrow, nine o'clock," Harry's mother said. "Must get these children to bed so they're fresh, but it was lovely to meet your brother. You must be very proud of him."

"I'm so glad," said Catherine. "I've been wanting to have Wills meet the new additions to our family."

She hugged Harold and the children, sending them all home with Cook's scones for breakfast in the morning.

Wills was waiting for her with their mother and Harry in the sitting room.

"So you went and got married," her brother said. "I'm sorry I wasn't here for the big event. And for Father's funeral, of course. How are you getting on, Mother?"

"Better, now that I'm in London," the baroness said. "I've been in touch with Madge Tutworthy who you'll remember. It is wonderful to see one's oldest friends and find they're just the same, only a bit wiser. You're looking well, Wills. The life obviously agrees with you. What are you going to do now that you've come in for the title and the Manor?"

Wills replied, "I don't see that much has to change. Unless you want me to hire a caretaker for the Manor. Will you be staying in London?"

"I really haven't decided yet," the baroness said. "I might. I need a change, I think."

"Then I will put my man of business on to finding someone to mind the manor. I don't want it to stand empty," said Wills.

Mother and son discussed estate business for a while before the baroness parted company and went to take a nap.

"I didn't know St. John was with you in Kenya," said Harry. "Is that working out all right?"

"Better than I thought it would," said the newly-minted Baron. He turned to Catherine, "How are you keeping busy, now that you're a married woman?"

"Well, there is Somerville, and just recently another murder. Not to mention a wedding and a spiffing honeymoon to Spain."

"Another murder?" Wills looked from Catherine to Harry and back again. "What member of the family is involved in this one?"

"Harry's uncle was killed on our wedding day, though we didn't know it at the time."

"Oh! I say, Harry. I'm dreadfully sorry to hear that. I was joking, believe it or not."

"It's not a joke," said Harry, and Catherine detected an edge to his voice.

"It's the most gosh-awful mess, Wills," said Catherine. "Full of family secrets and organized crime, not to mention those two lovely children you met."

"Tell me, then," invited her brother.

Catherine did. When she had finished her summary, she said, "It's really hard to describe Elisabetta Haverford without making her a caricature, but she is all that I said. And her father is even more so. Tomorrow we all go to court to decide the fate of those children. I don't even know if Elisabetta will appear. No one has seen her since she got out of jail."

"So you've got two crimes here," said Wills, confused. "Which one was she in jail for?"

"She took one of Jonathan's paintings to sell before he was murdered. We think she was frightened he was going to divorce her," said Harry.

"Could she have killed him?"

"Yes. But, so could Viscount Fawcett, a long-time friend of Jon's. He's under arrest now for stealing another work of Jonathan's—a da Vinci sketch," Harry added. "It's all a terrific mess."

"Yes, that's the second crime. I've managed to grasp that," said Wills, frowning. "And does this Elisabetta stand a good chance of getting her children back?"

"I don't really know," said Catherine. "She's not a terribly good mother from all that I can see, and Sarah Bascombe would be anyone's choice for a mother, by a long stretch." She grinned, breaking an odd tension in the room. "Look how nicely Harry turned out!"

Wills grinned back. "Well, I hate to break up this stimulating conversation, but I need to get back to the hotel and get some rest. I'm that tired, I'm afraid."

"Oh, but you must stay here, Wills!"

"All my luggage is at the Savoy. And Rafe is waiting to hear whether you went through with the wedding."

Catherine frowned. "I do hope you're kidding,"

"Nope. Afraid not. You owe me thanks for holding him back from coming here today. He's ready for a joust, I'm afraid." Wills stood and shook hands with Harry.

Dread all but swallowed Catherine. "Do me a favor and try to keep him sober," she said.

"Oh, he is. But he so wanted to tell you himself. And he is funding my work in Africa and helping dig some wells. He's not the idle rich man he used to be."

Still seated, Catherine put a hand to her head. "It needed only this. As if murder, grand larceny, and the Mafia weren't enough."

"Relax, darling," said Harry. "I'll take care of Mr. St. John, if you like."

If only he could!

"I wouldn't advise it," said Wills. "He doesn't like to be crossed."

"How underhanded of me to get married without his consent,"

said Catherine. She shook herself and stood, squaring her shoulders. "Never mind. I can handle Rafe."

* * *

Harry's temper exploded once they were alone in their bedroom. "Do you really suppose Rafe thinks he can win you back even though you're married?"

"I have one word to say Harry: Anne."

Catherine was amazed at the parallels in their situation. Harry's first love, Anne, who was also his brother's wife, had thought she could win Harry back on the strength of her status as his first love. And though Catherine and Harry had not been married at the time, they were celebrating their engagement. While Harry hadn't strayed, he had come under her spell once again, much to Catherine's distress.

"Oh, dash it, Catherine! You're not still holding that episode over my head!"

"No more than you're still holding Rafe over my head. I can't help what Rafe thinks any more than you could help what Anne thought."

Harry seized her by the shoulders and gave her a deep kiss. "So, you're saying, I owe you one?"

"Precisely. Let me worry about Rafe. I love you to bits, Harry. I certainly hope you're convinced of that. And I don't want to talk to or see Rafe ever again. He is firmly lodged in my mental and emotional past. A major mishap I was very fortunate to avoid."

He kissed her again. "I think I may take a little more convincing, darling. Why don't we go to bed?"

Chapter Eighteen

When Harry and Catherine arrived at the London courthouse where the custody hearing was to take place, they were a bit chagrined to see Elisabetta was there with her father and another man who appeared to be their lawyer.

Elisabetta acknowledged them only by inclining her head. But when the senior Bascombes arrived with the two children and the children's representative, Mr. Guthrie, she went over to them and made a big show of it.

She gathered both children to her, kissing and hugging them with fervor, babbling to them in Italian. Then it was their nonno's turn to come over and fuss over them.

Catherine said to Harry, "They should save it for the judge."

Said judge made his entrance and the court arose as the bailiff intoned, "All rise."

Catherine liked the look of him. He was neither plump nor skinny, his wig was pristine , and his face was mobile, not set in stern folds.

He spoke to Elisabetta's counsel. "Mr. Russo, I don't believe I've seen you appear in a family matter before. It was my impression that you specialized in criminal matters."

"My Lord, your memory is excellent as usual," replied the barrister smoothly with only the slightest hint of an Italian accent.

"But I do make exceptions for esteemed friends, such as my client, Mrs. Elisabetta Haverford."

"Very well," replied the judge, looking down at his papers.

A criminal lawyer for Elisabetta? I wonder if that bodes well for your parents," Catherine whispered to Harry as they sat in the courtroom.

The judge continued, "We are gathered this morning for the purpose of determining who shall have custody of two small children, Jonathan and Adriana Haverford, ages ten and eight respectively.

"This court has appointed Mr. Andrew Guthrie, a London solicitor knowledgeable about British law relating to families, as *guardian ad litem* for the children, to look after a children's rights and act in their interest exclusively in these proceedings. Mr. Guthrie is in the courtroom today."

Guthrie, impeccably dressed, stood and nodded to all present.

"The parties seeking to have custody of the children are the children's mother, Mrs. Elisabetta Haverford, ably represented by Mr. Tommaso Russo, on the one hand and the paternal aunt and uncle of the children, Mr. and Dr. Bascombe, represented by Sir Alistair Middleton, on the other. The necessity of a court intervention arose following the death of the childrens' father, Jonathan Haverford, some weeks ago. The appropriate authorities are investigating Mr. Haverford's death as a murder.

"As I have been informed by counsel, at the time of Mr. Haverford's death, the children were in England, spending their holidays with their father and his family following the completion of their first term in English boarding schools. Since Mr. Haverford's death, the children have lived at the home of their aunt and uncle, Mr. and Dr. Bascombe who are seeking custody of the children.

"Does each side agree to the accuracy of these facts as I have just stated them?"

"Yes, my Lord," issued from the mouths of two barristers simultaneously.

"And, the guardian ad litem?"

"Yes, my Lord."

The lawyer representing the Haverford's was bald and somewhat rotund, his grayish-white wig showing the effects of many years' use. The lawyer representing Elisabetta could not have been older than thirty-five years. His wig was snowy-white, partly covering a head of gleaming black hair, combed straight back.

The judge continued, "It is my further understanding that the children are currently enrolled for the upcoming term at the same schools they attended before the break. I understand that Mrs. Haverford, the children's mother, desires to take the children with her back to Italy, where she typically resides and, of necessity, would be withdrawing her children from these schools. It is my further understanding that Mr. and Dr. Bascombe wish to have their niece and nephew continue their schooling for the second term as their father planned prior to his untimely death and have made necessary arrangements to carry out those wishes, pay any necessary costs and so forth."

"Do counsel agree that I have accurately stated facts that are not in dispute?"

"Yes, my Lord," followed promptly.

"And the guardian ad litem?"

"Yes, my Lord."

"Very well," the judge said. "I am tired of listening to the sound of my voice. Mr. Russo, do you have any witnesses you wish to call?"

"I do, My Lord. I would call Elisabetta Haverford, the mother of the two children who are the focuses of this hearing."

Elisabetta walked forward confidently. On this occasion, perhaps at the direction of her counsel, she wore a black silk suit and hat with an emerald-green blouse buttoned-up nearly to her neck.

"Mrs. Haverford, could you please lift your veil while the oath is administered to you and thereafter as you are giving testimony?" the judge asked.

The woman lifted her veil and dabbed at an imaginary tear

before taking the New Testament in her hand and repeating the oath.

"You may proceed, Mr. Russo."

"Mrs. Haverford, we all understand that this is a difficult time for you and you are emotionally distraught, but I must ask you a few questions for the benefit of the court to assure the well-being of your children."

"Mr. Russo, feel free to ask questions directly. You will have an opportunity to make sentimental arguments to the court at a later time," the judge interjected.

"Of course, My Lord. Mrs. Haverford, until the end of last summer, where did your children customarily reside?"

"With me. In Italy. Always."

"And your deceased husband, Jonathan Haverford. Where did he see your children?"

"In Italy. Always."

"But you never went to Britain?"

"Never! I hate this place, Britain. My husband had to live here because of his business, but he loved Italy the best. My children love Italy the best."

"When did your children first travel to Britain?"

"This past *Settembre* when my husband forced them to come to this country for school. I did not approve."

Russo shuffled through his papers. "Mrs. Haverford, how do your children feel about attending their schools in England?"

"They hate it! They cry and cry! 'Mamma, please take us back to Italy! Please! We hate these English schools and these English winters and all these English children!' They hate their English schools! 'Take us back to Italy,' they say!"

"She's telling a desperate lie," Catherine whispered.

"But what a wonderful performance," Harry quietly responded. "Italian high opera in the dock."

"So you would like this court to give you, their mother, custody of little Jonathan and sweet Adriana so you can take them back to Italy, the place they love the most?"

"Yes! Of course, that is what I want! Back to Italy where they will be safe and happy! *Con la madre in Italia!*"

"Those are all the questions I have for this distraught mother," said Russo. She stood up and started to go back to her seat.

"Just a moment, Mrs. Haverford, opposing counsel may have some questions for you. Is that the case, Sir Alistair, do you have questions for Mrs. Haverford?"

"I do have a few questions for Mrs. Haverford, my Lord."

"Proceed."

"Mrs. Haverford, to the best of my knowledge, you have been in Britain for less than one month. Is that correct?"

"Yes. I do not like Britain, so I wish to stay only a short time."

"And during the time you have been in Britain, have you been arrested by British police?"

Elisabetta's father, Don Guiseppe, said something in Italian. Her attorney asked him to be quiet.

"I was wrongly arrested. I am completely innocent from any crime."

"And what charges were brought against you that resulted in your arrest?"

"*Lei è innocente!*" Don Giuseppe growled. "*La polizia è feccia!*"

"I must object to these outrageous questions, my Lord," said Russo as he rose. "They are being asked solely for the purpose of misleading this court and causing further emotional pain for Mrs. Haverford during a terribly difficult time in her life."

"Will my learned friend stipulate that his client has been arrested as a thief within the span of less than one month as a visitor in this country?" asked the Haverfords' attorney.

"I will stipulate to nothing that represents grave misconduct on the part of the Cornish police!" replied Russo.

The judge intervened. "Mr. Russo, regardless of her innocence or guilt for any crime, was Mrs. Haverford arrested as a thief by the Cornish police at some point in time after she arrived in England? A yes or no answer will suffice."

"She was, my Lord, but . . ."

"You have already answered my question, Mr. Russo. Let me ask another question that also lends itself to a yes or no answer. Does your client deny that she is guilty of thievery or any other crime for which she has been charged or arrested since her recent arrival in our country?"

"Yes, my Lord. Emphatically."

"Thank you, Mr. Russo. The court will take notice that Mrs. Haverford must be presumed innocent of any crime unless or until she confesses to a crime or is charged and found to be guilty of a crime committed here by a British court. Sir Alistair, you may resume your questioning of the witness."

"My Lord, in the interest of this court's efficiency," said Middleton, "I would like to end my questioning of Mrs. Haverford at this time but would reserve the right to recall her to the stand as necessary to provide the court with any further relevant information in this matter."

"Mr. Russo, any objections?

"No, My Lord." Russo looked relieved.

"Mr. Guthrie, does the guardian ad litem have any objections?

"No, my Lord."

"Mrs. Haverford, you are excused to resume your seat beside your attorney, but you may be recalled to give further testimony later in these proceedings. Call your next witness, Sir Alistair."

"I would like to call Mr. Oliver Brundage to give evidence."

"Mr. Brundage, please come forward and be sworn."

Oliver Brundage, a thin and aged man dressed in a morning coat walked forward slowly carrying a black leather dispatch case and completed the oath.

"Poor man. He looks like he's aged since he came to read Jonathan's will."

"Mr. Brundage, did you draw up Mr. Haverford's last will?" asked Middleton.

"I did."

"And when did Mr. Haverford execute his last will?"

"About four months ago."

"Was this his only will or was it a replacement for an earlier will?"

"It was a replacement for a prior will I drafted for him after the birth of his daughter some years ago."

"And did you and any other witnesses to the will watch while Mr. Haverford executed his will?"

"Yes. We did."

"Had Mr. Haverford created any other wills, perhaps with another solicitor, between the time he executed the prior will after the birth of his daughter and four months ago?"

"To the best of my knowledge, he did not. I have been Mr. Haverford's solicitor for the last twenty years, perhaps longer. I believe I am the only attorney who ever drafted a will for him."

"And did Mr. Haverford execute any other wills following his signature on that will you wrote, and he signed in your presence about four months ago?"

"Not to my knowledge."

"In Mr. Haverford's most recent will, did he make any changes with respect to his bequests to his wife?"

"He did."

"Would you describe those changes?"

"He reduced the amount to be paid to Mrs. Haverford on his death from 50,000 pounds to 5,000 pounds under certain circumstances which he thereafter presented."

"Did Mr. Haverford say anything about this substantial reduction in the amount his wife was to receive on his death?"

"All he said was that he was deeply disappointed by her behavior."

"What sort of behavior was Mr. Haverford on the part of his wife was Mr. Haverford concerned about?"

"He did not say, and I did not ask," replied Brundage.

"Do you have Mr. Haverford's will with you today?"

"I do not."

"And why don't you have his will?"

"Mr. Haverford requested that I keep the original in the will safe in our office for safekeeping. After learning of Mr. Haverford's death, I promptly obtained a death certificate and deposited the original of his will with the appropriate probate clerk's offices. I did retain two exact copies of Mr. Haverford's last will for my records and had them certified by another solicitor, Mr. Davies. I have brought one certified copy with me today."

"Would you hand me the certified copy?"

"Yes, I will," replied the solicitor, opening his dispatch case and reaching inside. "Here is one of the two certified copies of Mr. Haverford's will in my possession. I have also provided counsel for Mrs. Haverford and the sister of Mr. Haverford, Dr. Bascombe, copies of the will."

"Your honor," said Middleton, "I would like to offer the certified copy of Mr. Haverford's will into evidence, if counsel for Mrs. Haverford has no objections."

"Mr. Russo, do you have any objections?"

"I ask leave to briefly question Mr. Brundage before responding to your question your honor."

"Ask your questions, Mr. Russo."

"Is this usual?" whispered Catherine.

"I don't believe so," replied Harry. "If the lawyer who wrote the will and watched it being signed testifies that a copy is exactly the same as the signed original, that should be enough for anyone."

"Mr. Brundage, was Mrs. Haverford present when her husband signed this will?"

"No, I believe he said she was in Italy at that time."

"So she has no way of knowing whether this copy is the same as the one her husband signed?"

"Objection, my Lord," said Middleton. "Mr. Brundage has described precisely the way that thousands of wills are executed every month in London and also the manner in which thousands of wills of deceased residents of London are deposited with probate officials every month. Mr. Russo can go to the clerk's office and ask to examine the original of Mr. Haverford's will should he desire to do so."

"Your objection is sustained, Sir Alistair. Mr. Russo, if you have any specific concerns about the manner in which the will was executed, you will need to ask specific questions or make specific objections that might provide evidence that the will is invalid or improper under the laws of this nation sufficient to bring the validity of Mr. Haverford's will into question."

"I withdraw my question, my Lord."

"I like this judge," whispered Catherine. Harry nodded his agreement.

"Excellent decision, Mr. Russo. Are you finished with this witness, Sir Alistair?"

"No, my Lord."

"Proceed."

"Mr. Brundage," asked Middleton, "did you bring any other documents pertaining to the issue presently before this Court, the custody of the children of Mr. and Mrs. Haverford should Mr. Haverford die while they are minors?"

Brundage opened his dispatch case again and withdrew a large sealed envelope from it. "I did bring one additional item, an envelope Mr. Haverford left with me for safekeeping when he came to my office to execute his latest will."

"And what does this envelope contain?"

"I have no knowledge of what it contains. It was sealed when Mr. Haverford gave it to me in my office. His specific instructions were to keep it secure. He said I should not open the envelope but be ready to deliver it to his family or their representatives should he die before his daughter reached the age of twenty-one. Once his daughter passed her twenty-first birthday, I was to burn the envelope and its contents it without opening it."

"And you accepted this sealed envelope subject to those conditions?"

"I did."

"Where did you keep it. In your will safe?" asked the judge.

"Yes, my lord."

"Have your or anyone else opened this envelope, tampered

with it or done anything else to change it since Mr. Haverford gave it to you several months ago?"

"No." Brundage held the envelope up so the judge could see it. "I asked Mr. Haverford to sign his name across the sealed flap of the envelope so, if anyone did open it, that fact would likely be apparent upon a careful examination of the envelope."

"Is that his signature across the flap of the envelope?"

"It is. I am very familiar with his signature."

"And does the envelope show any evidence that anyone has tampered with it since Mr. Haverford delivered it to you?"

"No, it does not."

"Is it your testimony under oath that this envelope and its contents are exactly the same as when Mr. Haverford delivered the envelope and contents to you?"

"Yes."

"My Lord," said Middleton, "we offer this sealed envelope into evidence so the court may see what Mr. Haverford wrote concerning his possible death before his daughter reached the age of twenty-one."

"I object most strenuously, My Lord!" said Russo, jumping to his feet. "This is nothing but a badly concocted stunt to harm my client. The court should reject this so-called evidence and cause it to be destroyed."

"Are you saying we should destroy the envelope and its contents without examining them?" asked the judge.

"Absolutely. This is a travesty of justice, some sort of devious scheme perpetrated against Mrs. Haverford and her children to enrich her husband's family at her expense."

"And how do you or your client know what is in the envelope and how its contents may impact her?"

"That's just the point, your honor. We don't know. It's a nearly perfect trap for the unwary."

"Do you have a response, Sir Alistair?"

"I do, my Lord. The chain of custody between Mr. Haverford to Mr. Brundage to this court is iron-clad. Haverford hand-delivered it to Brundage who put it in his will safe and then brought it here to this court. An examination of the envelope shows no evidence that the envelope or its contents have changed or even been examined since that time.

"Mr. Guthrie, in your capacity as the guardian ad litem of the Haverford children, what do you think the court should do?"

"Open the envelope, my Lord. Mr. Haverford took unusual steps to make certain it was kept secure and would only be opened upon his demise. I don't see any way in which opening it would harm or disadvantage his children."

"Well, counselors," said the judge, "we shan't know whether the contents of the envelope include evidence that this court should consider or if they do not unless we open it. I suggest we clear the courtroom of all persons other than the parties, their attorneys and two individuals from the clerk's office to act as uninvolved witnesses to the opening. Let's also have a shorthand writer brought to make a transcript of what happens and what anyone present may say about the contents.

"Ladies and gentlemen," the judge said, "please clear the courtroom at this time. Bailiffs, wait outside and keep the doors shut until I order otherwise. A bailiff or a member of the clerk's staff will give ample notice to interested parties before this court will resume its consideration of the matters presently before it."

"A mysterious sealed envelope," said Harry as they left the courthouse and walked toward the first pub they saw. "I always thought probate was deadly dull."

"Your uncle always struck me as the soul of taste and discretion," replied Catherine. "An Italian wife and intimidating father-in-law from Sicily don't fit my picture of him."

"Which is even more evidence that, unlike my revered uncle, I chose wisely when I wed a sensible, intelligent and accomplished English woman who investigates murders."

"Be careful with your comments or I may need to tap my Cornish Mafia connections to keep you in order," said Catherine.

Chapter Nineteen

After luncheon, when the courtroom doors were opened, the judge looked tired, Harry's mother appeared to be quite upset and someone had tipped off the press and a group of reporters immediately pushed into the courtroom. Three policemen stood in front of the bench with two more on either side of the courtroom.

One of policemen loudly said, "Take your seats and be quiet, the court is in session." The crowd quickly filled all the seats, and several observers were standing in the back of the courtroom.

"Ladies and gentlemen," said the judge. "This Court, counsel for Mr. Haverford's widow, the mother of his two children, counsel for Mr. Haverford's sister and her husband who are seeking custody of Mr. Haverford's two children and the guardian ad litem have reviewed the contents of the sealed envelope the late Mr. Jonathan Haverford left with his long-time solicitor and the creator of his will, Mr. Oliver Brundage, for safekeeping.

"This court will not describe the contents of the envelope with any degree of specificity. As I discuss in general terms some of the contents of the envelope, I do not want to hear any audible response from any person in this courtroom. I have instructed the bailiffs and the several policemen you see in the courtroom that they are to immediately remove any person who makes a sound as I describe the contents.

"Does everyone present understand what I just said about absolute silence in this courtroom?"

Catherine saw one of the reporters whisper something to another sitting next to him.

"Bailiffs, officers, remove that man in the ugly brown hat from this courtroom immediately!" ordered the judge. "If he makes another sound before he is ejected from this courtroom, jail him. I repeat my warning that I expect complete silence from anyone else here who wishes to avoid being ejected while that man is removed."

The reporter was silent, but clearly unhappy about being hauled away. The courtroom door slammed shut behind him. Catherine wondered how he would explain that to his editor.

"Does anyone else want to make a comment concerning these proceedings and be ejected?" asked the judge, looking around the courtroom carefully.

"Hearing no response, I will continue. While not providing particulars, I will say that the envelope's contents included information obtained by private detectives Mr. Haverford retained in Italy to report to him concerning his wife's activities when he was not present. One or more of these detectives evidently took photographs of Mrs. Haverford that I will only characterize as scandalous. Some of these photographs showed Mrs. Haverford in compromising situations with men who were not her husband.

"Additionally, Mr. Haverford placed written reports from one or more of the detectives he had hired describing what they had seen, including additional activities not shown in photographs into the sealed envelope. These reports were accompanied by sworn statements from the detectives attesting that the photographs depicted actions and activities they had personally witnessed and were accurate representations of what they had seen and that their written reports were accurate descriptions of what they had personally observed.

"Mr. Haverford also included several sworn statements of his own. Some of these statements identified two of the men depicted in these scandalous photographs as men he personally knew to be members of the Sicilian Mafia.

"There was also a troubling assertion that Mr. Pinna, Mrs. Haverford's father is himself a major figure in the Mafia organization. There are additional documents that were in the sealed envelope that I opened, but I do not believe any further description is necessary at this time. Mr. Haverford left an additional sworn statement that, to the best of his knowledge, understanding and belief concerning his wife's actions, all materials relating to her in the envelope were true and correct.

"For the benefit of the children and to make certain the contents of the previously-sealed envelope held by Mr. Brundage are not damaged or accessed by any other person without the court's prior written consent, I am ordering that, immediately following the conclusion of these proceedings, the clerk of this court, accompanied by two police officers and counsel for each party should counsel wish to accompany the clerk, take sealed envelope and its contents across the street to the bank and deposit those contents into a secure lockbox located therein. Do either counsel or the guardian ad litem have any questions concerning the security of the lockbox? Apparently not. I hereby order the clerk and one of the employees in the clerk's office take the sealed envelope and its contents across the street and place them in a lockbox as the court has described. The lockbox will not be opened except upon the express order of this court. I will leave a written order concerning the lockbox with the clerk, should anyone desire to examine it."

"Mr. Guthrie, do you, as the guardian ad litem for the children wish to make a statement?"

"I do, your honor," Guthrie replied, standing up.

"Prior to this date, I have met and spoken with each of the children of Mr. and Mrs. Haverford, Jonathan Junior, and Adriana in private, where they are presently residing in the home of the sister of the deceased, Dr. Sarah Bascombe and her husband Mr. Harold Bascombe in Hampshire. The children told me that they enjoyed the home, their schools and the company of their aunt and uncle.

Mr. and Dr. Bascombe said they planned to have the children continue their education at their present schools or suitable alternative schools and were willing and able to pay all fees and expenses for the children's further education, continuing through university.

"During our private conference with the court that has just described, I reviewed the contents of the sealed envelope when the court provided them for examination by counsel and the guardian ad litem. I fully support the court's characterization of the contents of the sealed envelope as scandalous.

"Based upon all the information I have gathered, I believe it is in the best interests of the children, Jonathan Haverford, Junior, and Adriana Haverford, to be placed in the custody and under the care of their paternal aunt and uncle, Dr. Sarah and Harold Bascombe. I firmly believe that such custody arrangements are in the best interests of the children and further recommend that they should not be entrusted to their mother or leave England without this court's explicit written consent in advance of their departure."

"Thank you, Mr. Guthrie," said the judge. "Does counsel for either party have any questions for the guardian ad litem? Hearing no request, I will excuse the guardian ad litem, but ask him to remain in the courtroom until these proceedings conclude.

"Mr. Russo," said the judge, "As you learned after we finished our examination of the contents of the sealed envelope, it was my preliminary inclination to order that the current custody arrangements and schooling for the children remain as they have been previously established. After hearing the testimony of the guardian ad litem regarding his visit with the children, I continue to be inclined to continue temporary custody with their aunt and uncle and directing that the children continue with their schooling as they have begun it for the remainder of the school year.

"One of the principal reasons for my inclination is that it appears to me the continuation of the current arrangements will provide needed stability for the children and are in their best interests. Living with a medical doctor also assures the court that they shall receive prompt and proper medical treatment, should that become necessary. Does your client have any objections?"

Elisabetta, her father and the barrister all stood up and started to speak simultaneously. Don Giuseppe was the loudest, shaking his fist at the judge, and just barely exceeding the volume generated by his daughter.

The judge raised a finger, looking toward the back of the courtroom. Two strapping men wearing badges came forward to stand behind Elisabetta and her father. One put a heavy hand on the Don's shoulder. Their barrister spoke in rapid Italian to his clients and nearly had to force them back down into their seats.

"My Lord," said Elisabetta's barrister after some degree of silence returned. "We wish to object to this interference with the well-established rights of a parent to have custody of her child. As is obvious to anyone here, as the only living parent of these children, my client is distraught at the thought of being separated from them for longer than she already has been."

"So noted, Mr. Russo."

The barrister representing Harry's parents stood.

"Yes, Sir Alistair?" asked the judge.

"My Lord, I would remind the court that Mrs. Haverford has been placed under arrest since her arrival shortly after Christmas and that there are still outstanding criminal charges against her. She is merely out on bail."

Elisabetta and the Don exploded again with fists shaking and a torrent of angry Italian. Their barrister had even more difficulty getting them to quiet down and sit down again.

"I do recall the evidence, Sir Alistair. Mr. Russo, what is your client's formal response, in English, please, to my proposed order regarding the two Haverford children?"

Russo stood up and said, "My clients do not, of course, agree with the court's proposed order and believe it to be arbitrary and highly unreasonable to separate children of a young age from their mother. Other than noting the likely appeal of such an order should it issue, we have no other evidence or argument at this time."

"Very well, Mr. Russo. Sir Alistair, am I correct you have no further evidence or argument on behalf of your clients?"

"No, my Lord."

"Mr. Guthrie, as the guardian ad litem for the children, do you have anything further?

"No, my Lord."

"Very well," the judge replied.

"Dr. and Mr. Bascombe, it is this court's order is that you will continue to care for your nephew and niece as I've described unless and until this court or another with jurisdiction over the children orders otherwise. I intend to issue a temporary order promptly so the mother may pursue any extraordinary remedies she and her counsel believe are appropriate. After fourteen days, and considering any additional responses from counsel, I will enter a permanent order of custody so my brethren on the Court of Appeals or the Italian embassy or whomever else may have a horse in this race may take issue with my decision. My clerk will be sending out a copy of my temporary order to counsel for each party, likely by tomorrow's morning post and my final order on the schedule I've described. I'm not going to make any order for visitation by the children's mother at this time but may do so following notice to counsel in future."

The judge looked at Elisabetta who looked straight back at him. "To be absolutely clear to everyone, under no circumstances are the children to be taken away from England without this court's prior explicit written consent. Violation of this order will result in severe sanctions, including possible charges of kidnapping, against the party or parties who violate this order. Do you understand that Mrs. Haverford? Yes or no will do for an answer."

"Yes, I do, English judge," she replied.

"Does anyone have questions about this court's order concerning these two children?"

The judge looked around the courtroom before fixing his gaze on Elisabetta and her father one final time.

"Hearing no questions, we stand adjourned. Bailiffs, please assist those present in leaving the courtroom in good order. The bailiffs will inform any who are waiting outside this courtroom regarding other matters that the court will be hearing such matters following a recess of one hour."

"Ladies and gentlemen, be upstanding," said one of the bailiffs in a loud voice.

After the judge exited, the news reporters made a dash for the exits as a great many discussions erupted in the courtroom.

Chapter Twenty

With all the loud conversations in courtroom, the children looked confused. Sarah Bascombe went to them and embraced them both, then briefly spoke to them. She sent them to their mother to say goodbye. Catherine saw the conflict in Adriana's face, but Jon's revealed nothing.

Elisabetta hugged them, whispered something in Adriana's ear, then turned away to leave the courtroom. Guthrie also spoke with the children briefly, then escorted them back to Sarah.

How would it be to lose your father suddenly, then your mother and your grandfather shortly after? And going off with your father's sister whom you hardly knew?

There was no way those children would be anything but confused, no matter how their mother had treated them. Then there was Nanny. What did the Bascombes intend to do about her?

Apparently, Sarah intended to keep her for the time being, as Nanny came forward and accompanied the children as they left with the Bascombes. Nanny looked somewhat confused, herself. Catherine wondered how she felt after all the things that had transpired.

Catherine glanced toward Don Giuseppe and was frightened by his expression. His lips were bunched together, and his eyes narrowed. She felt anger coming off him in waves as he stood with clenched fists. But with two bailiffs standing behind him, he held his peace.

Catherine and Harry watched while the don walked quickly out of the courtroom with Elisabetta's barrister at his side, talking to him. No one concerned had heard the end of this. She worried the children would not be safe in the Bascombe's care as long as Don Giuseppe and Elisabetta were in Britain.

Harry caught up with his parents before they got to their Bentley. Catherine kept an eye on Elisabetta and her father who were conferring with their barrister. The children's grandfather kept looking back, his eyes sparking with threats. Catherine felt chilled.

How far would Don Giuseppe go to get those children? How naïve of us to think he would be dictated to by the English laws! There are problems ahead.

She hurried to where Harry was talking to his father. She heard the tail end of his conversation. ". . . Mary's house."

Harold Bascombe, Sr. was listening to his son, his face wooden.

"I wish Sarah hadn't decided to take Nanny. It will be like an enemy spy in our camp," Harry's father said, jingling his change and car keys in his pockets.

"I can understand why she did," said Harry. He put a hand on his father's shoulder. "She wants them to have someone familiar."

He said goodbye to his parents and shook hands with his little cousins. "We will see you before the beginning of your next term at school."

Adriana threw her arms around Harry's waist, crying into his shirt. The sight tore at Catherine's heart. Harry knelt and looked Adriana in the eye. "You are such a brave girl. I know things are different, but I honestly think they will be better. My mother is kind and gentle. And soon you will go back to school with your friends. We'll visit on special days when the family is invited."

He gently wiped her tears with his handkerchief. Seeing that his father had started the car, he said, "Time to go now, ducky. Say goodbye to your new cousin, Catherine."

Catherine bent down and kissed the girl's forehead. "I'm so happy to be your cousin! Have fun with your aunt and uncle!"

Harry walked with Adriana to the Bentley and tucked her in the back seat with a travel rug. "Goodbye now!"

The car slowly moved away as a great many locals were actively discussing the morning's happenings.

"Don Giuseppe looked murderous," Catherine said with a shiver. "Did I hear you say they're taking them to Mary's? Isn't she due any time?"

"Mary's family has a seaside cottage in Devon. It will be a bit cold this time of year, but not much worse than Cornwall. It's a quiet place with sheep and an old sheepdog and in a couple of weeks, they go back to school," said Harry, tucking his handkerchief away in its pocket. "For everyone's sake, I hope Mary can hold off the baby 'til then."

"Me, too," said Catherine. "But Devon is a good idea. Their nonno won't know where to find them. I understand your fears about Nanny though. I'm not certain what her relationship with the Pinna family is. But she's the one who told us that the children's mother hits them," said Catherine.

"I expect Nanny is grateful to be kept on by mother," said her husband. "I think Nanny has a close bond with the children, and I don't know what she would do if Elisabetta gave her the sack. Hopefully, she will see this as the best solution for all of them."

Catherine still felt as though the arrangement could fall apart at any moment. She shoved her hands into her pockets and bit her lip as Harry hailed a cab.

On the way back to the townhouse, Catherine tried to fight her unease. But soon she realized she had a different problem. A too-familiar Hispano-Suiza sat in front of the townhouse. It was red, not cream-colored like Jonathan's.

"Rafe is here," she said to Harry.

"The devil he is!" said her husband.

As they rode up in the lift, Harry's jaw was set, and she could almost hear him grind his teeth.

Cherry met them at the door. "Mr. St. John is here," she whispered.

"Thank you, Cherry. When is luncheon?"

"It won't be long, ma'am."

Catherine took off her hat and gloves, trying to decide what to do. She said, "I'll just go to my room and freshen up a bit." She looked at her husband. "What do you want to do, darling?"

"I think I'll go face the blighter right now."

She patted his cheek. "Remember murder is a capital offense."

Cherry followed her to her bedroom and helped Catherine change from her suit into a pair of trousers and a blouse. Rafe hated to see women in trousers. She applied some red lipstick which he also hated.

Cherry said, "It's time for luncheon, ma'am."

Catherine took a deep breath and went down the hall to the dining room. Rafe was bound to create some sort of fuss, but she was ready for him.

Harry and her former boyfriend were already seated but rose at her entrance. Despite his wild ways, Rafe still appeared to be in one piece.

She let Harry kiss her cheek. Both men said, "Hello, darling," at the same moment. Rafe looked over her trousers but made no comment about them. Instead, he said, "What on earth has happened to your head? What are those baldish patches? Is it an ugly new style?"

Catherine put her hand to her head. Bother. She should have kept her hat on. "Harry and I were in a car smash in October," she said dismissively. "Mother, how are you feeling, today?"

"I've enjoyed catching up with Rafe and hearing his stories about Africa. But how did thehearing go, dear?"

"The Bascombes have custody of the children, but the Pinna's are not happy. I'm a bit worried, to tell you the truth, but I don't think there's anything further to be done. Rafe, you look as though Kenya agrees with you." Tall and broad of shoulder, Rafe was still much more handsome than was good for him, even before he became so suntanned.

"It suits me down to the ground," Rafe replied heartily. "I still think you would love it there."

"It's not on the cards for the next several years, I'm afraid. My heart and my work are in Oxford. I'm writing a dissertation and tutoring at Somerville. Harry, darling, could you pass the rolls? I'm famished."

Harry complied and spoke up, "I don't know whether you've heard, but Catherine has taken a post at Somerville and is doing jolly fine work there. That and, as you know, we were married a couple of weeks ago. We're just back from a honeymoon trip to Málaga."

Catherine watched a scowl build on Rafe's face.

"How long will you be in London?" she asked as she buttered her roll.

"As long as it takes your brother to settle his business," Rafe said. "How long will you be here?"

"It's hard to say. Term starts soon, but we're caught up in some business we'd like to straighten out first." She turned to her mother. "Was there anything in the paper about the viscount's arrest?"

"You could say that," said the baroness, as Cherry placed a bowl of steaming bouillon in front of her. "It made the front page of *News of the World* together with an unflattering photo of the man. Do you think the viscount murdered Jonathan Haverford?"

"I don't know," said Catherine. Feeling cold clear through in the never-warm dining room, she was glad to see the soup. "It will depend on whether anyone saw him on the cliff that morning, I imagine. According to Harry's aunt, there were a number of people who were wandering around there at the time."

"You are involved in another murder?" Rafe asked, his eyebrows raised.

"Yes," Catherine said. "Harry's uncle was murdered on our wedding day, but we knew nothing about it until we returned from Spain. His body was only recently discovered. It's been a ghastly ordeal. And then, my father had his fatal heart attack right in the middle of it all."

"That sounds a bit much, even for you," Rafe said. "I knew about your father, of course. That's the reason Wills had to come home." He turned to Catherine's mother. "I'm so sorry. I should have expressed my condolences immediately. Was his death unexpected?"

"Not really," said the baroness, her voice clipped. "He was in a decline for the last year."

Harry entered the discussion. "I understand you are the main patron of Wills' endeavor. That must be very satisfying for you, St. John."

Catherine was thankful Harry was making an effort move past his anger with Rafe.

"It is satisfying," said her former boyfriend. "It's nice to be doing something besides taking up space on the planet. How is the world of Nineteenth Century Literature?"

"Spiffing," said Harry, obviously determined to see past the slur. "And Catherine is showing great prowess in her new role. She's writing and publishing energetically. Two books published to great reviews and she's working on the third. Her work on the War Poets is very apropos just now."

"Harry did a very moving reading of the War Poets during Michaelmas term and also when we were in Los Angeles teaching last summer."

Catherine used all her conversational skills to fill the rest of the meal with anecdotes from their summer abroad, including an account of the murder they had solved in Hollywood. Harry joined in with somewhat exaggerated accounts of her heroics. Since her mother hadn't heard these tales before it was entertaining for her, as well.

"None of this is greatly surprising," said Rafe. "I remember many a fantasy you enacted as a child around those castle ruins near the Manor. I assume that is where you derived your ability to scale walls."

"Yes," said Catherine. "And I remember you refusing to play the part of the hero who was supposed to rescue me!"

"From the sound of it, it's just as well you learned to rescue yourself," he said, smiling.

"Harry has been a huge help in that regard," said Catherine giving her husband a warm smile as she reminisced. Harry grinned.

Suddenly, she wanted to be alone with her husband, curling into his side as he gently stroked her hair. Being in the same room with Rafe's ego was always tiring. When they moved into the drawing room at the conclusion of the meal, she sat next to Harry and was frustrated that good manners forbade her cuddling with him right now. Evidently sensing her mood, Harry put an arm around her shoulders.

"Believe me, Bascombe, I get the picture," Rafe said dryly. "I don't really need a visual."

Catherine was instantly angry. "Why does everything have to be about you and what you need?" she asked Rafe. "I *like* Harry's arm around me. It's a comfort. I know we've not gone into the details, but I just lost my father. Not to mention we had a rather harrowing morning in court which I do not intend to discuss with anyone here. We aren't going to drop everything and enter your world, Rafe. We have plenty of our own concerns, believe me!"

Rafe recoiled as though he'd been slapped.

"Really, Catherine," said her mother in reproach.

Catherine stood. "I have work to do," she said for want of an excuse. "Good afternoon, everyone."

She left the drawing room and retired to her bedroom. She had no sooner sat down than Cherry appeared. "Will you be wanting anything, miss . . . er . . . ma'am?"

"Listening at doors, I see," Catherine said.

"Well, I had to know what was going on between you and Mr. St. John!" the maid said indignantly.

"Of course, you did," Catherine said, looking at her reflection.

She looked haggard, which was hardly surprising. "I'm sorry, Cherry. It must be a great strain to act the perfect maid when my mother is here."

"Not too bad," said Cherry with a cheeky grin. "I like your mother. She's what my mum would call spunky."

"Could you find me some aspirin? I have a monstrous headache." Catherine endeavored to get a knot out of her shoulder muscle.

"There's some in the bathroom cupboard. I'll bring it, but you need to take off your shoes and lie down. After the aspirin, why don't you take a little nap until Mr. St. John leaves? He's what my mum would call a bucket of bad news. You can't ever trust a man who is that handsome. Now then, I just get you that aspirin. You won't be any good to anyone if you can't manage those headaches."

What Cherry said was true. She'd been prone to headaches ever since her car crash in October. They came on with any added stress, and Rafe plus anything else equaled the worst sort of stress.

Catherine cast her mind back to sunny scenes from her honeymoon—a splendid antidote to Rafe. Despite all that was wrong in her world, she drifted off into a pleasant doze.

When she woke, she was surprised to find it was already time for tea. She hoped mightily that Rafe had gone. After putting herself to rights, she started to leave the bedroom when she saw a note had been pushed under the door.

She recognized the stationery. With a sigh, she picked it up. She had best read it now before Harry saw it. Then she could put it on the fire.

Dear Catherine,

You were perfectly right to push me out of your life. I was a dreadful ass. I realize you are married now, but I have made such an effort to change for you, I want you to know about it.

First, I have quit drinking. I've been sober for over a year now. I truly have. The clean air of Africa and the simplicity of my life there has been good for my soul. I see that I have wasted my life shamefully. I have many regrets about the past, but my greatest regret is how I treated you. Is there any way you can forgive me? You don't have to take me on again. I repeat, I know that you are married, and believe me that is a wound to my heart that will never heal.

So what do I want? I want you not to be disgusted by me anymore. I want you to trust that if there is anything you ever need, financial or otherwise, I will come to your aid.

I don't suppose I shall ever marry now. I will continue to live in Kenya, unless war should come again. In that case, I would throw myself into it with all my effort and try to make a difference. In the meantime, I shall try, along with your brother, to make a difference in Kenya by bringing healthy water to as many native villages as possible.

I hope you will have a happy life, but if you ever need me, I am here for you.

With all my devotion,
Rafe

Catherine read the letter twice, trying to make out whether Rafe *was* sincere or whether this was another of his manipulative ploys. In the end, she supposed she must give him the benefit of the doubt. He seemed to have accepted that he was no longer the most important person in her life. He also seemed to feel sorry for himself, an unattractive trait in any man. Harry would never indulge in self-pity.

In the end, she threw the letter on the fire. She didn't want Harry finding it by chance.

Chapter Twenty-One

When she joined the family for tea, she was glad to see that Rafe had left.

Tea started out as a cheerful pastime. It was lovely to have a cook.

"I rang the house in Devon just before tea," Harry told her, selecting a scone and covering it with jam. "The children weren't there yet. The caretaker's wife said they had been held up by a baby delivery. I rang Hampshire. They will leave as soon as they know Mary is all right. She had a healthy little girl.

"Mother is worried Adriana and Jon are going to have an abandonment complex, but she's going to do her best. It really was too bad of Uncle Jon to saddle her with the responsibility of children she didn't even know he had."

"I doubt when he wrote that will that he had any idea he would really die so soon. It was just a precautionary measure," Catherine said, helping herself to a watercress sandwich.

"Still, the right thing to do was to tell her about his family and give her a chance to make up her own mind whether she could take them on. Mother carries on, but she's not getting any younger, and she has her practice."

"Don't you think she would have said yes if he had asked

her? I do." Catherine looked at her mother. "What do you think, Mother?"

"I hardly took care of my own children, so I am the wrong one to ask. Now that you are grown, I have regrets."

Catherine was sorry she had spoken to her mother's feelings of inadequacy, but what the baroness had said was true. Before she could fashion a kind reply, her mother went on.

"I spent all my time running away from my feelings. Literally running away. I was never at the manor any longer than I could help. I grew to detest the place. But it wasn't you children in particular I was running from. It was the result of my bad decisions." She stopped to wipe her tears and blow her nose. "Now I'm regretting my regrets! You are such a fine woman, Catherine. The credit doesn't go to me, I know. But I'd like to spend this part of my life trying to make things up to you and Wills."

Catherine was surprised. All her life, she had thought that there was something wrong with her. She kept trying to be perfect, so her mother would love her.

Harry gave her a soft look. Part of her wanted to tell her mother that that ship had sailed, that she was no longer a needy little girl. But she found she couldn't. Instead, she took her mother's hand. "I'm sorry you were so unhappy, Mother. But all is well. How can you doubt it when you see that I am so happy? And Wills is doing so much good in the world."

But her mother wouldn't be consoled. She begged to be excused and left the room, having eaten nothing.

"Well!" said Catherine. "I never thought this day would come, but poor Mother. How awful to have those kinds of regrets!"

"Between her and Rafe, it's been a comeuppance kind of day," said Harry. "I think we need to bundle up and go for a walk."

"I am so very grateful for you, darling," Catherine said, once they stepped out into the foyer of the townhouse. "Thank heavens I never married Rafe!"

"I feel sorry for the poor fellow. I'm glad I'm not in his shoes," said Harry. "It's windy. You'll have to let me put my arm around you."

He pulled her in next to him with his wool clad arm.

"Yes. That's nice," Catherine said. "I hope Rafe will find someone else. I had a letter from him under my door today. I think he feels that if he shows me he's changed, I will take him back. He has blinders on."

Harry studied her profile. "I don't like the idea of his writing letters to you. He doesn't seem to have taken our marriage on board."

Catherine sighed. "No, I don't think he has."

They came to a bench in the square. "Sit down," she said. "I want to tell you something."

Harry complied.

"Do you remember a long time ago, my telling you that my feelings for Rafe arose because I didn't feel I had anyone to belong to?"

"Vaguely."

"I think I spoke about certain emotions in me just failed to develop. Or developed in a weird way. Hence my strong connection to Restormel Castle and my elaborate fantasy world. It was good for my writing, but not so good for my relationships. I didn't develop normal feelings."

Harry gave her a one-sided grin. "Are you saying your love for me is weird?"

"No, I'm saying that it's pretty normal, compared to my abject devotion to Rafe. Parts of me are still thawing."

He kissed her right in the middle of the square. "I'm happy to tell you I haven't noticed any lack of heat in our lovemaking."

She stroked the side of his face and looked deeply into his warm brown eyes. "No. I'm melting nicely. And I'm having random flashes of pure joy."

"I'm glad," Harry said. "I hope one day Adriana will have days of pure joy. What she's going through must be pure hell."

"Good friends help. Dot was my refuge."

"I give thanks to God for Dot," said Harry. "I know she really helped you when I was behaving so badly, as well."

"I wonder if Lady Tutworthy is Mum's Dot. I think I will give her a ring when we get back."

"Good idea."

* * *

Lady Tutworthy was graciousness itself when she took Catherine's call.

"I wondered that she seemed so unlike herself. If you think I can help, I would be happy to take her under my wing. There is a wonderful season of Opera this year, and she's always liked that. I can also get her together with some of the Old Girls from school."

"That sounds marvelous," said Catherine. "I'm sure she'd enjoy that! Thank you so much for your help. You probably know her better than anyone."

"Her parents were terrifically hard on her. I'm probably the only one who knows what she went through. There was another man you see. She loved him fiercely, but your father was a baron. Your grandfather sent the other man about his business."

The words sobered Catherine. Obviously, her mother hadn't had the best role model.

"That helps me to understand her a little bit better. I know you can help her. Thank you again."

"I want to help. Thank you for letting me know about this."

Catherine rang off and went to find Harry who was reading the evening paper.

"Darling," he said. "Listen to this: 'Viscount Fawcett, who was lately arrested for the theft of a Leonardo da Vinci sketch from recently deceased Jonathan Haverford, is now being investigated by Scotland Yard for Haverford's murder. The police are of the belief that Fawcett killed Mr. Haverford when he discovered the viscount's theft of the artwork. Anyone with any information about this matter is asked to notify Scotland Yard's Detective Sullivan.'"

"Well, we assumed that was coming," said Catherine. "What do you think?"

"I think it makes sense," Harry said, putting down the newspaper. "But being hanged for murder is a whole lot worse than a prison sentence." He rooted around his pocket, and finding his tobacco and pipe, he absently began to fill it.

Catherine sat next to her husband on the sofa. "If I remember correctly, your Aunt Patricia didn't see Viscount Fawcett walking down to the cliff."

"That doesn't mean he didn't do it," said Harry. "She also said she wasn't watching out of the window every minute."

Catherine said, "I don't think it is going to be an easy case to solve. There were too many people around the cliff that morning and they all have motives!"

"Bear up, love. Let's go pay Fox a visit in the morning. Maybe he will let us look through my uncle's papers. We may find something that has some significance."

"There's always Mr. Tomlinson, my man of business. We're due a report from him," said Catherine.

* * *

Tuesday morning found Harry and Catherine arriving at Mr. Tomlinson's office in the City in the midst of a rare snowstorm. She loved the snow, but Harry found it a nuisance.

Mr. Tomlinson greeted them with his usual sober countenance. "I'm afraid I haven't found much about any of the gentlemen you asked me to look into, except Mr. George Baxter. Viscount Fawcett's affairs have become public since his arrest, but absent the theft I would have said he seemed well off, financially. He keeps all his doings very confidential and doesn't use a man of business. Things are bound to be different because of the Depression, but he seemed to be on his feet. This is by way of an awful warning that things may be far different than they seem, even to someone like me with a fair knowledge of things financial.

"Milton lost one of his prize studs this winter, but he has two more, so I don't think it will seriously affect his business. He was clean.

"Now, Mr. Baxter is another story. He's strapped for cash. No wind of anything illegal, but he's borrowed more than he will easily be able to pay back."

"That could be a problem," said Catherine. "Harry's uncle appointed him trustee. But his lawyer is the other trustee, so hopefully everything will be all right."

"Mr. Baxter has a good reputation. That stands him in good stead," said Tomlinson.

Catherine stood. "Thank you so much, Mr. Tomlinson. I assume you would have informed me if I was having financial problems somewhere."

"Everything is going well," the man replied.

Their next stop was Jonathan's house/gallery on Notting Hill. The snow was piling up and the traffic was snarled, but they eventually made it.

Fox answered the door. "Good morning, Mrs. Bascombe, Dr. Bascombe. Please come in. What can I do for you?"

"We'd like to take a look at my uncle's papers, if you don't mind," said Harry. "We think it may help us find his killer."

"I've been doing that this morning," Fox said. "Please join me. I have come across something I think is of the greatest importance."

Harry and Catherine followed Fox back to Jonathan's office. Through the window, she could see the snow swirling in the wind and Fox had lit a fire in addition to the central heating. It was lovely.

"I found this. You'll want to read it first," Fox handed Harry a document. "I'm no expert but it looks to be a more recent will."

"The devil it is!" Harry paged through to the back where the document proved to have been properly signed and witnessed by the cook and the housekeeper. "Is that his signature, Fox?"

"It is. I'm very familiar with his signature. I've spoken to the cook and housekeeper and they saw him sign it and he told them it was his will."

"Dated the week before his death. Let's see . . ."

He began reading, passing Catherine each page as he read it.

"Ah ha! Elisabetta had reason to be concerned," said Harry. "He left her fifty pounds. That's it."

"Wasn't she here for a day, Fox, waiting for the children to arrive from school?"

"She was, and she made herself free of the office. I believe she saw the original will and stole it. The one you are holding is Mr. Brundage's copy. It was in an envelope in my quarters."

"What in heaven's name was it doing there?"

"I was given it the day he left for Cornwall with instructions to deliver it by hand to his solicitor. But the children arrived and I'm afraid it went out of my head. It was a terrible lapse on my part."

Catherine could read the man's lowered brow and bunched mouth. Agonizing over this lapse, he said, "Do you think this will change anything? Besides Elisabetta's bequest, everything else is the same. He doesn't give her any parental rights, but it says he won't include his reasons in a document that is likely to become public. He refers to the sealed envelope."

"Mr. Guthrie and Mr. Brundage need to see it right away," said Catherine.

The man looked more agitated than usual. His eyes jumped between Catherine and Harry. Finally, he cleared his throat. "I will take it today, of course," Fox said. "If I had been privy to the contents, Mrs. Haverford's arrival would have made it doubly important to deliver it, but I didn't know what it said until I came across it today. I feel like I failed him."

"Well, no harm done," said Harry. "We'll just ring Mr. Brundage and tell him about it."

Catherine spoke up. "He's taken her rights away altogether

with this will. He doesn't give a reason, but we have that in the 'secret envelope' which he still refers to in this document."

Fox found Brundage's telephone number in Jonathan's address book which lay on the desk blotter. Harry rang and delivered the message about the new will to the clerk and said that Mr. Fox would be bringing a copy to him that afternoon.

"Elisabetta must have been angrier than Medusa with a headache," Harry said to Catherine. "This gives her an urgent motive to make away with Jonathan before he finds out she stole the will."

Catherine said, "If ashes could be read, I imagine we'd find it in the grate in the fireplace."

"We need to make another phone call. To DI Duncan," said Harry. "He needs to know about this immediately. Probably before we send it to Brundage."

Fox was sitting now, holding his head in his hands. "If only I had known . . . I could have prepared the major so he would be on his guard. She wouldn't have had a chance to murder him."

"We don't know that, Fox," said Catherine gently. "He wouldn't have expected her to come up behind him with a knife."

Chapter Twenty-Two

To say DI Duncan was furious about the suppressed will was an understatement. He cut off Fox whenever he tried to speak, pounding on the desk.

"Do you realize that your carelessness is responsible for your employer's murder? That it still might be responsible for his murderess escaping? I have no time for your excuses. I have to find the woman while I still can!"

He went straight to Haverford's telephone and rang the rooming house where Elisabetta had been staying with her father. Obviously, she hadn't disappeared as far as the police were concerned. However, the policeman found that they had left their lodgings just hours before, taking their suitcases.

DI Duncan cursed roundly and then without missing a beat, called his office and began issuing orders to close the ports, the boat trains, and the airports to women of Betta's description. He still held her passport so she would be travelling on a false one. Next, he put in motion an alert to all police stations in the kingdom.

Catherine and Harry sat mutely, witnesses to this titanic effort to stop the wanted woman from escaping the law.

When the DI paused for a moment, Catherine said. "Mrs. Haverford may be in touch with Mr. Brundage, Jonathan's solicitor about claiming her money under the old will. Harry and I can take the new will to his office and explain what is being done."

"Yes, yes. Do that," said Duncan.

Catherine refolded the handwritten document and slid it into a fresh envelope from the desk drawer. After sealing it, she wrote the address taken from the torn envelope, and nodded to Harry. They left.

Mr. Brundage greeted them with surprise and invited them to be seated in his office.

"Have you heard from Mrs. Haverford this morning?" asked Catherine.

"Yes, as a matter of fact. She rang. She wanted a check for the first installment of her fifty thousand pounds. She said she was leaving town. I told her she needed to sign the waiver giving Jonathan's family power to raise the children. She intimated that the court's decision yesterday decided the matter for her. I must admit, I felt a little sorry for the woman. I said I would talk to Mr. Baxter, the other trustee and try to move things along.

"She was quite angry that she couldn't get her hands on it right away. My solicitude vanished at that point. I am not accustomed to being spoken to in that manner. I told her that these things took time and that we would need the approval of the court before dispensing the funds."

"Well, it turns out that was a fortunate thing, sir," said Harry. He explained about the new will and delivered it to him. The solicitor read quickly through the document and looked up. "By Jove! And you say she knew about this?"

"Not only knew about it but stole the original. It has probably been destroyed."

"Well, this will must be filed with the court immediately," Brundage said. "A new probate course must be initiated."

Catherine recounted Fox's story of his failure to deliver it before Jonathan's death, adding what the man had told them about his lack of understanding about the importance of the envelope's contents.

"Do the police know about this?"

"Yes. We rang them immediately. Of course, this heightens Elisabetta's motive for killing my uncle before he could find out she had destroyed the will," Harry said.

Brundage paged through the document and checked the signature page. "So now she really is on the run."

"Yes. The police are livid. They're pulling out all the stops," said Catherine.

Mr. Brundage slapped his desktop and rose to his feet. "The children! She might try to take the children! They are her only bargaining chip."

Catherine's heart leapt in alarm, and she grabbed Harry's arm. "I didn't think! Oh, Harry, you must ring your parents!"

"The devil! Of course! Mr. Brundage, your phone?" Harry asked.

"Of course. They live in Hampshire?" Brundage asked.

"Yes. I must put a trunk call through."

"Tell the exchange that it's an emergency!" the solicitor said.

At length, Harry had his mother on the phone. "The children! Where are they?"

"They're out riding, why?" Sarah Bascombe asked.

"You must go after them and leave for the beach cottage immediately. Take Mary and the children with you if you must. Keep Adriana and Jon by you and don't trust Nanny. We will be down and can pack up your things and follow you. Elisabetta's missing and wanted for murder. She and her father will probably try to take Jon and Adriana. You need to be gone!"

"Oh heavens! What's happened? Oh, never mind. First things first. They don't have much. I must get off right away."

Sarah rang off, and Catherine realized she was twisting her hands in her lap.

"Is there anything else we can do?" she asked. "Your poor parents!"

"No. We just need to get down there and get their things together. I only hope they get away in time."

"Has it occurred to you that it might be a good idea to notify Scotland Yard that Elisabetta may show up at your parents' home? They could arrest her there," said the solicitor. "If you like, I could take the matter in hand so you can be on your way."

"Oh, this whole thing is making me a dimwit!" said Catherine. "Of course! Yes, if you could do that, it would be enormously helpful. Thank you so much, Mr. Brundage."

The two of them went back to the townhouse. They found Lady Tutworthy there, visiting with Catherine's mother. Catherine explained the situation to the baroness.

"We must pack up a few things and then be on our way," Harry said after quickly summarizing the situation.

"A new will! Oh, heavens. Yes, yes. I can see she might have destroyed it. Oh dear. Oh dear. Yes, you must go. Heavens," dithered Catherine's mother.

They excused themselves and left the baroness explaining the whole complicated situation to her friend.

Because Harry's Morris was still in Oxford, they had to take the train to Hampshire.

Once they were aboard, Catherine sat kneading her hands together and biting her lower lip. "I only hope they got away!" she said to Harry as the miles passed.

"I hope the Pinna's run straight into an ambush by the police!" said Harry.

"I'm glad about the will, though," said Catherine. She began to chew her thumbnail, a habit she had broken in boarding school. When she realized what she was doing, she put her hand back in her lap.

Harry must have decided she needed diversion, so he said, "Are you making any changes to your curriculum this term?"

"Oh, Harry! You know I can't even think of that right now!"

"All right, how about this? Do you think Dot and Max will work out?"

"You mean get married? I have absolutely no idea. There are

a slew of things against it, but they seem very committed to one another. That's all I can tell you about that."

"What shall we do for the Long Vacation this year?" he asked.

"Oh, Harry! I don't know. Nor do I care at the moment."

"Kenya? South America? Sweden? Italy?"

The thought of going anywhere but Hampshire had no appeal for her at

She grabbed her hair and pulled it. "Stop trying to distract me! It's only making me cross."

"All right. Try this: how do you think Elisabetta and Don Giuseppe are going to get out of England and back to Milan?"

She paused in her hand wringing and gave the matter some thought. "If I were them, I think I'd go to Scotland for a bit. Until the furor dies down."

"Not a bad idea. You ought to mention it to Scotland Yard. It's a straight shot on the train, and they could go to ground in some little Scottish village with a view where visitors wouldn't cause comment."

The porter came by with the afternoon edition of the newspaper, and Harry took one, handing the first section to Catherine. She lost herself reading about the case in *The News of the World*. The editors played up the organized crime angle. Particularly the Mafia angle. Some enterprising journalist had also gotten hold of a picture of Elisabetta modeling a swimsuit.

"Well, *News of the World* is keeping up with their reputation—crime and sex on the front page."

"Cherry will eat it up and your mother will be disgusted," predicted Harry.

The news did make the trip seemed shorter. When they got off the train, they were met by Harry's brother James who was living with the parents for a while to escape the gossip and brouhaha of his divorce.

He looked smooth and handsome as usual, but Catherine noted new lines in his forehead.

"Did they get away?" asked Catherine immediately.

"Just barely. It was probably only ten minutes before the Mafia turned up. They left as soon as they realized they had missed the children. Of course, I wasn't any help at all. I must say Uncle John chose a looker, but her temper put me in mind of a sailor."

"Yes, well, he certainly lived to regret it, and the latest development is that there is a warrant for her arrest," said Harry. "I don't suppose they dropped any hints about where they were going next?"

"The police asked me that already. They have been and gone. Our dear aunt-in-law is a downy bird, and she and her father, who was masquerading as a concerned grandfather, were out of here shortly before the authorities arrived. It's been like a train station here."

"Well, we're going to rush off, as well, once we get everyone packed up," said Harry. "It's a good job they didn't stop to do it themselves or they would have been caught by the not-so-loving Mama."

Catherine was immediately calmed by Harry's childhood home. Even though the day was dreary, the bright colors of the abstract paintings on the white walls brought cheer when one entered the front hallway. The entire house was furnished in the Art Deco style of leather and chrome with colorful accents throughout.

The children's rooms were easy to find and pack up. They hadn't really had a chance to completely unpack yet. Catherine put their soiled clothes in pillowcases and packed the rest of their things in their school suitcases.

Her mother-in-law was a different story. After half an hour, she had only packed the basics, and none of her toiletries or undergarments. Unfortunately, Sarah had taken her maid with her to Devon. All Catherine could do was to pack what she would have taken were she Harry's mother. Harry was finished with his father's things much faster than she was.

The winter day was growing dark by the time they boarded the train for Devon. They ate dinner in the dining car while rain slashed against the windows. It was the gloomy essence of a typical winter day in the West Country. Sunny Spain could be on a different planet.

Harry had picked up a pack of cards at his parents', and after dinner they began playing Gin Rummy. Harry had won a good bit of cash from the distracted Catherine by the time they reached the coastal town near his sister's cottage.

They sat huddled in the cold railway waiting room after Harry had put in a call to the cottage saying they had arrived.

The children were in bed by the time Harry and Catherine had been picked up and driven by his father up to the cottage in the Bentley.

"How are they?" asked Harry.

"It's yet another change for them. Jon seems to have a spirit of adventure about the whole thing, but I'm afraid Adriana has regressed to her thumb-sucking again. Poor child. Every time she turns around there is another jolt. She did so like the horses and the puppies."

It was no worse than Catherine had feared.

"This place is very cozy," she said after they arrived, looking at the overstuffed furniture draped with handmade quilts. There was a fire in the large fireplace and the chess set on the occasional table showed evidence of a game begun. "It will make them feel better to have their things."

"James told us that you got out just in time," said Harry. "Elisabetta and her father arrived only ten minutes after you left. The police missed them, though. They didn't stay long."

Sarah Bascombe put the back of her hand to her forehead. "I'm relieved they missed us. I don't know what we could have done. Do you suppose Don Giuseppe has a gun?"

"I don't doubt it," said Harry. "I expect he has a way to get his hands on one. Too bad the police missed them. I wonder where they're going now."

"I can't imagine they'll be able to leave the country very easily," said Harold Bascombe after his son told him about the new will and all the precautions Scotland Yard was taking.

"I don't see Don Giuseppe leaving without his grandchildren. Maybe Elisabetta would, but he won't," said Harry.

"Is Nanny here?" asked Catherine suddenly.

"Yes. She's actually been a great help with the children. She knows what they like to eat and that sort of thing."

"How does she feel about Elisabetta losing the children?" asked Catherine, pulling a beautifully embroidered pillow onto her lap.

"She's the one who told me that it's Don Giuseppe who wants them back. Elisabetta would have been perfectly happy to let Jonathan have them, although she did genuinely dislike the idea of boarding school," said Sarah, stabbing at the fire with the poker.

"Any guesses as to how the children feel about Elisabetta?" asked Harry.

"Any child is attached to their mother, no matter how poor a caretaker she is," replied Sarah. "They are always going to feel abandoned," said Sarah. "And I can't even imagine if she gets hanged because she killed their father. That will be a nightmare they'll never forget. They won't know what to do with their feelings."

"You are going to be of long-term importance to them," said Harry. "Are you really prepared for that?"

"I'm just going to take it one day at a time," said Sarah. "Mourning the death of their father, outlandish behavior by their mother who is suspected of murdering him. I really don't know how they will bear it. We'll see how things develop."

"On some of their school breaks, they can come to us in Oxford, if that appeals to them," said Harry. "Jonathan would have liked that."

"You're right. He had a great deal of respect for education and how it shapes one's life."

"I really admire you for taking this on," said Catherine. "I just wish Jonathan would have discussed it with you. Told you about his family."

"I wish he had, as well. It was such a shock!"

Catherine and Harry chose to have an early night in the cozy room under the eaves they had been given. There were quilts here as well.

"Who does all the quilting?" she asked her husband.

"My sister. She always has a quilt going. Mary is a real homebody," Harry said.

"I would love to learn how to quilt," said Catherine. "I'm hopeless at embroidery and it would be nice to have a hobby like that that I could pick up on winter evenings."

"I'm sure Mary would love to teach you."

Catherine and Harry held each other tightly that night. Catherine reckoned they had a long way to go before this case would be over with. Where had Elisabetta gone?

Chapter Twenty-Three

On Wednesday, Catherine and Harry spent the day taking windy, cold walks on the shore, exploring the little seaside village—mostly shut down for the winter—and eating excellent, if heavy, food as prepared by the Bascombe cook.

Everyone was highly strung and a bit irritable except Harry's mother. She sought out the children and showed them Harry and Mary's old games. They played Snakes and Ladders, Happy Families, and coaxed the adults to join them for a game of charades. Nanny did the children's laundry, mostly kept to herself, writing letters and knitting. Catherine wondered what the woman thought of them. What did Italians do to pass the time? Would Sarah Bascombe keep her on? Nanny was probably wondering that, though she seemed serene enough.

By the time the children had gone to bed, Catherine was ready for some alone time with Harry. As they lay in each other's arms in their cozy room, she asked whether he thought Nanny would stay on if she were asked. Harry thought she would go back to Italy.

"I've been observing her these last few days," Catherine said. "In her way she is passionately devoted to Jon and Adriana. She doesn't show it as much when she's around Elisabetta, but she's very good at anticipating their needs, and when she thinks no one is observing her, she is affectionate, particularly with Adriana. She may be the only reason the children are not worse off than they seem to be. I have never seen Elisabetta be particularly affectionate with them."

"Thank heavens for Nanny then," said Harry. "Mother's job is hard, but if you're right, Nanny is helping in her own way. It's good to see her out from under Elisabetta's shadow. I think that woman makes Nanny nervous."

"She makes *me* nervous. I simply can't imagine what kind of marriage your uncle had!" said Catherine.

"Divorce is illegal in Italy, remember. And it's only legal here in cases of adultery. It seems that he just barely got evidence of that," Harry said, trailing a finger round her ear. "I'll bet you anything little Jon told him about all the other men."

"How sad. I wonder what kind of young man he is going to grow up to be after spending half his childhood under those circumstances." Catherine rolled onto her side so her ear would be away from his tickling fingers. She, in turn, ran her finger round his ear. "Thank heavens they have your mother and father."

"I think I'm ready to go home to our own little place," he said. "What do you think?"

"I have a feeling we haven't heard the last of Elisabetta and her father. They and that barrister of theirs seem very resourceful. How about if we stay here one more day?"

"There are some caves nearby," said Harry. "Because of the ocean patterns, tides, and so forth near here they are more accessible in the winter. I think the children might like to see them."

Catherine shivered. "Caves give me the pip. You can take the children. There's a quilting store in the village. If I'm to be a quilter, I'd like to start with a simple project. Your mother said she'd get me started if I'd like to try. I'll go there while you go to the caves."

"Well," Harry said, "That settles tomorrow. Now what do you think we could find to do tonight?"

"I don't know," she answered. "Have you a good book?"

Laughing, he caught her in his arms.

* * *

Catherine sat by the window underneath a lamp in The Quilting Bee, a little shop run by an American woman from Ohio who had moved to Devonshire. Having already picked the kit she wanted to try—a simple wall hanging for Mary's cottage—Catherine was now endeavoring to choose from the bolts of fabric. She studied them in the meager sunlight. The colors and patterns were all so enchanting, how could she pick just four?

The door opened and she was vaguely aware of two people entering the shop. Catherine didn't look up from her project.

In less than a minute, she felt something hard poke her sharply in her back through her coat.

"I beg your pardon," she said, thinking she had gotten in someone's way. The pressure didn't relent but became sharper. Whipping her head around, she found herself confronting Don Giuseppe in a guise she had never seen. His features were set in a grim mask.

"There is a pistol at your back," said his daughter in soft, menacing tones as she stood behind him. "Stand up slowly and walk out the door without saying anything to anyone."

Catherine froze, rooted to the spot. Gripping the fabric in her hands, she tried to process the words. Elisabetta, Don Giuseppe *here? With a gun?*

She said the first thing that came into her head. "How did you find me?"

"Don't worry about that. Walk out the door. Let us be on our way," said the woman, her beautiful features hard and not the least bit charming.

Catherine's heart raced, and her legs felt like they would fail her.

"We go now," said Elisabetta. "Don't make a sound."

Catherine walked ahead of the Don. Elisabetta put her arm

around Catherine as though she were a friend, but in actuality her grip was like iron.

"Ma'am?" The proprietor called. "Ma'am, is anything the matter?"

"We are going for coffee with our good friend. She will be back later to finish her shopping," the Italian woman said in a cheery voice. "We are so glad to see you, my dear," Elisabetta continued as they walked out the door.

A car was idling in front of the shop. Don Giuseppe opened the rear door and prodded her inside with his pistol. Catherine obeyed, her mind racing. Until she was sitting in the back seat, she didn't realize she still clutched a swatch of cotton fabric.

What's going on? Where are they taking me?

Elisabetta smiled and waved at the woman in the store then got behind the wheel. She asked, "Where are the children?"

"With Harry. You'll never get them away from him," Catherine said.

"He'll give them up." Elisabetta said. "You will see. Our plan is made. You are going with us. I know all about you, now. The newspapers wrote all about your crime-fighting. But you've never faced the Pinna Family before. For centuries, we have been persuading people to agree with us. Once you understand, you will agree with us also."

Catherine's mind finally began to work. How could she escape? Don Giuseppe was old, but he seemed powerful. Especially with a pistol in his hand. They had reached the cottage.

"Tell me, are Harry and the children inside?" Elisabetta asked.

It flashed into Catherine's mind that she would take a bullet if it meant saving the children, but in this case, it wouldn't do the least bit of good.

"They are down in the caves with Harry. They could be hours," she replied.

"Then we will wait hours," the Italian woman said. "We'll just sit right here and wait. What shall we talk about?"

"How about the fact that you murdered your husband?" Catherine suggested.

The woman gave a mirthless laugh. "Ha! I didn't, as a matter of fact. Believe me or not, I am innocent. I wouldn't kill the father of my children. I suspect it was the viscount, or maybe Jonathan's good friend George Baxter? Another good choice is Milton. I don't trust any of them."

Catherine was startled. It must have shown in her eyes, for Elisabetta continued, "I didn't even go down to the cliff. I was with Adri, trying to help her. She was miserable, poor thing. She doesn't . . . didn't like it when my husband and I fought, and we had words that morning."

Silent, Catherine gave this some thought. Could Adriana be forced to lie by her mother and Nonno? She had absolutely no idea. But what if Elisabetta's story is the true one? What if it is one of Jonathan's party of friends? I don't trust George Baxter and the viscount has already proved he is capable of grand larceny. But murder? And how about Roderick Milton? He is certainly a dark horse. Whatever the truth, however, kidnapping me and the children will not help Elisabetta's case.

Catherine remained mute. Her captors began to communicate in rapid Italian, evidently devising their plan.

It seemed ages before she heard Harry's voice as he shepherded the children up the steps from the beach. Catherine's mind raced as Elisabetta opened the car door.

Catherine reached for her car door and flung it open. "Harry! Run!" She screamed using all the power in her lungs and ran toward them. She fell down as a shot rang out behind her.

She threw herself full length on the ground. Harry and the children ran to her. Pulling her up into his arms, he said, "What is going on here? Are you hurt?"

Elisabetta answered. "That was just a warning shot. I have come for my children." The don exited the car and came around behind them, still wielding the pistol. Harry, help Catherine back into the automobile." She spoke rapidly in Italian to the children.

They didn't obey her.

Adriana cried, "No! I don't want to go back to Italy with you!"

"Papa has a pistol aimed at your dear wife's back," she said to Harry. If you don't let my children come with us, she won't live until your one month anniversary. What a pity that would be, but you should never have meddled. Help her into the automobile."

She turned to her children "Bambini!" Elisabetta's tone was now syrupy sweet. "Look who is here! Nonno! We're going to leave this horrible, cold England! We're even bringing Catherine with us!"

The children were silent, their faces pinched in confusion. Catherine couldn't imagine what they were thinking.

In a moment of vulnerability, Jon tugged on Harry's coat sleeve. "But I don't want to go! I want to stay here with Aunt Sarah and Harry!"

Catherine wished Elisabetta's back wasn't to her, for she would love to read the woman's face.

Now Elisabetta went forward, knelt down, and put her hands on Jon's shoulders. "You know that you have important business back in Italy. Nonno is depending on you! You will be the head of the family when he is gone. He needs to teach you, to train you!"

Jon hung his head. At the same time, Catherine became aware that Adriana was crying. She tried to hide herself in the folds of Harry's coat and put her thumb in her mouth.

"Get in the car, Jon. I must speak to your sister." She yanked Adriana out from behind Harry. "Now, little signorina, you are always telling me how nice Catherine is. Won't it be fun to travel with her?"

"But I lub Harry!" she sobbed. "And Harry lubs Catherine."

"Get in the car, *bambina*," her mother said gently. "Maybe Harry can visit if you are good."

Reluctance in every movement, Adriana climbed into the car next to her brother.

Elisabetta addressed Harry, "Your wife will be our hostage

until you pay me my fifty thousand pounds out of my husband's estate. You will give it to Mr. Russo when you have the money."

Catherine thought she was going to be sick. The don looked at her with satisfaction.

Elisabetta jumped in behind the wheel and slammed the car door. She switched on the motor, it caught, and they were off speeding down the dirt road.

Catherine felt her heart breaking and her eyes dim with tears as she watched her husband recede from view out of the back window. She didn't believe Elisabetta. This was the Mafia. Only death awaited her once her role of hostage was done.

No! I can't think that way! I will find a way to escape. I must keep my wits about me.

* * *

Nonno conversed with the children in non-stop Italian, his tone cajoling as he spoke from the back seat. After what seemed like hours, Elisabetta spoke sharply in Italian. With a final sniff, Adriana stopped crying.

They were approaching a small harbor. Catherine's heart sank. She had hoped they would try the boat train which she knew was under surveillance. Surely they wouldn't take a yacht all the way to Italy.

Her heart went out to the children. Jon's lack of spirits hurt her most. He was keeping his grief inside, as always, but she knew it was costing him. It must be the price he was willing to pay for peace and freedom from abuse.

How many people had the children's nonno caused to be killed? He seemed to be a caricature of a Mafia don. But she hadn't done well to underestimate him or Elisabetta. She must take them seriously. There was a reason the great operas were in Italian. They were about the big emotions: love, hate, betrayal. They would be ridiculous if they were sung in English. But Elisabetta and Don

Giuseppe were not ridiculous. They would have no problems with this script. They were Sicilian. Melodrama was in their blood.

The harbor was set against formidable cliffs, making escape impossible, even should she get away. She could never outrun the car, and there was no place that offered escape other than the road they had traveled.

It was late in the winter afternoon when Elisabetta finally parked. Catherine consoled herself with the idea that it would be better to get where they were going before attempting a communication with the Bascombes.

The harbor was little more than an inlet with a dozen or so small pleasure crafts along two separate piers. There was the inevitable pub and bait shop, but little else in the way of businesses. Somehow the Pinna's had managed to find and secure the loan of a boat. Or were they stealing it?

The don steered Catherine at gunpoint onto a paneled cabin cruiser and down to a tiny cabin with a narrow bench/bed. Don Giuseppe gave Elisabetta the pistol and went up to the bridge. Elisabetta locked Catherine's door and left her to rail against her helplessness.

Was there a captain on this little boat? Or did Don Giuseppe know how to pilot a cruiser and plot his course to Italy?

When the boat's engine caught and they began to move out of the slip into the channel, Catherine looked out the porthole and tried to figure out which direction they were headed, but without reference points, the matter was practically hopeless. Everything in her told her they were going West, but surely that couldn't be. Maybe when the moon rose, she would be able to determine something.

Meanwhile, Catherine was left to think about Harry and quell her hunger pains as best she could. Harry would never be able to find her, so it was up to her to make an escape strategy. She wouldn't survive in the water for long in this season, so jumping overboard was not an option. If she only had a weapon, she could incapacitate Don Giuseppe . . .

Chapter Twenty-Four

Her captors evidently had some compassion as the don brought her some bread, cheese and soup, and a bottle of water for supper. She was able to visit the "head," which sailors called the WC, while he waited outside.

Back in her cabin, Elisabetta was awaiting them, "Don't give us any trouble, or there will be no more food."

His words brought home the fact that she was a prisoner, though her cell might be a little unusual. How strange that organized crime had infiltrated her life and Harry's. At first, the Italian drama had seemed almost humorous, but that had been before the don showed himself as anything but a loving grandfather. Now she was fast understanding that the man might have feelings for his family, but he was also someone else entirely. All his grandfatherly love for the children had vanished, leaving a flat-eyed, pinch-mouthed killer with one desire only—to threaten Catherine with his nasty looking pistol. He wanted her to visualize him pulling the trigger and discharging his weapon into her body. She knew he could take her life in a split second if she failed to remain compliant.

Sleep was impossible. Her mind was a cyclone of worries, questions, and fear all turning on the reality of that pistol. She couldn't imagine what Jon and Adriana thought of the threat against her. And how were they coping with this latest and sudden uprooting?

Jon was hiding his fears behind anger. Was he wondering what Harry would do in his shoes? The boy was being forced to grow up too soon, faced with problems he could not solve. How rotten it all was! Did he and his sister think Harry had let them down? Or were they imagining that he would overcome all obstacles and be awaiting them when they docked? Or that she would somehow free herself and them? If only that were possible.

To avoid obsessing about gruesome scenarios, Catherine fell to thinking about the case of Jonathan's murder. Had Elisabetta murdered her husband, or did Catherine only want to think that because the model was such a cruel, self-involved person? Was there a reason other than extortion to account for her kidnapping? Did she know something she shouldn't about Jon's widow? She couldn't think of anything worse than what she already knew. Did the Pinnas know that the police were holding another suspect—Viscount Fawcett? Kidnapping her at this point was a tactical error. Now the police would be looking at Betta and the don as suspects in the murder again.

Elisabetta and Don Giuseppe were proving themselves to be violent and capable of murder. And Elisabetta had destroyed the will. Catherine felt certain Jon's wife had done so with the intent of profiting sometime in the near future.

She unscrewed her water bottle and took a long drink. She explored the drawers underneath the seat/bed and found a fitted sheet, a duvet, and a pillow. The only other drawer contained a pair of men's flannel pajamas. Just as she was thinking of changing into this welcome find to keep herself warm, there was a knock at her cabin door.

"Well, I can't keep you out!" Catherine shouted.

"It's Jon," came the loud whisper. "You can open the door. I found the key to unlock it."

Her heart leapt. "Well, aren't you the clever one!" she said, opening the door and giving him an exuberant hug. "Come in!"

The boy entered and sat on her bench. "You'll be glad to know we're not going all the way to Italy in this boat. Nonno said that was too obvious, and we should probably be caught."

"I shouldn't mind being caught," said Catherine, "But I must admit, I'm not that excited about being shut up in this cabin all the way across the Mediterranean."

"Don't you want to know where we're going?"

"Do you know? Do tell, Jon!"

"Ireland."

Her heart fell. Ireland. No one would ever suspect they would go west.

"It's a place with a funny name. Something 'sherry,'" Jon informed her.

Ireland. Well, at least it had the virtue of being closer than Sicily. "Do you know how long it will take for us to get there?"

"Mama said we should be there by morning."

A thought occurred to her. "Who is piloting this boat, anyway?"

"A rum fellow who I think is halfway drunk."

Though his words were scornful, there was fear behind them. *He's trying so hard to be grown up.*

"What has your mama said about why she's locked me up?" Catherine asked.

"She says you want to take us away from her. That you're wicked."

Catherine wished she could do away with the sadness in his eyes. "And what do you think?"

"I never realized it, but she forgets that we hear her when she's shouting at other people. She thinks we only hear her when she's talking to us in that smarmy voice she uses," said Jon thoughtfully. "I heard her say that she's taking you so the lawyers will pay her the money she's supposed to have."

"That's what I heard, too. Now did your Aunt Sarah explain about what happened in court?"

"Yes. She said the judge told her Adri and I could live with her and Uncle Harold."

"He did. Now, listen. The judge also said that if your mother did what she's doing—taking you away—it would be kidnapping. She'd get a life's sentence in jail for kidnapping. It's one of the worst laws you can break." Catherine stopped for a moment. The other thing would be terribly disturbing to Jon, but he needed to know what they were dealing with. "And perhaps I shouldn't tell you this, but she is also running from an arrest warrant. The police think she killed your father."

The boy frowned as his eyes grew big. "Crikey. Do you think that's true?"

"I don't know, Jon. But I do appreciate that all of this is hard for you to take in. I'm so sorry." What kind of scars was this poor boy going to have when this was all over?

But he just straightened his spine and squared his shoulders. "I need to know these things. Even if they're hard. What is going to happen to you if they don't pay the money? Is Nonno going to shoot you with his pistol?"

She was quiet. What should she say? "I hope not," Catherine said. "But that's not your problem to solve. It's mine."

His grave face suddenly came alive as his eyes sparkled. "I will find a way to go to the police! I'll tell them we've all been kidnapped!"

Catherine felt a jolt of alarm. "Jon, no. It's too dangerous for you."

"I heard Mama and Nonno talking. When we get to the place in Ireland with the funny name, they're going to keep you locked up on this boat. I will find a policeman and bring him to you, so you can talk to him."

Catherine ran a hand through her hair. *Can he really do this?*

"I don't need your permission, Cousin Catherine. I can do it. I know I can!"

She hoped very much that Jon was more intelligent than the average ten-year-old.

At that moment, the door flew open and a seething Elisabetta stood there. "*Giovanni! What are you doing here?*"

"I thought Catherine would be lonely," he said promptly. "She is."

"You're supposed to be in bed. Come now. And give me that key you found. Do I have to lock you in, too?"

Catherine watched as the boy went, outwardly docile at least. Tears started in her eyes as she watched his brave posture. Could he do it? Was she a wretch to hope that he succeeded? What would Harry say?

Harry. Oh crikey, she missed Harry. A chill overcame her and she began to tremble. To Don Giuseppe life was cheap. She realized that he had probably killed before to gain his ends.

This is not happening. It's too unreal. I am not being held captive with my only hope resting with a ten-year-old boy.

She examined the door to her jail. It was decorative rather than secure. Made of one plank of teak, it had a simple lock on the door handle. When her captors had left the boat, she ought to be able to break it down. Her jailers were putting a lot of faith in a doorknob lock. At five feet five inches, 110 pounds, she didn't look strong enough to take out a door, but somehow she would manage.

Nothing could be done until the others had left, which she presumed they would do in the morning when they reached their destination. She might as well lie down and try to get some sleep.

Her heart was heavy in her chest as she made up her bed. She decided against the pajamas. She was exhausted but her nerves wouldn't settle.

She spent the night becoming more and more convinced of her peril and praying that poor Jon would not suffer for trying to do what he proposed.

What use would Elisabetta and her father have for her once the ransom was paid? She would certainly be an inconvenient witness to their deeds. Wouldn't they consider themselves better off if she had a convenient accident and fell into the ocean?

Would she never see Harry again? Would they never have a life together in that charming little Oxford house her father-in-law had purchased for them?

For some reason the latter thought was finally enough to drive her to tears. However, gradually the tears morphed into anger. What right had a criminal and his narcissistic daughter to take away her life? To rob Jon and Adriana of a chance to get a good education and to grow up in a home with loving parents like Harry's? No rights! Catherine vowed she would make it as difficult for the Pinna's to carry out their plans as possible. She would fight to the last. And maybe, just maybe Jon's plan would work.

* * *

The next day was long. A storm blew in and set the boat rocking in its moorings. Normally, Catherine was a good sailor, but this was not a normal day. The violent rocking of the boat made her ill. There was a basin in her cabin where she vomited, but the stench was overwhelming. Watching the hours crawl by on the lovely little watch Harry had given her, she wondered if Jon could be successful. No food or water appeared, and she gradually grew aware that she was alone on the boat.

Late in the afternoon she heard a racket outside her door. It sounded like someone was using an ax to break it down. Hope blossomed inside her. In a very short time, a red-faced Irish policeman was standing in front of her. Behind him stood Jon with a big smile on his face.

"Cousin Catherine? I'm Murphy. This boy tells me you've been kidnapped."

"Yes! Thank you so much for coming!" Catherine put up a hand to try to smooth her hair. "Have you been in touch with Scotland Yard?"

"Yes. By telegram. They put us in touch with your husband in Hampshire. He is on his way to get you. He's flying into Waterford and driving down. Courtmacsherry is not the easiest place to get to. Now, let's get you off this boat and sitting beside a nice cup of tea . . ."

"But Jon's mother and grandfather . . ." she protested.

Everything was suddenly moving very quickly. Jon had been lucky in his policeman!

"Ach, not to worry. I have them all sewed up in my wee jail."

"Already? How did you do that?"

"We'll save that story for another time. For now, let's say the big Italian fellow had never had a tussle with an Irish copper.

"Now, I can tell that you've been sick. Let's get you out of this place."

"Wait 'til you hear, Cousin Catherine!" said Jon. "It was wizard!"

Catherine's head was spinning at her sudden freedom. She was beginning to think that this policeman *was* a wizard.

"And where is Adriana?" Catherine managed to ask.

"She's having a kip at my place with my good wife. Plumb worn out, she was."

"Oh, I *am* glad. I've been so worried about her!"

"Come along, my dear," said Mr. Murphy, extending a meaty hand. "There's time for tea and a biscuit or two while we wait for my superintendent."

The tea and biscuits were served to Catherine in the tiny stone police station not too far from the little harbor. A thick steel door guarded the one-room jail.

"This here is a fine young man. Now, his mam . . ." the policeman began, nodding toward the corner where Jon and Adri were playing cards.

"Best not to speak of her just now," warned Catherine, revived by several cups of tea, but feeling grubby and in need of a bath. It would be horrible if she had to greet Harry this way.

"You're right," said Murphy, looking a bit shamefaced. He seemed to be having almost as much fun as Jon. Didn't he realize how dangerous his captives were?

"What's going to happen with Elisabetta and Don Giuseppe?" Catherine asked, beginning to realize she was hungry for more than a biscuit.

"My super is going to take charge. He should be here shortly.

I haven't a clue what he'll do. Scotland Yard is anxious to get its hands on them.

"Now, my lady is fixing stew and soda bread for supper."

"That sounds divine," said Catherine. "Jon, you deserve a medal for rescuing me. How can I ever thank you?"

"Let me come and visit you and Harry sometimes," the boy said, eyes alight.

Murphy's superintendent arrived at mealtime, and Catherine suspected he might have planned things that way. Mrs. Murphy was a grand cook with a happy smile. She had Jon and Adri helping her in the kitchen. Catherine partook freely, glad her queasiness had passed now that they were on dry land. The woman had made enough for an army. Some of the stew went over to the jail, as well.

When the superintendent had taken his fill, they moved into the small sitting room which was crowded with furniture covered in floral prints. The children stayed in the kitchen with the comfortable Mrs. Murphy feasting on apple crumb pudding.

Superintendent Higgins was a large man with a heavy face and keen blue eyes. "Well now, suppose you tell me how this all came about—your kidnapping. I can understand why a mother would want her children, but why would she encumber herself with another woman?"

"Extortion," said Catherine. "She wanted to hold me hostage until we gave her fifty thousand pounds from her husband's estate."

"Ah! Another mafia specialty. Extortion. She is quite an enterprising woman. Too bad for her she's mothered an honest, brave boy."

"My husband, Harry, says Jon takes after his father, Jonathan Haverford, who was recently murdered. Apparently, he was a splendid man. I wish I'd known him."

Superintendent Higgins said Scotland Yard had briefed him on Jonathan's murder. The rest of the interview consisted of Catherine conveying the information covered in court—both the inquest and the custody hearing, as well as the full details of Catherine's kidnapping. She was weary when she had finished.

"So what do you think? Did the woman kill her husband?"

"There are other suspects, as I have said. She seems to be the most likely to me, but my judgment is obviously affected by my kidnapping."

The only things that sustained Catherine through her exhaustion were the knowledge that she was free and that Harry was coming to collect her.

"Ah, well. It's sure an' I'd like to know how this will end. I expect the folks in London will let me know," said the superintendent, rubbing his hands together.

She asked, "What will you do with Mrs. Haverford and her father?"

"It is my inclination to turn them over to the Yard without any fuss. They are Italians who committed no crimes in our country, other than crossing our border with a kidnapped woman, and incarcerating her overnight. It doesn't make sense to try them or to spend money imprisoning them for a far lesser crime, but that decision will be made by powers higher than me. DI Duncan and his sergeant are coming across by Royal Navy Coastguard tonight. We can expect them here in the morning when they will take custody of the prisoners. I imagine the coast guard will take them all the way down the Thames to London, where they will be incarcerated and tried. From what I understand, Mrs. Haverford has a good chance of being tried for murder, as well. Neither one of them is likely to return to Italy until they're dead."

Catherine was completely overwhelmed by the thoroughness of this superintendent. To her embarrassment, she began to cry. "Thank you so much. It's not everyone who would have gone to bat on the evidence of a ten-year-old boy. I'm absolutely certain they meant to kill me."

"Aye, that boy deserves a shiny medal, he does," the superintendent replied. "And maybe a letter from the King."

Chapter Twenty-Five

It was nine o'clock that evening before Harry arrived in Courtmacsherry. The children were in a trundle bed, asleep, but Catherine, after a very satisfactory bath, was sitting up with Mr. and Mrs. Murphy. He had finally told her the story behind the arrest.

"I had Sonny O'Hara, the proprietor of Courtmacsherry Guest House, call Mrs. Haverford downstairs for a telephone call. She was a bit suspicious I think, for who would be ringing her? As soon as she reached the telephone, I popped out and clapped the handcuffs on her wrists. 'I arrest you, Mrs. Elisabetta Haverford, for the kidnapping of Catherine Bascombe, Jon Haverford, and Adriana Haverford.'"

"Sonny brought his shotgun which was a help. Fair shocked she was!"

"I can imagine! How did you entrap the don?"

"Well, yon woman began a howl like you canna believe. I was waiting for him at the bottom of the stairs. He saw Sonny's shotgun and I fixed those handcuffs on him before he knew what was happening. 'Twas all vera satisfactory! Italians! They yowled like cats in a tussle all the way across to the jail. Then they began to tell me that I would be in a fair lot of trouble for believing what a lying ten-year-old boy told me. It was my greatest pleasure to tell them I had a telegram from Scotland Yard authorizing their arrest. That made them quiet at last."

"So I should think," said Catherine. "Jon's father would be very proud of him."

When Harry walked into the small sitting room, Catherine fairly leapt off her chair and ran to him. He clasped her close, stroking her hair as she laid her head on his shoulder. "Oh, my darling, this has been the worst and then the best day of my life!" he said.

"Mine, too. I don't know if you realize it, but it was all Jon's doing. Well, he had a great deal of help from Murphy and Superintendent Higgins, not to mention Scotland Yard, but Jon put it all in motion."

"Imagine! Uncle Jonathan, whatever realm he inhabits, must be very proud of him. I can tell you now Jon shall have a new horse and whatever else he desires," said Harry.

"I think he has his reward. He is very proud of himself. And very relieved that he will be able to live with his Aunt Sarah and go to school in England."

"Now. Let me introduce Jon's wizard, Murphy, and his good wife, Mrs. Murphy."

Harry shook hands vigorously with Catherine's hosts. "Harry Bascombe," he said. "You have my everlasting gratitude."

"Harry, there must have been someone in England helping Elisabetta. Where did they get the car and the boat? How did they know about this place?"

"I suspect Russo, but he may have just been helped by a fellow don who is in London riding out the Mussolini years. There are a few of them, apparently. Sir Alistair told me that Russo is from Sicily but studied at Cambridge. He got his law degree there. I imagine he was recommended to Don Giuseppe by those same contacts."

"The Mafia is obviously a useful thing. There are probably dispossessed members all over Europe," said Catherine.

Mrs. Murphy intervened, "I'm imagining that you haven't had supper, Mr. Bascombe. There's lamb stew and soda bread."

"I don't want to be any trouble," said Harry.

"It's just waiting for you," the good lady said.

"That sounds topping, if you will all join me in the kitchen," said Harry.

* * *

Once Harry had eaten and was filling his pipe, he began to tell them his part of the story.

"We went back to Hampshire, once Catherine and the children were taken, but not until we had rung DI Duncan and told him what happened. He was livid, of course. We had no idea where you had gone, but he increased the resources monitoring the boat trains to the Continent.

"Before we left, I also grilled Nanny. She was acting strangely. It soon became evident that she was angry enough to spit nails. She eventually broke down and told me that she had a telephone number where she was able to reach Elisabetta. Nanny rang her, told her that we were in Devon, and gave them the direction.

"Once she told me, I became incensed. I hammered her with questions about their plans. She wouldn't say another word. All she did was cry. When we all got to Hampshire, we found that DI Duncan was already there. I requested that Scotland Yard arrest her as a conspirator in the kidnapping and formally interrogate her. Detective Sergeant Sullivan came and did the honors, carrying her in handcuffs back to London. She's in jail there. From what I gathered; her allegiance isn't so much to Elisabetta as it is to Don Giuseppe."

"Hmm," said Catherine. "I wonder why that is. There must be a story there. After all, she's lived with Elisabetta for years. I think Nanny could be a member of his extended family."

When it was apparent that both Catherine and Harry had begun to run down, she said, "It's off to Courtmacsherry Guest

House for us, darling. The Murphys have kindly housed the children."

When they were finally alone in their comfortable room at the guest house, Harry fairly ravished Catherine with kisses.

"I really thought I'd lost you forever," he said, holding her so close she could scarcely breathe.

"I couldn't think how an escape was even possible, but Jon had it all figured out. I don't think he realizes he's only ten."

"I expect great things of that boy. It will be good for him to be mentored by both my parents. My father's a 'wizard' in his own way. He took a medium sized sheep farm and built it into a small wool business, bought more farms, expanded the business, etcetera until he became one of the largest wool merchants in the country."

"Yes. I know. Now, I think it's time for us to stop talking," Catherine said in her smokiest voice. "I need reassurance that you're real."

"Enough said," Harry replied.

* * *

It wasn't until the next day at breakfast that Harry told her that it was Rafe who had flown him to Ireland.

"That was good of him," said Catherine, spreading strawberry jam on a crumpet.

"He's going back to Kenya today, so he had to make it a round trip flight," Harry explained. "He's really involved with Wills' company, you know."

"I'm so pleased. It could be the making of him." She took a bite and chewed thoughtfully. "I haven't decided whether having too much money or too little as a child is the worse handicap."

"He was quite disturbed by your situation. At least you were rescued before he had to leave. If not, I think he would have gone in shooting. He's still in love with you, darling."

"He came to it too late, Harry. You know that. It wasn't until

I put my foot down that he stopped taking me for granted. Now he's all primed and ready for a real adult relationship."

"You're probably right. So, to change the subject, how should we get home? Plane or ferry?" Harry asked.

"We're not in any hurry now that Elisabetta is in custody. Let's take the ferry boat train. I'm still not crazy about flying, and I'm not certain how the children would take to it after all the trauma of the kidnapping."

* * *

Everyone in Hampshire was thrilled to see her and the children. Even Catherine's mother was there, having gone down from London for moral support when her daughter had been kidnapped. She had stayed on for the pleasant company after the rescue was announced. The baroness had been accompanied by Cherry who had been camped out by the wireless all day long waiting for news.

Greetings were warm and effusive. Catherine could see that her mother had aged just in that short interval. The baroness didn't stand as tall and her skin had lost some of its usual healthy color.

Sarah Bascombe told Catherine privately that her mother was actually looking better. She was riding every day, and since horses were her passion, this was a good thing.

"It's not just your kidnapping that aged her. She really hasn't recovered from your father's death. It will take a while," said Sarah "Something strange has come up. I don't know quite what to make to make of Adriana. She overheard us talking about the murder unfortunately. She says she's positive her mother didn't do it, but that no one will believe her. She just told me when I put her to bed that she is quite certain that she was with her mother the whole time they were outdoors that morning that Jonathan was killed. She says her mother never went down to the cliff. Do you think I should call Scotland Yard? Will they take a small girl's testimony into account? How do we know her mother didn't put her up to it? Adriana really doesn't like to displease her mother."

Catherine very nearly cursed. "You're sure Adriana knows what she's talking about and how important it is?"

"You and Harry should talk to her again. You may have more insight into her than I do. I'm inclined to believe her because she doesn't seem to hold any special fondness for her mother."

"We will do just that," Catherine assured her. "Once she's had a good night's sleep." Everyone wanted to be where Catherine and Sarah were, by the fire in the morning room.

Catherine's mother brought her embroidery, Harry carried the newspapers, and Harold poked at fire which wasn't burning the way he liked.

Catherine struggled to remain in the moment. She asked herself for the hundredth time, if not Elisabetta, who could have killed Jonathan? It had to have been one of the "Bachelor Trio" as Catherine was beginning to think of them. Most likely the viscount.

"Have you dealt with the press all right, Baroness? Have they been too bothersome about the kidnapping?" asked Harry. Catherine realized she hadn't even thought about that.

"It's been horrid," Catherine's mother said. "If it hadn't taken you so long to get home, they'd still be camped out here. Something else juicy must have happened by now. But they will be out there tomorrow once they realize you're home, mark my words."

"And Nanny is still in jail?" asked Harry.

"Yes, and she will continue to be," said Harold. "There is no one to bail her out. We're certainly not going to. Not after what you have been through, Catherine. I hope she serves a nice long stretch for conspiracy in your kidnapping."

"In other news, Patricia is joining us while she looks for a flat in London," said Sarah. "It appears George was able to find a buyer for her Bronzino surprisingly quickly. She's getting a good price for it, and since she's got no reason to remain in Scotland she's decided to settle in London. She's arriving tomorrow."

"My goodness. A full house," said Catherine's mother. "I had best make my way back to London now that we've had our joyful reunion. But thank you so much for putting up with me."

"Absolutely not!" said Sarah. "Not only do we enjoy your company, but the horses haven't been so well-exercised since the children left."

"We've plenty of room for everyone," said Harold. "This house was built for a Victorian household, and we're not that many."

"And it will be good for the children to be around so many adoring adults," said Sarah, helping herself to more tea. "I think they need to be smothered in love for a bit. Tea, anyone?"

The others all declined. "How do you think they seem?" asked Harry, taking out his pipe.

"Their rescue was so spectacular, one would think the whole thing a grand adventure," said Catherine's mother with a smile. "Oh, to be a child! But they have had their eyes opened about the Don, after seeing him bully and threaten Catherine."

* * *

When they were finally alone in their cozy bedroom, Catherine told Harry what his mother had said about Adriana.

"So, her mother could be innocent after all! The devil!" exclaimed Harry, stopping with his pajamas only half buttoned. "Though I don't want to, I'm afraid she must be right. She hasn't struck me as a child who takes liberties with the truth."

"But you realize what this means?" Catherine asked, settling herself under the duvet. "We're back to Jonathan's friends for suspects. Who do you think it can be?"

"Tell you what," said Harry, climbing into bed. "We need to speak to Aunt Pat again. I can't remember who went down to the cliff and when. Remember, she was watching out her bedroom window."

"I'm so tired, Harry," Catherine said, cuddling up close to her husband. "Let's leave it 'til we talk to Aunt Patricia then."

Harry pulled her close and kissed her. "I think that's a brilliant idea."

The following morning, Catherine and Harry found Adriana out with the two-week-old black and white puppies by the barn. Harry knelt beside her as Catherine sat on the gate.

"Your aunt has told us that you have something really important to say about your mama," said Catherine.

"Um-hmm," said the girl. "I like this one best, Cousin Harry. He's the smallest one, so I call him Junior."

"So you went out with your mama on the morning that your father was killed?" asked Harry.

"Yes. I wanted to go for a walk, but I wasn't allowed out by myself because of the cliff. She said she wanted a walk, so we went together," said Adriana. "How old does Junior have to be before I can take him for a walk?"

"Give his little legs a chance to get longer," said Catherine. "He'll grow fast, and then he'll want to go walking all the time!"

"And your mother stayed with you the entire time you were outside?" Harry asked.

"Yes. I keep telling Aunt Sarah that, but I don't think she believes me. We went in the house together and Mr. Fox made us both some hot cocoa."

It certainly seemed like the truth to her, Catherine thought. Unable to resist the burrowing little bodies, she knelt beside the girl and fondled a black and white mix. "What breed of puppies are these, do you know?"

"They're border collies, Uncle Harold says. He's such a nice man. He reminds me of my father."

CHAPTER TWENTY-SIX

When they returned to the house after a brisk walk, Harry's father said, "You'll want to see the morning paper, I think." He handed it over to his son.

He and Catherine sat on the sitting room sofa and looked at it together. "Nanny Says She Witnessed Victim's Wife Commit Murder," Harry read the headline aloud.

"Of the two people, Adriana and Nanny, who do you think is telling the truth?" Catherine asked. She realized she was quite exasperated with Nanny even though that was too small a reaction. They were dealing with life and death here, but sometimes it seemed as haphazard as a game of skittles.

"Read a little further," said Harry's father.

"Ah. That explains it," said Catherine. "She traded this statement for clemency on the accessory to kidnapping charge. She says she was loyal to Elisabetta until Elisabetta betrayed her. Now she doesn't think she owes her employer anything, so she decided to tell the truth. Crikey!"

"Here's Nanny's name. Francesca Sassari," said Harry. "The paper says she's now at an undisclosed location to be kept safe until the trial."

"I think the fact that she 'told the truth' in order to get quit of the charges against her makes it very suspect," Harold said.

"The police are still holding her until they can get further corroboration, at least," said Catherine. "Or maybe it's a kind of protective custody to keep her safe from the Mafia."

"What time is Patricia coming?" Catherine asked Harry's mother who had just returned from visiting a patient in a nearby village.

"Soon, and I haven't had a chance to pack up Nanny's things. Patricia is going to be staying in that room. The sheets are clean, fortunately. I didn't want to leave the clothing for the maid."

"You sit down," said Catherine. "Which is the right room? I'll take care of it."

"It's the room at the top of the stairs on the first floor, darling. Thank you so much. I was called out in the middle of the night. Miscarriage. Very sad." Sarah looked drained.

Catherine was secretly happy to have a chance to snoop in Nanny's things. Perhaps she would find a clue.

She was disappointed, at first. She did learn a bit more about the woman's character, however. Francesca had some very stylish clothes. A feather boa. Even trousers! Catherine loved trousers. She had several pair herself. When she picked up a matching strawberry-colored jumper to fold, something fell out and hit the floor.

Picking it up, she saw it was a group picture. The people's faces were so small, she couldn't make them out, but with individuals of all ages, it appeared to be an extended family. She was relieved the glass hadn't shattered, for it obviously meant something to Nanny Francesca. It looked like it was taken in a vineyard, possibly in Sicily. There! Wasn't that Don Giuseppe in the back row? Was he a relation? That would explain the nanny's partiality to him. Possibly Elisabetta was a cousin of hers.

Hmm. Interesting. Her refusal to name Elisabetta as the murderer until now is probably because she is a close relative. Italian family ties are strong.

Catherine put all the clothing in a box provided by Sarah, positioned the photograph in its ornate frame on top, and closed the box. Her mother-in-law hadn't told her what to do with it, so she took it with her downstairs and placed it in the cloakroom on the shelf next to the outdoor hats. Catherine would ring DI Duncan in the morning to find out where Francesca Sassari was staying so she could deliver the clothes. It would give her the chance to interview the nanny about her confession.

Patricia had arrived and was having a snack in the kitchen with the children who were helping the cook make biscuits for tea. When she saw Catherine enter, she insisted on being told the entire story of the kidnapping.

"It could have been much worse," said Catherine when she finished. "I have reason to think that they just planned to leave me there, locked in that stolen boat with no food or water. The drunken captain must have been hired in England. He disappeared once we docked in Courtmacsherry."

Catherine sat down next to Harry's nephew and patted his knee. "Jon is my hero. He brought a policeman to rescue me. The same policeman who arrested his mother and grandfather. It was a good days' work. I have high hopes for Jon."

"I should say!" said Patricia.

Jon beamed.

"On the train, I read about the nanny and her supposed evidence against that Elisabetta," said Patricia. "It also said she was in jail for being complicit in your kidnapping."

Catherine said, "Her confession is certainly suspicious." She told Harry's aunt about Adriana's account of her mother.

Since the girl was right there, Aunt Pat was sensitive enough not to question the veracity of Adriana's version of the facts. She did raise an eyebrow, however.

Catherine remembered her intention to question Patricia about what she had seen that morning. "If I recall correctly, you also saw George Baxter walk down to the cliff when you were still in your room. He has denied ever going near the cliff that morning. I would like to confront him with your evidence."

"Yes," said Sarah's sister. "I did see him. He was walking

quickly. But when I got to the cliff a while later, he was nowhere to be found."

Harry walked into the kitchen in search of his wife. Hearing his aunt's statement, he asked, "How long was it after you saw him that you left the house to go down to the cliff?"

"Oh it would have been twenty minutes or so. Not less than that, anyway. He was walking in the direction of the cliff where Jonathan's body was found." Patricia jumped up, obviously done with the topic. "Has anything been done about Jonathan's funeral, do you know?"

Harry said, "They're motoring the remains over from Cornwall today. Because of all the publicity, mother decided to just have the family to do a short graveside service tomorrow. There will be a full memorial service for Uncle in St. George's in London this spring."

"Who is coming to the funeral?" Patricia asked.

"Just the family, Fox, Baxter, and Milton," he said.

Sarah wandered into the room. Creases marked her forehead. "Mary's got a case of mastitis, poor thing. She won't be coming, which is a shame, because we want to see that little one."

"There will be plenty of time after she gets well," said Catherine.

Harry suggested to Catherine that they go ride the horses while they had some time. They took their leave of the sisters. "Glad you're here safe, Aunt Pat," said Harry.

"Mother's out there riding. Somewhere," Catherine said on the way to the barn. "It's lovely that our parents have become friendly. Mother feels so at home here, but I'm hoping it's not a burden for your mother."

"Of course not. We have a household of servants. Mother needs to be able to rush off at a moment's notice to see one of her thousands of patients. I remember one time she left forty guests in the middle of a formal dinner when a farmer called and said his wife was about to deliver. Off she went. Everything proceeded well—at the party and at the delivery."

They spent the afternoon riding to a nearby ruined abbey and exploring it. Harry described what identities he'd given to the barely detectable ancient rooms when he had been growing up. They sat in what Harry had decided was the dining room on the convenient ruin of a wall.

"There certainly seems to be a world of difference between your mother and your aunt," Catherine said, picking at the crumbled stone of the wall with her gloved hand.

Harry tossed a loose rock between his hands. "Yes, Aunt was the eldest and by far the favorite of my grandfather's. He was a doctor, you know. Uncle Jon was the middle child and my mother, the youngest. Jon and Pat were kept on a short rein, according to my mother, but no one really noticed mum, so she had an idyllic childhood running about the estate with my father, who was then just the son of the sheep farmer whose land ran next to grandfather's."

"Oh, goodness. So they've known each other donkey's years! What about Aunt Pat and your Uncle Felix? When did they meet?"

"She met him at Oxford. They married and then both did their medical studies in Edinburgh. Too much competition there, I think. I don't know why, but Aunt Pat has never been a comfortable person, just the opposite of my mother. She always has an agenda, if you know what I mean." Now Harry juggled two rocks between his hands.

Catherine mused as she watched her husband, "Maybe now that she's retired, she will relax a bit."

"One can hope," said Harry with half a laugh. "She's really not a bad sort, if you get on her frequency. She's very good to have as a bridge partner, for instance. And she's a wizard at planning parties and decorating for Christmas.

Catherine felt that this was faint praise. "Did she not want children?"

"I don't think she was able to have them, but she was besotted with James—mum's firstborn. When he was little, she took him about all the museums in London. She takes credit for his success as a pathologist. James and Pat are still thick as thieves. He has her work ethic which is really the secret to both his success and the failure of his marriage." He added a third rock to his act. "Let's see if I can remember how to do this." In moments he was juggling the three rocks. Catherine applauded.

"Let's walk again," Catherine said. "This wall is making my bones cold. We should probably be getting back for tea, anyway. Tell me more about your Mum. I can't see how she turned out so different from Patricia."

"She actually has a very strong personality, but it's just directed differently. A lot of it probably comes from marrying my father. She avoided the debutante track. She learned to care for those less fortunate than she was at a young age. Do I really need to explain all the ways she is wonderful? You've seen it for yourself."

"You're right. She's extraordinary but not outwardly flashy. It means so much to me to have her acceptance. I never felt that from either of my parents. Thankfully, my mother seems to be changing. Plus, I married the most perfect man in the world for me."

"Of course you did."

They mounted their horses and made for home.

* * *

While they were gone, Nanny had rung. Harold had told her that they wouldn't be able to bring her clothes until after the graveside service the next day. He had taken down her address.

Catherine said, "Thank you, Harold. I'll take them to her after the service since I have some questions for the woman. You know she's a bit of an actress. At the inquest, she was such a sweet little thing—butter wouldn't melt in her mouth. But that is not the same woman who is accusing her benefactor and closest friend of murder. She may even be related to them." Catherine pulled off her riding gloves and handed them to a waiting Cherry. "When I was putting together the box of her things this morning, there was a photo. It looked like one of those family shots with several generations together. Don Giuseppe was standing in the back row."

Harry said, "I'd be willing to bet he's not going to waste any time before finding out where the police have stashed Francesca Vassari. He doesn't want her to live to testify against his daughter."

The children arrived in from playing outdoors and were busy washing their hands under the housekeeper's supervision.

"I'm sorry we had to cancel the neighborhood reception we had planned for you and Catherine, Harry. Perhaps we can have one during the Easter hols," said his mother.

"That would do splendidly, although Catherine and I have been talking about going abroad again." Looking at his wife, he winked.

She thought that he must be thinking of making another magical trip to Málaga. The Spanish beaches sounded heavenly at the moment. The fog had rolled in during tea.

Adriana, looking forlorn, came over to her and sat on the floor at her feet, "Will you play Snakes and Ladders with me?" she asked.

Catherine was touched by the softly plaintive request. The little girl had been through so much. She'd lost everyone who was familiar to her—mother, father, grandfather, even her nanny. She said, "Of course I will, lamb. How is Junior?"

She put her head against Catherine's knee and looked at the floor. "He always misses me when I'm gone. I hope he won't die."

"I don't think he will," Catherine said, a lump in her throat. She stroked the girl's glossy black pig tails. Who had done her hair today? Who was going to do all the little things nanny used to do for her? "Would you like to go back out to see Junior, or would you rather stay inside and play the game?" Adriana's eyelids were drooping. The gentle, rhythmic stroking of her hair was putting her to sleep. She didn't answer, so Catherine kept smoothing her hair.

She knew so little about children! But right now, Adriana

needed connections with people who wouldn't leave, who she could trust. And in just a few days, it would be back to boarding school. Too much turmoil for an eight-year-old.

Harry came over and sat next to Catherine on the sofa. "You've put her to sleep."

"Yes. Do you think you could carry her up to the bedroom? I'll lie down with her for a while. She's tired, but she needs me to be with her, too."

"Let's put her between us on our bed," he said. "She'll get plenty of love that way." He gathered the slight figure into his arms, and Catherine followed them up the stairs.

* * *

When Catherine woke up from a refreshing nap, she found Adriana awake, curled against her while holding on tightly. Harry was sitting up next to the bed reading a novel he would be teaching in the new term.

Catherine bent so she could kiss the top of Adriana's head. "Well, precious, did you have a good sleep? You were worn out."

"I did. I don't sleep too well at night."

"A lot of things have been happening to you. Sometimes your mind needs to stay awake to try to make sense of everything. Do you miss Italy?"

"Not too much. Mama and Nonno were always fighting about the friends she brought home. She said he couldn't keep treating her like she was still a little girl."

"I think you'll like living with your aunt and uncle. They don't fight. And you'll be able to visit us at Oxford. We'll come down here to visit sometimes, too."

"What kind of things did you do when you were eight?" asked Adriana.

"We have a huge castle ruin by my home in Cornwall. When I was home from school, I used to love to climb all over it. I pretended that the castle was still the way it was in olden times. I was a fierce warrior sometimes. But most often I played like I was a beautiful princess. My brother, Will, was the king and our friend, Rafe, was a knight. We played for hours."

"Your mum let you stay out that long?"

"She was almost always gone with my father on a trip somewhere. But that was all right really because I had Rafe and Will. I didn't really know what it was like to have a mother and father home all the time."

"Like me," said Adriana.

"Yes. But now, you're lucky, because you are going to have an aunt and uncle all the time, and guess what!"

"What?"

"You're have a new baby cousin! You will meet her any day now. Do you like babies?"

"I don't know anything about people babies, but I like baby puppies."

"It's like that, only better. Why don't we sit up. I'll do your hair in a French braid. Do you like that?"

"Yes, please." The girl still sounded sleepy and Catherine hoped that her body was daring to relax after all the turmoil.

Chapter Twenty-Seven

It wasn't until after dinner that Catherine judged that the time was right to ask Adriana again about her outing to the cliffs with her mother on the day her father was killed. She had wanted to make sure that Adriana was feeling more secure about her place in the world.

They were sitting on the carpet with their legs crossed, putting together a puzzle of London. "Did you and your mum often take walks in Italy?"

"No. Not unless we were on holiday. Then the whole family took walks. My favorite was to walk along the seaside."

"I like that, too," said Catherine.

Jon was arm wrestling with Harry, and the rest of the adults were playing bridge.

"Are you positive your mum stayed with you? It's rather important. What did you do? Wasn't it cold out?"

"It was. I had to jump up and down to keep warm. Mum and me kept saying we wished we had worn our trousers."

"Do you like wearing trousers? I do!" said Catherine.

"Me, too. I have three pairs!" crowed the girl.

"What color are they?" Catherine asked

"One pair is plaid, black and green. One is red and one is blue."

Red trousers. Why is that important?

"Do you remember what colors your mama has?"

"Oh, all hers are black. She says black is her best color. I don't think black is my best color."

Red trousers. That's it! Patricia said Elisabetta was wearing red trousers that morning when she saw her on the cliff path.

"Now. I'm going to ask you an important question. Does your mama have any red trousers?"

"No. I just told you. Only black."

Catherine sat with the Tower Bridge puzzle piece in her hand as the truth hit her. Patricia Buchanan had seen a woman in red trousers walking down the cliff path after Jonathan. The nanny owned a pair of red trousers. I saw them, packed them. Was it Francesca Sassari on the cliff path and not Elisabetta? What color was her hair?

Patricia was sitting on the sofa right behind Catherine, knitting. "Aunt Pat, did you see what color that woman's hair was who followed Jonathan down the path?" she asked.

The woman paused a moment, closing her eyes, her knitting in her lap. "Let me think. No. I couldn't tell what her hair looked like. She wore a scarf. A red one what matched her trousers. But I only saw her from the back."

Not exactly a convincing sighting then of either woman.

I need to talk to George. He could be the murderer just as easily. Tomorrow after the graveside service.

* * *

Because a memorial service was going to be held in London at a later date, the graveside service was small, beginning at ten o'clock. The clergyman had set up chairs, but it was far too cold to be comfortable. Catherine pulled her fur around her more tightly and turned up her collar against the cold fog. Adriana sat in the chair beside her, and they held hands in Catherine's lap. Harry joined with five local farmers in their Sunday best who acted as pallbearers, carrying the casket to the grave from the old-fashioned horse drawn hearse. Adriana seemed fascinated by the fittings on the gold-tooled hearse and its four black horses in their gold-tooled harness. They watched as casket was lowered into the six-foot deep grave at the feet of Catherine, Adriana, and the rest of Jon's family.

The words out of the Book of Common Prayer seemed inadequate for the circumstances. Surely a death by murder should be memorialized differently than a peaceful death from old age. Jonathan's life had been cut short by violence

George, a possible murderer, was standing right across the grave from her. Even more surprising was that Viscount Fawcett was next to him.

Catherine watched as George stared down at the casket obviously moved. His lips were pinched as though to keep himself in check. His eyes were troubled and wet. He kept using his handkerchief to wipe his nose. She had already noted, when he shook her hand before the service, that he had been drinking. The viscount was stony-faced. Catherine wasn't able to isolate a single emotion from his appearance. Was he still a suspect in the murder? Was he out on bail in connection with the theft charge?

Sarah was the only one of the observers who openly wept. Catherine noted that Fox looked suspiciously red-eyed. Perhaps he was blaming himself for failing to save the "major's" life a second time.

". . . Ashes to ashes, dust to dust." The vicar concluded. A clod of dirt fell on the casket, and Catherine found herself near to tears. Who had done this terrible thing? As they stood and sang "Rock of Ages," she felt herself emerge from tears into anger. She and Harry would find out who did this.

In the Bentley on the way back to Harry's home, she held a subdued Adriana on her lap. The girl hadn't wanted to be separated from Catherine. Jon had gone with George and Roderick Milton in his flashy Lagonda.

Back in the Bascombe home, Sarah's cook had provided a

generous spread of cold meats and cheese, several kinds of cake, scones and raspberry jam. There was heated rum for Hot Toddies and hot lemonade for those who preferred it.

The fire felt lovely after the foggy mist of the cemetery. But Catherine shivered at the thought of the cold grave. She sat on the sofa with a tray of food on her knees for her and Adriana who still stayed close to Catherine's side.

"Isn't this hot lemonade lovely?" she asked the girl.

"I'm glad it has lots of sugar," Adriana said. "And chocolate cake is my favorite."

"What did your father like to eat?" Catherine asked.

"He loved any kind of pasta! Especially ravioli. One day he taught me how to make it. You have to put the dough through the pasta maker nine times! It has to be thin enough so you can read a newspaper through it!

"I never knew that!" said Catherine. "Tell me some other things you used to do with your father."

She listened while the girl told her of their trip to Florence—just the two of them—and how he had bought her gold earrings on the Ponte Vecchio. She lifted her hair so Catherine could see the miniature gold flowers with jade centers that she wore. She talked of their trip to Murano Island where they watched glass workers make the stunningly beautiful Murano glass, and another trip to Burano Island to see the legendary lace-makers.

"I loved to go on gondola rides with him in Venice."

"It sounds like he was a wonderful father," said Catherine. "You are a lucky girl. My father just died, and I don't remember one thing that we ever did together. It is getting hard for me to remember him, but you will have those wonderful memories all your life."

Adriana gave a smug little smile, and then in an instant, she sobered and asked, "Cousin Catherine, is my father really in the cold ground now?"

Catherine had been dreading this question, but she must stumble through the best she could. "I have always thought that our soul—the part of us that thinks and loves and feels—is the most important part of us. When we die, our body and soul become separated. Our soul is waiting somewhere—I like to think it's with Jesus. It's waiting to be resurrected."

Adriana's bottom lip stuck out as she looked doubtful. "And when will he be resurrected?"

"Sometime in the future. No one knows when it will come, so we must make sure we are ready for it by making good choices in our lives." She smoothed the girl's long hair. "But, everyone makes mistakes. The vicar can tell you how to make that right. It's called repentance. There now. Doesn't that make you feel better?"

"It sounds very complicated," said Adriana.

"Then I haven't explained it very well. Would you like to talk to the vicar? He seems like a very nice man. He introduced himself at the graveside service."

"I don't know," said Adriana shyly.

Adriana sat quietly, seeming to be thinking this over. It was quite a lot to take on board for a little girl grieving over her father. An idea began to form in Catherine's mind. She needed to talk to her mother-in-law.

* * *

After Adriana had gone out to visit the puppies, Catherine told herself that she must also make an opportunity to speak to George Baxter and Roderick Milton before they left for London. She had to find out about the viscount.

She found them along with Harry sitting in the conservatory smoking cigars which seemed a bit irreverent after their best friend's funeral. Harry was smoking his pipe, and they were all drinking hot toddies. The room was heavy with humidity and the scent of green things growing. The windows were opaque with condensation.

Harry said, "Don't look so disapproving, darling. Jonathan's shade is probably here with us, you know."

Catherine sighed. "Is this men only?"

"No," said George Baxter. "Of course not. Groups of men at a funeral tend to be maudlin if left alone. We were just discussing all the trouble Fawcett is in. I've known the fellow, or thought I've known the fellow since we were practically nippers. This has been a shock, to say the least. But at least he's quit of the murder investigation."

"Yes," said Harry. He turned to Catherine. "Turns out the cook was his alibi. He came down early from bed and drank coffee and smoked over the newspapers all morning."

"We should make a chart of who was there and when," said Catherine. "I've been talking to Aunt Pat." She saw the blank expressions on Baxter and Milton's faces. "Dr. Buchanan from Edinburgh to you. I have a new idea."

Catherine sat on the last chair. They were sitting in a circle around a water feature which was still for the winter.

She continued taking charge. "Aunt Pat was looking out the window that morning, as you recall from the inquest. She saw a woman in red trousers walking down the cliff path after Jonathan went down." She looked at Jonathan's friends' faces. They were both attentive but didn't seem at all nervous. Of course, she imagined they were excellent card players. "We previously assumed that woman was Elisabetta. But, according to Adriana, the only trousers her mother owns are black. And the woman had a scarf on her head, so her hair was covered." She told them about Nanny's red trousers. "So, I conclude that it was Nanny, not Elisabetta who went down to the cliff that morning. Did you see her Mr. Baxter? When you went down?"

George fidgeted. "Well, I guess if Dr. Buchanan saw me, the cat's out of the bag. It's a bit embarrassing, but I've had a spot of bad luck. People sometimes hesitate to buy pictures in this economy, don't you know? Jon said he would give me a loan just to tide me over until I made another sale. I'm in old pictures, you know, like Jon was. Fact is, I had just made a sale the day before. I'd been trying to get him alone so I could let him know I'd made a good sale which should set me up nicely for the next little while, so I wouldn't need the loan after all. My man of business let me know the night Jon was at that dinner for the wedding party."

Harry cocked an eyebrow. "You do realize your skittishness about your finances could have landed you in the dock?"

Catherine watched as Baxter's ears turned red. He scowled. "Don't want to get it around that I was treading water, now, do I?"

"Well," said Catherine, "Now that we know you were there, did you see Uncle Jonathan?"

"No. I was surprised. I couldn't locate him. He wasn't anywhere to be seen. Couldn't think of where he'd got to. His car was there at the cottage. I checked when I got back to the cottage. I wasn't lying when I said I needed to get back to London. I was to deliver the painting I sold. I was jolly anxious to get my hands on my payment."

"Did you see Francesca? That is to say, the nanny?" asked Harry.

"No. She wasn't around, either. I would have noticed her. Especially in red trousers," Baxter answered.

"It seems to me that poor Uncle Jon must have been dead by then. I wouldn't have thought Nanny had the gumption to say 'boo.'" said Harry. "We shall have to tell this to DI Duncan, Baxter."

"But what if he thinks I did it?" the man queried.

"In these matters, it's always best to tell the truth. Convenient recollections aren't always accepted at face value," Harry told his uncle's friend. "But it looks far worse for Nanny than it does for you. She is very attached to the children. She probably thought killing Uncle would have put paid to any business about them staying in England for school."

"If she did it, it may be that her way of solving problems was tainted a bit by growing up with the Mafia," said Catherine. "I believe she's somehow related to the Pinnas. I found a photo in her things. It showed her in a nice little group that included Don Giuseppe."

Sitting quietly, smoking as though they were discussing nothing more important than horse-racing, Roderick Milton had said nothing up to this point. Now he entered the conversation. "It sounds like you've got this thing sewed up. Now you just need to find out where the police have stashed Nanny so you can get her to confess. Or do you know where she is?"

"She called and talked to Harold. She wants her things. She left an address. I was planning to go take them to her this afternoon," said Catherine. "She's somewhere in London."

"Whoa, baby!" said Harry his face resembling a thundercloud. "You're not going to see that woman alone!"

"You'll come with me, then?" Catherine asked.

"Of course," he said emphatically.

"I was counting on that, actually," she said with a smile.

* * *

Harry's father lent them the Bentley, with the idea that Catherine would drive it back while Harry picked up his Morris. As it happened, she was very glad they were together to begin with. The address where Francesca was tucked away was not in a London neighborhood Catherine would have approached on her own. It was in a rundown block of flats near the docks.

The nanny had a uniformed policewoman minding the door. Before he would allow them to meet with Miss Sassari, he frisked Harry and searched Catherine's handbag. Then he accompanied them up the steps and stood beside the door where he couldn't be seen inside the room.

The nanny did not invite them in. She spoke to them from a narrow opening in the door.

"Miss Sassari, we'd like to speak with you for a moment," said Catherine

"I have nothing to say to you."

Catherine decided to use shock tactics. "Have you no reason to give us for why you killed our Uncle Jonathan?"

"I didn't kill him!" Her voice was high and hysterical. "I didn't even see him! I wanted to plead with him to send my babies back home to Italy, but he wasn't even there." The nanny began to cry. "I know Elisabetta killed him! She saw his new will leaving her next to nothing! She burned it."

"You are lying. Adriana was with Elisabetta that morning when they took their walk down near the cliff. She has no reason to lie, Miss Sassari, unlike you," Harry said. "She says her mother never left her."

Francesca looked down at her feet. "She *must* have done it! She wanted him dead before he could make another will. She told me that."

"So you didn't actually see her do anything to him, then?" asked Catherine.

"No," the nanny said in a low voice.

"We shall be telling the police," Catherine said. "You did it, didn't you?"

"You have no proof," Francesca said, her eyes sparking. "Because I didn't do it. I saw one of Mr. Haverford's horrible friends. I can't tell them apart. I doubt that he saw me. He was coming down to the cliff and I was leaving. I ran off along the cliff path in the other direction. But Mr. Haverford was already gone. He wasn't there, I tell you!"

"Well, someone killed the poor man. Elisabetta is the only one other than yourself who has a motive," Catherine told her, running her hands up and down her arms. It was beastly cold, and she was aggravated because, against all reason, she believed the nanny. The young woman dropped her voice and appeared to be scrutinizing her fingernail. "There is someone else. Don Giuseppe."

Catherine was stunned. Harry said, "You're saying Don Giuseppe was about Cornwall then? At the cliff?"

"He came along with us from Italy. He stayed away at first, until Betta had the children. Jonathan didn't like him to be around them. I don't know if he was at the cliff, but I would not be surprised."

Catherine fell silent, looking at Harry. He gave a whistle.

"I don't understand why he came at all," said Harry.

"I think he wanted to be sure that Betta got the children. She really didn't care that much one way or the other about them, but she can never say no to the don."

That figures. "Did you see him that morning?"

"No. Just because I didn't see him doesn't mean he wasn't there. He's strong and quick. He also knows how to use a knife."

"You must tell the police, Miss Vassari. Elisabetta didn't kill her husband. She has an alibi, but you don't. Did you look up the path when you first saw that Mr. Haverford wasn't there?" Catherine asked,

"I did see someone," she said, thoughtfully, still unwilling to let them enter her room. "Just a little . . . a little peek. A brown coat and a brown shoe, just going around the big rock. It is huge. You can't see around it."

"Could you tell if it was a man or a woman?" Harry asked.

"Not for sure. I thought it was maybe a man." She licked her lips and squinted as though trying to see something far away.

Catherine was afraid this was just another attempt to steer them elsewhere. "It is in your interests to help us."

"The brown was dark. Like midnight mink."

"So it was fur?" Catherine pressed.

"It might have been. I remember wishing I had a coat. It was freezing and I had come out with only a jacket. Anyway, for some reason, I thought maybe it was Mr. Haverford. But now we know it wasn't. He'd gone over the cliff. Now I'm afraid that the person who did it saw me."

Catherine had to give her credit for quick thinking. Had she truly seen Jonathan's murderer? She handed the woman the box she had set down on the doorstep. "Here are your things. What kind of shoes did the person you saw wear?" she asked.

"Thank you for these. I don't know how you call the shoes in English. You tie them up."

"Hmm. Oxfords. Yes. They could be a man or woman's. Did you see a trouser leg?"

"I must have," Nanny said. She closed her eyes for a moment. "It's all just a brown blur. The trousers must have been as brown as the coat."

Harry asked, "Did you tell the police about this?"

"No. I didn't really remember it. It was just a second's glance."

"Well, I certainly hope they find who did it soon, because as far as I'm concerned, you make the best suspect," said Harry, his tone flat.

The policewoman stepped into view. "Put your coat on, Miss Vasari. We're going into the station where you're going to have a little talk with Detective Inspector Duncan.

Chapter Twenty-Eight

Harry and Catherine decided to see Detective Inspector Duncan in person before they went back to Hampshire. They called at Scotland Yard and were lucky that the policeman was in.

"What can I do for you this morning?" he asked. "Have you brought me the murderer's head on a silver charger?"

"No, unfortunately," said Catherine. "You're going to be seeing Francesca Sassari again. She requested that we bring her clothes to her. She confessed that she didn't really see Elisabetta kill Mr. Haverford, but said she knew that she did it. She also dragged the don into it. Apparently, he arrived in England when they did. Your policewoman at the door heard it all as well. She's bringing her in."

Duncan slapped his armrests. "Wonderful. Now I'll have to jail her again on the accessory to kidnapping charge. What do you think about the don? Think he could have done it?"

"I'm afraid so. She suggests the don might be the culprit. He apparently lay low because he knew Mr. Haverford didn't like him. He was here to continue the pressure on his daughter to take the children. Apparently, she wasn't all that keen."

"Ah ha! Well, that's some good news. I'll have to put the thumb screws to him. Anything else?"

Catherine told him about the possibly spurious clue of the Oxford clad foot.

"Sounds like something she read in a book," he said. "I like the idea of the don better."

* * *

By the time Catherine reached Hampshire once more, it was dark. Harry had taken the train to Oxford to pick up his Morris and would be coming down to Hampshire that evening. Sarah was replenishing her doctor's kit in the utility room when they came in.

"Could I talk to you about Adriana? I have an idea," said Catherine.

"Go right ahead. I'm listening," said Sarah.

"I'm worried about sending her off to school when she's so grief-stricken and unsettled. Boarding school is difficult under the best of circumstances. Are you even certain that they will have her? The daughter of a man who was murdered with her mother in prison?"

"Oh! What a dunce I am. I hadn't even thought that through. I was just going blindly ahead with Jonathan's plans," said Sarah, snapping her case shut.

"Remember when we were doing our last inquiry and we had the opportunity to interview the headmistress at Bishop's School for Young Ladies here in Hampshire?" asked Catherine.

"Why yes. And I told you I was doctor for the school. Why didn't I think of that? It would be the perfect place for Adriana. She could even be a day student, if she wanted! Then in later years, if she wanted to go elsewhere, we could try boarding school again. By then the scandal will have died down. Excellent plan. Shall you put it to the child, or would you like me to?"

"Why don't I just sound her out. If she shows interest, you can take over. You know more about the school than I do," said Catherine.

"Right! Splendid. Now, we're going to have an early dinner.

Jon and Adriana were happy to see Catherine and Harry. By the girl's red and puffy eyes, Catherine could see she had been crying. Jon seemed somber as well.

Both Roderick Milton and George Baxter had departed for London, however Catherine's mother and Harry's aunt were still there.

While the others had before dinner drinks in the drawing room, Catherine took Adriana to the sitting room. She cuddled the girl to her side as they sat side by side on the leather sofa.

"How is Junior?" Catherine asked.

"Is it true that Nanny *pushed* my father off the cliff?" Adriana asked.

Catherine held an expletive to herself. "Who told you that?"

"It was something I overheard my aunt say to your mother. They didn't know I was listening. I was hiding behind the drapes. I wanted to disappear for a while."

"Why did you want to disappear?" Catherine asked, pleading internally for time to think of an answer to Adriana's question.

"I wanted to go someplace where I didn't have to be brave every moment. I miss my father so much. I was pretending he was away on a trip to feel better for a little while. But I can't really pretend for very long about him. I just realized today that he's never going to come back from this trip."

"I understand. You're just trying to feel better for a little while. It's all right to try to feel better. No one likes to feel sad. You need to know that it's all right to feel the way you do. Maybe you can even talk about it with your brother. Are you close to Jon?"

"Not really. I tried, but it feels like he's more than two years older. And boys are different than girls I think."

Catherine thought about this for a moment. She said, "Boys feel the same things you do, but people expect boys not to show it as much as girls. I suspect that's why he's been running from one thing to another. Every time he starts to feel something, he runs away and starts doing something different to try not to think about it. I don't know if he'll ever let his guard down enough to talk to anyone about what he feels deep down."

"Oh." The single word was like an arrow through Catherine's heart. If only she could think of the right words to say. Instead, she kissed the top of Adriana's head.

"I don't know why I didn't think of this earlier. Would you like to go to school here in Hampshire? There's a school here called Bishop's School for Young Ladies close by. You can live here at home and be a day girl or you can board there. They let you choose."

For the first time she saw a light in Adriana's eyes. "Oh! I should like that. I want to stay home with Aunt Sarah and be a day girl! That would be perfect. I didn't want to tell anyone, but I didn't want to go back to that boarding school. Everyone would be whispering behind my back about my father's death and my mother being in jail."

Catherine felt a surge of relief. "And there's something else you need to know. These feelings you're having now, they aren't endless. They will lessen over time. If you were just stuffing them inside, they would come out in various unhealthy ways as you got older. Though you may feel like you're coming apart, you are actually a healthy, normal eight-year-old who loved her father dealing with some grown-up feelings in the best way you can."

"I'm much happier already, knowing that I can stay here," said Adriana, letting go a huge sigh of relief.

By the time the children had gone up to bed, Catherine was feeling tired herself but ideas were spinning through her head and she felt she needed to nail them down.

"Harry, let's do a timeline of who, when, and where," she said as they were relaxing in the sitting room after the tea tray had come and gone.

"Good idea, darling," her husband said.

"I'll help, too," said Patricia.

"Perfect," said Catherine. Going to the desk, she drew a piece of paper out of the middle drawer.

255

"Too bad Elisabetta has an alibi. Jonathan was going to divorce her, you know. He told me so when we were driving down to Lostwithiel for the rehearsal dinner."

"Well, that's interesting. I suppose you told the police," said Harry.

"I did, as a matter of fact."

"All right." Catherine asked Patricia, "Have you any idea what time it was that you saw Jonathan leave Caravaggio House for his walk along the cliff?"

"It was around eight a.m. and scarcely light," Patricia said. "I happened to be at the window. I was wondering whether I might get some exercise before going down for the wedding."

"All right," Catherine said again, writing this information at the top of her paper. "Next? Was it George or Nanny you saw next?"

"Oh, it wasn't for a while. Half an hour maybe. That was when I saw the woman in red trousers. I thought it was Elisabetta."

"No. Nanny," said Catherine. "So that was at about 8:30. Then George?"

"Right," said Patricia. "He came along about ten minutes later, just before I left my room."

"And, did you go for a walk?" asked Harry.

"Yes. A very quick one. The only person I saw was George. He was looking for Jon. I decided it was getting a bit late. The wedding was at eleven, so I was planning to leave at about 9:30. I had to pack up my things. I planned on leaving for Scotland from Lostwithiel after the wedding breakfast."

"Next, we need to know who was back at the cottage and when. Did you see anyone about when you went downstairs?" asked Catherine.

"Young Jon. He was having breakfast—pancakes." Now that I think of it, Lord Fawcett was sitting at the table in his dressing gown smoking and drinking coffee."

"And what time was this?"

"I imagine it was going on for nine o'clock."

Harry was carefully packing his pipe. "So no Elisabetta, no Adriana, no George, and no Nanny," he said.

"Right. They all came straggling in over the next half hour." Patricia tapped a nail on the rim of her teacup. Catherine reflected that she was enjoying being the center of attention. "Let's see if I can remember the order," Patricia said. "Yes. George was first. He was looking for Jonathan. Went up the backstairs in search of him.

"Adriana and Elisabetta came in last. So, Francesca must have come in during the interval. That's the lot. I left for the wedding at 9:30," Patricia finished.

"Did you give this to the police?" Catherine asked.

"I would have, if they'd asked."

Harry shook his head.

"Well, this seems to indicate that it was Francesca who was likely the murderer. George found no one there when he went down later," said Catherine, tapping the timeline with her fountain pen.

"She has no alibi. She has motive and opportunity. No reason to think she might not carry a switchblade for self-defense," said Harry.

"She claims it was probably Don Giuseppe. We just found out from her that he 'may have been' in Cornwall that morning," said Catherine.

Catherine blotted her timeline, folded it in half, and placed it in her pocket. "Well. It's been quite a day. I'm ready for bed."

* * *

When Harry came up to bed, Catherine was sitting and staring at the paper timeline in her hand. "Something bothers me about this, but I'm not sure what."

"You'll think of it," said Harry with confidence as he leaned down to give her a kiss.

"We're running out of time to solve this thing," she said.

"So you're not satisfied that it is the malicious Francesca?"

"Not satisfied enough to see her hang." She ran her tongue over her bottom lip. "Would you mind terribly making a jaunt to St. Ives? We can take the train if you like."

"What's on your mind?" Harry asked.

"I don't know. I just need to walk through everything in person, I think. Times, distances, and so forth."

"Jolly good. No need to take the train. I have the Morris now. We'll spend the night in the cottage tomorrow night. Maybe inspiration will have struck."

She kissed him. "You're a brick," she said. "I love you so much Harold Bascombe, Jr."

"Would you care to show me how much that is?" he replied as he began kissing her shoulder.

Chapter Twenty-Nine

Catherine and Harry left the house at nine the next morning with a basket picnic full of good things to eat on the drive to Cornwall. They passed the time with rambunctious performances of songs from their school days. Harry also entertained with tales of all the unpunished mischief he'd gotten up to at school. Then they fell to discussing their plans for the term that lay ahead in just a few days, speculated on whether or not Wallis Simpson would ever become Queen, and the significance of the rumblings Franco was making in Spain.

"I think we took our honeymoon at just the right time. People who should know are predicting a Civil War," said Harry.

"Yes, I know," said Catherine. "Hard to pick sides in that one. Stalin from afar versus Franco up close."

"Some of my school friends would actually pick up and go over there to fight against Franco. Doesn't matter to them who's on the other side."

"Hmm," said Catherine. "You know I hate war, past, present, or future. Let's change the subject.

It was four o'clock in the afternoon by the time they pulled up to the cottage.

"There it is," Harry said as he and Catherine bumped over a

rough single-track road better suited for an oxcart than an automobile.

It was late afternoon, but the gray clouds along the Cornish coast diminished the light as a brisk wind made waves through the long sea grass and on the gray ocean that extended to the horizon. Everything seemed to have remained the same since their last visit. The gray granite walls of the cottage looked as if they would outlast anyone now living and no storm that roared in from the Celtic Sea or any internal storm generated by murder would change that.

"Did I tell you that Uncle Jonathan added quite a bit of space to the original cottage?" he asked. "Unless you know that, it's hard to discern where the old ends and the new begins. I still have good memories of this place, but it doesn't seem as welcoming since his murder."

"I wonder if the trustees will keep it or sell it," Catherine replied.

"Don't know," Harry answered. "I expect they'll wait a few years while Jon's children grow to see how they feel about the cottage." It was already growing dark, so they decided to put off their investigations until 8:00 o'clock the next morning when Aunt Pat's account began. Catherine wanted to see exactly how much light there was at that hour.

"Let's get out and see if we can walk along the cliff path to the place the police believe he was pushed off."

Wrapping their woolen scarfs securely around their necks, they walked along the cliff path, braving the strong wind from the ocean. Catherine was reminded how beautiful the Cornish coast was and mourned for Harry's uncle that he would never again see this sight he had loved so much. This time of year, there wouldn't be many visitors, but come summer the cliff paths would be filled with holiday makers. If it were offered for sale, Jon's cottage would be snapped up by a wealthy London banker or a Birmingham industrialist and go out of the family. Harry had mixed feelings about this.

"I think this must be the cove where Jon's body was discovered,"

Harry said, placing a protective arm around Catherine as he moved them closer to the cliff's edge. At the bottom of the sheer drop, Catherine could see, amidst several large boulders, just a bit of a sandy shore that must be near the entrance to the cave where the body was found.

She knew Jonathan had been stabbed and was dead or dying before being pushed, but, absent that, a fall from this height would have certainly killed him by itself. The sound of waves crashing against the rock would have made it difficult, likely impossible he or his attacker said anything before he was stabbed and pushed.

"Have you ever wondered why the murderer bothered to stab him?" asked Catherine. "I think the murderer must have been enraged at him for some reason and in that moment, stabbing was not enough, so the push followed," she said. "I wonder what triggered such rage. It's almost maniacal."

Turning to look back at the cottage, Harry said, "It would not be the easiest job to recognize the murderer from the cottage."

Catherine replied, "Well, even my thickest wool skirt and stockings are not going to keep me warm for much longer. Let's get out of this wind."

They had an early dinner at the Italian restaurant and Catherine had Shrimp Scampi again. Harry ordered lobster and they enjoyed a quiet dinner alone for the first time since their honeymoon.

They slept well in the cottage's best guestroom, curled together under heaps of quilts. They woke to the sound of the sea. It was half past seven, and cold as ice. Harry stacked kindling in the well-swept fireplace and started a fire, while Catherine added coal to the Aga stove in the kitchen and got it going so they could heat milk for morning cocoa to warm them up. She toasted leftover bread from the picnic basket and ferreted out marmalade from the pantry. They ate this small repast by the warmth of the Aga in the kitchen.

At eight o'clock, they visited each of the guest rooms. Halfway into January, there was just barely enough light to see. In mid-December when the murder occurred, there would have been only a sliver of moonlight and possibly quite a bit of fog at eight a.m.

The bedroom at the top of the stairs faced the same way as the kitchen windows—away from the cliffs. The second bedroom faced the sea and the cliff path; however the window was deeply inset from the exterior surface of the granite stone walls. The stones blocked any view of the relevant section of the footpath where the murderer would have walked. "He wouldn't have been seen from this window," Catherine thought.

"Just to make sure, let's open the window and see if that provides a better view," she suggested.

"I doubt that even a fresh air fiend would savor a blast of mid-December morning air off the ocean, but I will open the window and you can look out, if you like."

Releasing the latch, he pushed the window up as far as it would go.

"Be prepared to grab me!" Leaning out, she could almost see the cliff path. Harry put his hands around her waist. She overbalanced. "Aii!" she screeched. Harry pulled her back quickly and held her safely in his arms.

"Little hellion!" he said fondly.

She laughed, but quickly sobered. "You realize your aunt could not have seen the path unaided, even if the light was good."

The third window brought no better view of the path than any of the others had.

When they entered the fourth bedroom, Catherine said, "Last chance, but this is a small window.

Harry looked through the window toward the cove.

"Look for yourself, darling," he said.

Catherine looked through the window and discovered that the house's largest chimney blocked the view of the path and the cove. Even leaning out of the window, no one could see Jonathan taking the path or anyone following him.

Somberly, they looked at one another. "She was lying," Harry said. "Aunt Pat was lying. And there's only one reason she would have to lie."

"I know what felt wrong," said Catherine. "It was just too neat." She sat heavily on the bed. "All the times were perfect. But with the wedding happening that morning, I doubt that your uncle would have spent that much time outdoors. We can't rely on her for anything she said she saw. It was her alibi. But she had to have been first on the scene. She may even have arranged to meet him for his morning walk.

"I'm having trouble believing she killed her own brother," said Harry, sitting down beside her.

Catherine put an arm around his shoulder. "She was desperate, darling. And she said Jon told her he was going to get a divorce. I'll bet he told her about the new will, too. When they were driving down to the Rehearsal Dinner the night before. It never occurred to her he would create a trust and leave almost everything to his children."

"She must be degenerating mentally," said Harry. "Think of everything that has happened to her recently. She lost two wonderful jobs—teaching at the college and practicing medicine at her own Women's Clinic. The only reason I can think of for that was that she either made some major mistakes or had become impossible to work with. And then, the divorce, after all these years. Things would have had to have been awfully bad for Uncle Felix to have divorced her."

"All that rejection must have accelerated her decline," Catherine replied, drawing her husband closer to her. "It makes me sick to think of her murdering her brother and then calmly coming to our wedding and celebrating all day."

"What a shock the will must have been to her," Harry said.

"*It was a shock. You have no idea!*" said an indignant voice. "That my own brother would treat me so thoughtlessly!" Patricia stood in the bedroom door, shaking with rage. She was holding a shiny silver scalpel in her hand.

"What do you think you're doing Aunt Pat?" asked Harry as

they both stood up. Catherine could see he was trying to calm the woman down with an almost fatherly tone.

"I followed you, of course. I overheard your comments. You're too clever by half. Both of you. It's past time for talking, I think."

The woman lunged at them. Before Harry could block her, she slashed Catherine's arm with the scalpel. Then Harry smashed into his aunt, immobilizing her wrist. The scalpel dropped. He drove her back into the granite wall of the room. Patricia's head collided with the stone, and she collapsed to the floor, unconscious. Harry picked up the scalpel and slid it into his jacket pocket.

He turned toward Catherine. She stared where he was looking and saw that she was bleeding copiously. He scooped her up in his arms, stepped over his motionless aunt, and started down the stairwell.

"Tourniquet," Catherine said, breathlessly. "Your belt."

Putting her down gently on the top step, he propped her against the wall. He removed his belt, looped it several times around her arm above the wound and pulled it tight. Applying his handkerchief to the bloody cut, he said, "Try to press down on the wound to help staunch the bleeding."

He took her in his arms like a rag doll and carried her down the stairs and into the kitchen where he lowered her with care onto a chair. After checking to make certain the belt was still tight, he grabbed the telephone and dialed the exchange.

"Emergency," he said. "Ambulance and police to Caravaggio House. There has been an attempted murder and medical care is needed urgently. This is Harry Bascombe."

* * *

When the police arrived, Harry recognized DI Ross from early in the investigation.

"The murderer is my Aunt Patricia. She confessed just now. She's on the second story of the cottage." He handed the DI the scalpel. "Weapon. She carved up Catherine and we got into a tussle. I bashed her against a wall. She was unconscious when I left her."

As the police ran up the stairs, the ambulance crew came in through the open door. They were able to stop the bleeding and bandage Catherine's arm.

As a nurse started an IV in Catherine's good arm, she heard Patricia's wild cries coming from upstairs. DS Ross and another policeman had her restrained in addition to the handcuffs around her wrists.

The ambulance crew followed the police followed out of the cottage door. The police had their hands full wrestling Patricia into the police van.

When the ambulance door shut, all the tension left Catherine's body and she slumped against Harry.

* * *

When Catherine awoke in a hospital, Harry was at her side.HaH

He kissed her gently on her cheek. "You were fortunate that Aunt Patricia missed an artery in your arm. The doctor who stitched you up said you should be able to leave after the IV in your arm finishes its job."

"Aunt Patricia?

"Locked up tight. Your only job now is to get some additional rest."

* * *

"What made you suspect your aunt?" DI Ross asked, as Harry brought in a medicinal pot of tea for all of them.

Harry explained. "It was Catherine's idea. She got to wondering how much Aunt Pat could really have seen at 8:00 am a month ago. She suggested we come down here and look out the cottage windows to determine if we could even see the path."

"Blimey! That's something any dumb copper should have thought of. We never suspected your aunt for a moment. We didn't even question her! All that stuff about windows and people on the path came out at the inquest. We took it for gospel."

"No one thought of checking except Catherine. We were all fixated on the Mafia connection. We even suspected Don Giuseppe might have done it."

"Well, DI Duncan up at the Yard is going to be very glad to have this case behind him!" said Ross. "I read about the kidnapping. Nasty lot, those Italians. Very happy you're recovering well, Mrs. Bascombe."

Catherine tried to heave a sigh and coughed instead. "As am I," she said.

"I'll have Sally, my stenographer come up the cottage to take your statements, so you can stay cozy and wait for Mrs. Bascombe to recover her strength. I imagine you'll be staying on in the cottage for the night?"

"Yes," said Harry. "I don't think Catherine's up to a journey home, just yet."

"Good thinking. When Sally gets the statements typed, she can bring them back here to have them signed. Now, before I go call Duncan at the Yard, is there anything I can do for you? Do you have anything to eat?"

Catherine piped up. "I could eat a horse, but I'll settled for some fresh crab from the Sloop Inn."

DI Ross laughed. "You've discovered our secret vice here in St. Ives! I'll send Sally along there before she comes here with her steno pad."

When the policeman had left, Harry said, "I don't think we can put off calling the parents any longer. Are you up to it? My mother will want to talk to you to make sure you're all right. I hope she's not too devastated about her sister."

Harry was right. His mother was chiefly concerned about Catherine's wound. When Catherine had reassured her with an account of her treatment, Sarah Bascombe said, "I'm not as surprised about Pat as you might think. I worked out that she was lying a long time ago, but I didn't know why. I didn't think she was the murderer, though."

"How did you know she was lying?"

"She has a tell. She's had it since childhood. She gives her head a little shake, almost a twitch. I'm sure when I've had a moment to recover from all the awfulness of the last month, I'll feel shattered to have lost both my siblings in this awful way. It's far too much to take in. But my balm will be Jonathan's children. They make it easier to bear."

Shortly after the conversation with Harry's mother, DI Duncan called and talked to Harry then insisted on speaking with Catherine.

"I want to hear you've retired from all your detecting, Mrs. Bascombe. What with the Pinnas, Signorina Sassari, and now Patricia Buchanan, my jail cells are nearly full. Good job Fawcett is out on bail!"

"I am ready for a little peace in my life, Inspector. I promise I will do my best to not to send any more murder suspects to you," Catherine replied.

* * *

Before began their drive to Hampshire, Harry wanted to visit the place where his uncle had experienced his last moments. They walked out and watched the sea roll in and crash at the foot of the high cliff.

"I'm going to miss Uncle Jonathan," he said.

"He was a lovely man," Catherine replied. "It's hard to see how he and your mother could have sprung from the same parents as Patricia. Do you know, she was determined to carve my heart out? I instinctively put up my arm to fend her off."

Harry drew her to him. "She had the devil's own strength. I had a job pulling her off you, darling."

"She had a morbid fixation on your uncle's money. I think she truly believed it belonged to her." Catherine snuggled her face into her husband's chest.

Taking the back of her head in a possessive grip with his large hand, he said, "Darling, I've got you. Forever and ever. You're going to be all right."

"It was almost like she thought she had some sort of divine right," she went on.

"She had a screw loose in the old brain box, as Bertie Wooster would say. She was crackers."

"I certainly hope we are finished investigating friends and members of our families, if we're going to continue in this vein."

"We ought to make it a policy from now on. Speaking of murders, too bad someone hasn't knocked off Hitler."

Catherine gave a small sigh. "One can hope."

Pulling back Harry looked down into her face. "Also too bad the term's starting. I could do with another honeymoon."

"Having our own little house in Oxford will seem like a honeymoon," Catherine said.

"What shall we name it?"

"Something like 'Pilgrim's Rest,'" she suggested.

"No, darling. A name like that would jinx us for certain."

Catherine laughed. "Crikey, I think you may be right."

THE END

Other Books by G.G. Vandagriff

Fiction

Catherine Tregowyn Mysteries
An Oxford Murder
Murder in the Jazz Band
Murder at Tregowyn Manor
The Hollywood Murders
Death of an Earl
Murder in the Family

WOOT TV Series
Breaking News
Sleeping Secret
Balkan Echo

Regency Romance
The Duke's Undoing
The Taming of Lady Kate
Miss Braithwaite's Secret
Rescuing Rosalind
Lord Trowbridge's Angel
The Baron and the Bluestocking
Lord Grenville's Choice
Lord John's Dilemma
Lord Basingstoke's Downfall
Her Fateful Debut
His Mysterious Lady
Not an Ordinary Baronet
Much Ado about Lavender
Spring in Hyde Park (anthology)
Love Unexpected
Miss Saunders Takes a Journey

Historical Novels
The Last Waltz
Exile
Defiance

Women's Fiction
Pieces of Paris
The Only Way to Paradise

Alex and Briggie Murder Mysteries
Cankered Roots
Of Deadly Descent
Tangled Roots
Poisoned Pedigree
The Hidden Branch

Non-Fiction
Voices in Your Blood
Deliverance from Depression

Other Books by David Vandagriff

I Need Thee Every Hour:
Applying the Atonement in Everyday Life
Deliverance from Depression

ABOUT THE AUTHORS

G.G. VANDAGRIFF is the author of over forty books, in many different genres. She is most at home writing historical fiction, be it mystery, romance, or family sagas. Currently, she is writing in the Golden Age of Mysteries—the 1930s. This is a period she is very familiar with as it was the focus of her undergraduate and master's studies in the history, politics, and economics of Europe during the interwar years.

She and her husband live in the foothills of the Wasatch Mountain range in Utah. They raised three children and now have seven grandchildren. In addition to writing, she enjoys reading and traveling.

She is the winner of the Whitney Award for best Historical Fiction of 2009 for her epic novel, *The Last Waltz*. You can reach her through her website, http://ggvandagriff.com.

* * *

DAVID VANDAGRIFF is a recovering lawyer. In addition to co-authoring mysteries with his wife, G.G., he is the mind behind the blog, The Passive Voice, which documents the emergence of self-publishing and the new world it has created for authors.

A graduate of Northwestern University, he received his law degree with honors from Pepperdine University, where he was selected for the Law Review.

David was a regular columnist for The Journal of the American Bar Association for several years, focusing on the use of computers and related technologies in the law office.

His favorite part of this stage of life is his grandchildren, which surprised him and everyone else. Visit him on his blog at The Passive Voice. http://thepassivevoice.com

Printed in Great Britain
by Amazon